DEDICATION

I DEDICATE THIS BOOK TO MY FAMILY

Back Row L to R: Mason, Dylan, Susan, Michael, David,
Melissa, Megan, Peyton
Front Row L to R: Ellie, Mary, Mike, Lauren, Dawson

THE
LOVE OF A FAMILY
IS LIFE'S
GREATEST BLESSING

ACKNOWLEDGEMENTS

My never ending thank you to **Karen Coulter** for teaching me how to write.

Thank you to **Marilyn Clark,** my main editor for COBWEBS A'PLENTY. You are editor, mentor, beta reader and brainstormer and friend. Your love for reading gives you great knowledge that I am so thankful you share with me. Couldn't have done it without you!

Thank you to my Beta Readers, who are an integral part of this journey: **Marilyn Clark, David Koma, Megan Koma, Mike Koma, and Cathy Patterson.** I know how much work it is to be a Beta Reader. I appreciate you all so much.

For the cover I thank **David Thompson,** the brilliant artist who allowed me to use his print and thank you to my sister, **Cheri** (Maffei) **Wolff** for her input and advice.

Thank you to my husband, **Mike,** for supporting my addiction to writing and sitting alone for hours on end while I write. You always said do what you love. I do. I love you.

To our sons, **Michael and David**, my daughter-in-laws **Susan and Melissa,** and my grandchildren **Megan, Mason, Lauren, Dylan, Peyton, Ellie, and Dawson** for unending faith and support. Thank you, David, for your tech support.

To the families who allowed me to share their tragedies: **Darla**(Doms) **Travis,** the **Brochetti** Family, The **Nagy** Family, The **Lias** family, **Larry Pompelia, Debbie** (Nelson) **Kreutzer, Charles Schrecengost, Glenda Burns, Kay Schrecengost, Gary Devivo.**

2

For pictures and history: **Mary Jane** (Otte) **Woodward, Gene Hockenberry, Linda** (Hill) **Gaston, Beatrice** (Milicia) **Peace, Cindy** (Milicia) **Rearick, Carol** (Rearick) **Hall, Joe Chobody, Marion Lucas, Cindie** (Lucas) **Macko, Darla** (Doms) **Travis, Debbie** (Nelson) **Kreutzer, Jim Patterson, Charlie Boyer,** The **Brochetti Family, Nancy** (Cogley) **Serbin, Wilbur Griffith, Chauncy and Janice Moore, Don and Pat Dixon, Joanne Kreutzer, Janet and Denny Hellgren** and **The Shannock Valley All Class Reunion Facebook Page**

Thank you to my siblings, **Donna** (Maffei) **Dentler, Jolene** (Maffei) **Formaini, Rick and Tom Maffei, Cheri** (Maffei) **Wolff** for good memories.

Thank you to **Will Spera** who lent me yearbooks from 1941 through the 80's, and thank you to my brother **Tom Maffei** for having collected them all in the beginning and putting them in good hands. It was so much fun going through them.

Thank you to **Joe Malec Photography** and his son, **Jeff Malec,** who gave me permission to use the pictures.

To my photographer: **Ian Heitman,** thank you.

Thank you to my book designer, **Jen Clark.** You were amazing to work with. And thank you to Author, **Janice Dembosky** for pointing me in your direction.

To all who gave me your memories. You are too many to mention. You know who you are. I hope you enjoy reading your experiences in my book. I write my books on true memories. You make it possible for me to create the story. Thank you!

CHAPTER ONE
BUCKET OF BLOOD
May 31, 1958

"Dead as a doornail." Policeman Hoot Gibsen tells the bar owner, Mr. Skrow. "Done got his throat cut!"

People are gathered outside the building where the *The Bucket of Blood* keeps their liquor. Men are peering inside to look at the dead body. "He's in there layin' by the wine barrels. Blood everywhere."

"How'd he git there?" Mr. Skrow scratches his bald head as his glasses slide down his nose. "So much blood. Hard to know who he is!"

Hoot looks down over his bulging belly, putting his hands in his pockets. "Somebody's gotta know him. Small town like this n'all. Who had the keys to this building?"

"Ain't no keys!" Mr. Skrow says. "Never needed keys!"

Hoot looks towards the parking lot. "That old pick-up truck there belong to anybody you know?"

"I've seen it before." Mr. Skrow replies. "I cain't think who it belongs to."

"Stand back there, men. Don't need you messin' up the crime scene!" Hoot orders the men trying to peek inside. Mr. Rusnica and a couple of fellows step back.

Sneaky James is still looking at the man. "Hell, dis here is Kiser Wilson! He lives in da country out dere at Owl Holler, on a farm. Never done nothin' bad to no one. Who'd wanna to kill him?"

"You know him?" Hoot asks.

"Hell ya! I bin out dere buyin' hay for my horses from 'im for years. I picked up two bail jist yesterday. He had a niece livin' with him. His brother's girl. Name was Ellen or Helen, somethin' like that. He told me that just before I got there, that the girl took off. She was walkin' back to her old man's place in Rose Valley. She had got mad at Kiser about somethin'. Kiser was plannin' to go down there to his brother Fred's place to check on her, bein' Fred is kind of a drunk. I know Kiser was worried 'cause of that. I wonder if he ever made it!"

Mr. Skrow seems surprised. "Kiser? He was in the bar last night fer not more than half hour. He drank a Coca Cola and left. Said he was headed to Rose Valley. You sure it's him?"

Sneaky lifts his beaten baseball cap and wipes his sweat from his forehead. "As sure as a squirrel eats nuts! It's a shame, a damn shame!"

Hoot makes everyone get out of the way as he ropes off the entire building. I hear the whistle of the ambulance coming to take the dead man. "You girls better git outta here! Dis ain't no place for kids!" He waves us away.

Jax grabs my arm and we run back onto the street. I look back at the crowd of men gathered, as I run. I'm scared, and troubled. Troubled bad!

I never knew Numine could be so interesting! I come here to visit my friend, Jax. Our walk today through Numine was sure not simple. Not with murder happening!

When I turned eight this year, Dad said I could go to Jax's house, "If you behave." He says. Mom always makes sure my skirt matches my shirt, but I insist on wearing just flip flops on my feet. My glasses never stay where they belong on my nose, and my curly hair is always wild.

This is my third time to Numine. We were just walking through town like we did last time I visited, when we happened upon the drama going on at *The Bucket of Blood*. It is a bar. It is an old building. The broad porch with peeling paint, and the crooked roofline make it appear as if the place is about to fall over. The steps going to the porch are tilted. To the right of the door is a bench seat from an old pick-up truck, a spit-toon, and a tin bucket filled halfway with sand and the rest with cigarette butts. Last time we passed here we heard the jukebox playing and people chatting, and sometimes arguing. But, not today.

I have so many questions, as we walk. "Did you know that man that got killed, Jax?"

"Nope. Don't know 'im!" She skips onto the cement curb and off again, onto the road.

"Well, what do you think, Jax? Is the murderer around her somewhere. Is he?"

"How the heck would I know, Sophie!"

I try to get my mind off it as we walk. It's a beautiful sunny spring day. The forsythia spills over the embankment touching the road. As we pass the forsythia, a garden snake slithers from below it across the road in front of me. Snakes don't scare me. Jax is a bit of a sissy though. She is skinny as a noodle and always wears white fold down socks with her worn tennis shoes. Her blonde hair is tied back in a messy ponytail that is not quite in the center. She squeals like a baby when she sees it. "A SNAKE!" She jumps off the road onto the grass.

"Come on, Jax. It isn't going to hurt you. It's just a snake!"

"Just a snake to YOU, Sophie! You know I hate snakes!"

Just then my flip flop comes apart and I feel the gravel from the road on my soft foot bottom. "Hold up, Jax. That is, if the snake doesn't get you first!" I sit on the cement curb to brush off my foot. I push the little rubber hicky-ma-do back through the hole in my flip flop and squeeze my foot back into it.

"You're not funny, Sophie. Not funny at all!"

"Whatever, Jax!" I stand up and brush the dust off my skirt. We never get mad at each other. We stick together like mud. 'Specially in mud.

I hear someone humming. Glancing down the street, I see Shin Rabbits sitting in the dirt near the steps at Dimaio's Grocery Store. Shin is a town legend. I talked to him last time I was here walking with Jax. He was outside the show building. He is always somewhere. He wears a round hat with a brim. His thin hair is greasy brown. It flows from beneath his cap to just below his ears. His once white dress shirt is soiled from wear. The dirty collar peaks out from under his black cloth jacket with threads showing through and the cuffs hanging half off. The suspenders that hold up his pants are barely attached. He is humming as he drinks from a bottle within a paper bag. His face is red from the sun or perhaps from what is in that bag. He stutters and slurs. He smells like garlic, mixed with whiskey. Dad always says that garlic makes a man wink, drink, and stink. That is true about Shin. He seems to be a friendly fellow though.

Jax says I shouldn't believe everything he says. "He'll scare you; you'll have nightmares!"

"No, I won't, Jax. I'm not superstitious! I'm just a little stitious!" We both giggle. Shin sees us.

"Hey g-girls!" His lips turn into a grin as he wipes his eyes with the back of his hands that look like they haven't been washed in a week.

"Hey, Shin!" I push my glasses back up my nose. "Did you hear? There's a dead guy in Skrow's building where he keeps his liquor! His name is Kiser Wilson."

"Kiser? From out Owl Hollow?"

"That's what Sneaky James said! He said he was just a farmer, never caused no one any trouble."

Shin laughs and takes a drink from the brown paper bag. "Well, somethin' got him killed. It 'ill come out, you'll see."

I see he is thinking. His eyes wrinkle at the corners as he closes one eye and looks upwards to the sky with the other. We wait. He takes another swig and leans closer to us. He winks. "You ever seen the g-ghost that hangs out in the ice c-cave over y-yonder, past the b-boney dump?"

"Ghost?" I ask. "No!"

"Yep! G-ghost. Ain't foolin' ya!"

"Did you see it, Shin?"

"Sure d-did! Even sh-shook h-hands with it!"

I think he is lying. "You can't shake hands with a ghost!"

"Who s-says!" he replies. "You ever t-try it?"

"I think you are just trying to scare me, Shin!"

He smiles and I see his rotten teeth with two missing. "You l-look into that ice cave and see for yourself. It ain't very b-big, you see. But as you l-look into it, the hole w-will open up w-wide and the g- ghost will let you in." He tips his bottle up for another swig. "You g-girls git home now. Seems like nothin' g-good goin' on at this end of t-town."

"See ya next time, Shin! Next time I come to Numine!"

"Yay, N-Numine!" he laughs.

Jax and I pass the Company Store. She picks up a stone and throws it at an already broken window. "This here closed a couple years ago. It's where my mom got most everything. The Post Office was in there too. It moved down the street now. There was a gas station over to the side there. The top floor was the post office and the store office. They sold shoes up there too. The left side was dry goods and on the right was groceries. You had to go down the stairs to the basement if you wanted the butcher shop."

I skip up the steps and look in the window. "How do you remember all that?"

She laughs, "What I don't remember on my own, my mom talks about."

"We had one of these in Yatesboro. A company store, I mean. Ours burned down a few years back."

9

We've already passed three churches and there is another one I can see up the road. "You people in Numine must be religious! You got a lot of churches for such a small town."

Jax laughs. "Guess so! Do you know, when the coal mines are working there is always a *humming* over the town. Do you hear it?"

We stop and stay silent. "Yes, I hear it, Jax!"

She hops over a tricycle lying on the sidewalk on its side. "Dang kids. Need to pick their stuff up!"

Our next stop is the Numine Elementary School. We sit down on the front steps.

Jax looks up to her right. "That's my classroom up there. I don't like my teacher. She's mean!" She hops down off the steps. "You take what you get, right? Let's keep going!"

To our right we come to a low brick building. "This here is the show building, Sophie. I'll take you there sometime for a movie. It only costs twenty cents to go! When you walk in the door here, the floor goes straight downhill. Sometimes, though, we get on the bus Jack Nagy sends up to take us to the Rural Valley Liberty Theater."

"That's where I go, to the Liberty Theater. Did you know it used to be an Opera House and Grange Hall?"

"No, I didn't. An Opera House in Rural Valley? Ain't that somethin'!"

We cross the street to a large white building. "What's this, Jax?"

"The Grandview Hotel. This here hotel came about almost forty years ago Mom said. Peter and Sara Smeltzer own it."

Two older fellows are sitting on the front steps chewing snuff and spitting. "Hey girls!" The one guy hollers. "Did ya'll see what was happenin' at *The Bucket of Blood*?"

"Sure did! Kiser Wilson got killed!" I tell them. "Did you know him?"

The man spits another brown stream of spit and tobacco onto the grass. "A murder in Numine? Kiser? Yeah, I know him. Nice feller. Who'd wanna kill a nice feller like that!"

"I don't know, but it's awful. The killer could still be around here!"

He laughs. "Ain't no killer gonna hang around. He'd be long gone by now."

That makes me feel a little better. We turn around and head toward Jax's house, but she wants to go to the tipple first. The train runs by the tipple. As we walk, Jax tells me about Numine. "There was once a skating rink, a poolroom and a restaurant on Main Street. The Ku Klux Klan were around once too. When NuMine Presbyterian Church was built in the 1920's, they called it *The Church that Coal Built.* My mom told me that the day when they dedicated the church, that the Ku Klux Klan showed up. She said she was little but remembers being scared. I'd be scared too! They dedicated St. Gabriel's the next year. Mom said they didn't show up for that one."

"I never understood the Ku Klux Klan, Jax. You know they did awful things. My Nonna calls them devil men."

"That's a good word!" Jax laughs.

We stop to let three boys speed past us on their bikes. As we get near the tipple, we stop to watch the coal cars climbing up the track and tipping their load of coal into the tipple. I see the boney dump burning. Jax walks towards it. "This burns day and night! Same as the one in Yatesboro. Hey, Sophie, did ya' know they used to call Numine MOONSHINE CITY? Did ya' ever taste moonshine, Sophie?"

"Gosh no."

"Me neither. A friend of my mom's, Vivian Ash, told us that she went to one of the cellars where they were making moonshine and brandy once. She took a straw and stuck her head into the bucket of brandy to get some. The fumes of the brandy nearly killed her. My mom thought that was hilarious. She said to her, 'Wouldn't that be nice reading in the newspaper the next day, WOMAN DROWNS IN A BUCKET OF BRANDY.'"

"That's hilarious, Jax! What did Vivian say?"

"She said it would be a great way to die."

The Show Building years later. It still stands

The Grandview Hotel in Numine

CHAPTER TWO
DINNER AND CHATS
SAME DAY

I love eating at Jax's house. Sometimes, her mom makes fries in lots of grease and gives us a whole bowl of ketchup for us to dip them in.

We get back to Jax's house in plenty of time for dinner. I take my flip flops off as we hit the grass. The feel of the cool grass is pleasing to my feet. Her company house is like all the others on the street. The same front porch, the same beaten wood on the outside. The window's halfway up allowing the soft wind to blow the sheer curtains inside. The outhouse still sits at the end of her garden, with the half-moon carved on the door. Just a keepsake now.

Her Dad is home from the coal mines. He is tall and he has a mole on the side of his face that is interesting. We go around the house to the back. He is standing in just his underwear, using the garden hose to wash his coal dirt away. I turn my head away quickly. "Hey, girls! I'll be done here in a minute." He sees my embarrassment.

Jax isn't embarrassed. "Hi, Dad! There was a murder in Numine today!"

"Murder, Jax? Where? Who?"

"At *The Bucket of Blood*. They say it's Kiser Wilson. Someone cut his throat. He's in that building where they have their wine barrels."

"Kiser? That don't make no sense to me. He's just a timid old farmer. Wouldn't hurt a fly! You sure it was him?"

"Sneaky James said so, Dad. He was in there where he was layin'."

He swiped off with his towel and tied it around his waist. "What else do you know? Did the police say they know who did it?"

"No, Dad. They don't seem to know nuthin'."

He walks towards the back door shaking his head. "A murder in Numine! Poor Kiser. Oh my. Oh my."

By the time we have the table set, he is done. His cheeks are rosy from the hot water of the shower, as he sits down to eat. He is a nice man, but a little boring sometimes. He loves basketball. "Did you girls know that just last year, the Shannock Valley Basketball team won the West Regional Title AND the W.P.I.A.L. Championship? That Wicki Long was SOME player. Yes, he was! I can name all those players on that team. There was Wicki, then there was Matyus, Haky, Shirey, Smith, Marken, Franceschi, Krecota and Tom Krizmanich. There was a Smith, Mueller, Shirey, Yanik, and Larry Boyer too. Jim Sibley coached them. How many people you think can name a whole team like that?"

"No one, Dad. Just you!" Jax replies, turning her head to me, smiling as she winks.

He is so proud of the facts that he knows. "I know even the managers of the team. It was Zuchelli, Sotak, Hockenberry, Keller and Craft. That Wicki Long was one tall fellow! Too bad he graduated!" He reaches for more mashed potatoes. "Wicki plays baseball on the ballfield here in Numine sometimes." He looks at me. "You know the field don't ya, just down there left of the tipple and all."

"We know the field, Dad." Jax says as she butters her bread.

"Last summer Wicki had five homeruns in one game! Yay, Numine!"

"Yay, Numine?" I ask. "Does that mean Numine won?"

"Not necessarily. It's just a sayin' that Tim Kuhta started long ago. When you play baseball here in Numine, you end the game by hollerin' 'Yay, Numine!' It grew on people and most everybody uses it anytime they talk about Numine."

Sounds a little corny to me, but that explains why Shin said *yay Numine!*

"Did you know Wicki's dad was murdered at the Sagamore Hotel a while back?" he says, as he shoves a spoonful of potatoes into his mouth.

"He was? Who killed him?"

"Never found out, I guess. Or maybe just nobody tellin'. You know they call that hotel 'The Knife and Gun Club' don't ya?"

"No, I didn't. I've never been to Sagamore."

"Well, you gotta git there, girl! It is a town much like our Numine. You know, here in Numine, way back in the day, there was nothin' here but farmland. Then the Coal Vein #5 opened, and men were employed, and overnight the farmlands were transformed into this town you see now. They rented us all these houses. Included electric in the rent too! Same thing happened in Sagamore!"

"Is Sagamore as big as Numine?" I ask.

"Maybe even bigger! It's got the biggest tipple in the world. And they've got the Sagamore Hotel there. They had a theater and an Opera House once too. Heck, they employed over 800 men at one time, and produced over 600,000 tons of coal! They got a restaurant up there next to the hotel that all the teenagers hang out at, just across from the Sagamore Hotel."

"You sure know a lot of stuff, Mr. Cravener." I hear TOOT, TOOT! Dad is here for me. "Gotta go, Mr. Cravener. You can tell me more next time!"

I run out the door and jump in Dad's car. "Did you have a good time?" he asks.

"Guess so." He looks different and smells like powder. "Did you get a haircut?"

"Yep, just came from Al Russo's Barbershop."

"Dad, did you know they found a dead guy at *The Bucket of Blood* today? He was in that building where they keep their liquor."

"No, I didn't. Dead? You sure?"

"Heard it with my own ears. The policeman was there telling Mr. Skrow that the man was in there by the wine barrels with his throat cut! His name was Kiser Wilson."

"Kiser?" Dad seems puzzled. "You sure it was Kiser Wilson?"

"I'm sure. There were men there that knew him. Do you know him, Dad?"

"I do! He has a farm out there in Owl Hollow. Not the type of guy someone would be after." He turns and looks at me. "You were there, Sophie? What were you doing there? You know the rules. You can come up here to Numine, on the condition that you behave yourself. An eight-year-old girl should not be anywhere near a bar!" He seems mad.

"I know, I know." But I rarely behave myself.

"Then explain yourself to me!"

I had to think fast. "We were just walking to Jax's friend's house. Just passed there, that's all."

"Okay, Sophie. But next time you find a way to get there that you don't pass the bar!"

"Actually, Dad, there's a path behind the Brewer house we can take that we won't pass the bar."

"Good. You go that way next time."

He believes me. There is no path. Dad is so easy to fool. I have a little voice that lives in my head and never pays rent. My little voice tells me to do things. It lies for me sometimes. I can't shut-up that little voice.

18

Long, Matyus, Haky, Shirey, Smith, Marken, Franceschi, Krizmanich, Krecota.

Long, Captain

Willard Long, Captain

A baseball game on the baseball field near Tipple in Numine

Overview of Numine

CHAPTER THREE
HELP!
June 8, 1958

Dad is up at the crack of dawn. He always says, "Early to bed, early to rise, makes a man healthy, wealthy and wise."

I got up early too. It's been a week since I visited Jax. "Can I go to Numine again today, Dad?"

"If you behave yourself!"

Gosh, I get tired of hearing those four words. "I will, Dad. Do you think you'll ever stop saying that?"

He laughs. "Probably not!"

Today, Jax and I are walking to the end of Numine, where the Numine road meets the road to Dayton. It is a long walk, and Dad would not approve. But what he doesn't know won't hurt him.

As we pass Numine Elementary School I see there is a cracked window on the top floor. "They need to fix that, Jax."

"I know, but that's only one window. Do you know that last year a guy from here broke several windows?"

"He did? Why?"

"Well, he didn't mean to, really. His name was Walter Bohan. He was in the Marine Corps and was flying a Navy Cougar Jet. He was stationed in Columbus, Ohio, so it wasn't much of a trip for him to fly over his hometown for us all to see him. We were all outside watching. He went past here towards Yatesboro, then came back and did a roll.

It was awesome! It was so loud, it made my ears hurt. Then, all of a sudden, we heard windows in the school breaking."

"Holy crap. Did he feel bad?"
"Don't really know if anyone told him." She skips over a small log and keeps going.

As we walk, we pass the Show Building on our right, then the Zamperini bar a couple doors up. There are three men standing at a car arguing about something. One throws his cigarette down angrily and goes into the bar.

"What do you think that's about, Jax?"

"Who knows! Seems like when people drink, they find stuff to argue about. It don't have to be much!"

We keep walking. I notice a one room school on my left. "What's that?" I ask.

"Oh, that there? That's the old Cassidy School. Lots of kids went to school there. It's been closed for years. Frank Bohan bought it, but he hasn't done anything with it just yet. Let's go inside!"

The front door is unlocked. It is a big wooden door, with glass above it. As we walk inside, it smells of dampness and old wood. There is still a blackboard, and student desks sitting helter skelter. There are two empty beer cans laying on the floor and cigarette butts beside them.

We run to the blackboard and with the one lonely piece of broken chalk left there I write "Sophie and Jax were here."

"It's creepy in here." I tell her. I start sitting at the desks, going from one to another.

Jax is pretending to be my teacher. She taps the desk with a ruler she has found. "Here, here children. We are going to do a lesson. Sophie, what did you bring for show and tell today?"

It's hard not to laugh, she is being so silly. "I brought snot. Can I show it now?"

"You're disgusting!" She goes back to opening the drawers of the teacher's desk.

I lift the top of the small student desk I'm at. A pencil and paperclip. I go to the next. An empty gum wrapper. The third desk, as I pick up the lid, I see a pencil and a piece of paper. On the paper is one word. "HELP".

"JAX! Someone needs help!"

"Oh, Sophie. You are so dramatic! Who would need help?"

"I don't know WHO! But SOMEONE DOES! Someone was in here and wrote this note! When did this school close?"

"A long time ago!"

"Do other people come in here?"

"Well, maybe. I saw Twigs Peat at the post office yesterday. He said he was up here on Wednesday looking for old bottles in the yard and there was a guy in here. He hollered at Twigs to get out."

"A guy? What guy? Who was he?"

"Twigs says he's just an old hermit from Smeltzer Hollow. They call him Boofer. He lives in a broken-down trailer in the woods up there. He's crazy as a soup sandwich."

"Well, he was in here, and now this note. It could mean something, Jax! We can't just ignore it!"

"Okay! Okay! I'll ask Twigs where Boofer's trailer is. Next time you come up we'll go there. Wear your walking shoes!"

I'm satisfied for now. I put the note in my pocket and we head for Jax's house.

I think about the note. Who is it that needs our help? Then, I think about Kiser Wilson. I can't stop thinking about him. A lonely old farmer. Both things swarm in my mind like bees swarming their hive.

Dad picks me up before suppertime. "Did you have a good day?"

"Guess so." Yet, everything is bothering me. Kiser being killed, the note in the old school. Just everything.

"Seems like something's bothering you, Sophie."

I must make something up, so he doesn't know I was in that school, so far from Jax's house. "I was just wishing Jax would play cards. I wanted to play cards and she didn't."

"You can lead a horse to water, Sophie, but you can't make it drink."

Gosh, I wish he would speak English! He has so many sayings! I don't know what most of them even mean!

The Cassidy Schoolhouse

CHAPTER FOUR
THREE LITTLE GIRLS IN A TIN TUB
June 9, 1958

Nighttime comes quickly. My dreams are troubling. I dream about the dead man. It is a strange dream. Shin Rabbits is sitting by the man, combing the man's hair. As I watch, I smell the dampness of the wine barrels and the stench of dried blood. Then I hear a door slam. There is a dark frightening figure standing there. Suddenly, I wake up and sit straight up in bed, letting out a squeal. I realize I was awakened by Julia slamming the bathroom door. It is sprinkling outside and that was the dampness I smelled. I am so relieved that it was just a dream. A faint breeze touches my cheek through the window. It is Sunday. Must get ready for church.

I crawl out of bed to use our bathroom. "Come 'on, Julia, let me in!" I holler. She refuses to answer. She knows that her silence gets under my skin. "Julia, hurry up!"

Dad hears the racket and comes up, carrying his coffee cup and newspaper. "What's going on!"

Julia finds her voice. "Sophie is rushing me, Dad, and I just got in here!"

"Now, Sophie. Be patient. You can wait your turn."
He turns and walks back down the stairs, reading his
newspaper out loud as he walks. "President Eisenhower
announces the United States launched its first satellite.
Ain't that somethin'!" Dad's morning newspaper is
important to him. And as far as our bathroom problem, the
truth is that parents are not really interested in justice. They
just want peace and quiet.

Once he is gone, I lie with my cheek on the floor,
where the crack is big between the bottom of the bathroom
door and the floor of the hallway. I holler to Julia. "Cookie
Pennsy will be in church today, and she is WAY prettier than
you!"

My little brother, Sammy, just woke up. He is soon
four. His real name is Samuel Donald. We call him Sammy.
He is standing in the hallway wiping his eyes.

The bathroom door suddenly opens and Julia shoves
me hard. I fall on my bum. She is a year older than me, and
she is strong.

I glare at her. "You better watch out! I'll put you in
an iron lung!' Julia is scared to death that someday she will
be in an iron lung. We see them on television with people in
them. It is people who got polio.

"I'm not scared of anything, Sophie!"

I get to my feet. "You are too, you liar. You're
scared of everything! Donna Ondich told me you cry when
the sirens blow and you must get under your desk at school!
You're a BABY!"

I run back to my room and slam the door. I plop onto my bed. I hear mom come for Sammy, as she tells Julia to wind it up. As I stare at my ceiling, I think about things I am afraid of too. Polio is one of them. It hit in 1952 and people died. Who says the same thing won't happen to me? I'm scared too when the whistles blow and we get under our desks at school, but I'll never tell Julia I am.

My door opens. It's Ruby. She is laughing. "I heard it all, Sophie. I think you lost this time."

"I didn't lose anything! Julia is a brat and she hogs the bathroom!"

"It's empty now. Get yourself up and get in there. We have to go to church."

Ruby is seventeen now. She always settles the fights between me and Julia.

Ruby is my earliest memory. We used to live next door to Ruby, with our own real parents, Jay and Stella Fischer. Ruby always played with us girls. She was playing with us this one day when my parents wanted to go to Dayton for corn. I remember Ruby saying, "I'll watch them, leave them here. They are having fun."

Ruby filled a tin tub with water for us to play in. Julia was just five and I was four. Our other sister, Dutch, was there too. She was six. Her real name is Delilah, but we call her Dutch.

My parents never came home that day. They were hit head-on by a drunk driver in front of Reefer's Store in Numine. They were killed. The other driver took off on foot. The car he was in was stolen, and was full of empty booze bottles. My mother's purse was gone, so the drunk robbed them before he ran. They never found out who it was.

Reefer's Store

It's funny the things I remember from that day. I remember the water in the tub was cold. I remember standing in the grass laughing. Dutch was hogging the tub. I can still feel the cool grass on my feet. I even remember the suits we wore, with the little ruffle across the top and the straps going up and around our necks. But I don't remember my parents. It doesn't seem right that I don't remember the people who gave me life.

I have a memory of Sam and Patsy hugging us, telling us everything was going to be okay. I remember being sad. So sad. Dutch and Julia cried hard. I must have too.

Surely, I did.

We had nobody but our Nonna and Nonno, and one uncle. Nonna and Nonno were too old to care for us. Their only son, Zio Dom, couldn't take us. He wanted to, but his wife, Zia Ulla, told him no. She didn't want us. I heard someone telling Patsy that Zia Ulla never liked my dad, because he was German and Protestant. I suppose she didn't want little light-haired German Presbyterians running around. It was just as well. No one in their right mind would want to live with Zia Ulla. She is a witch.

I remember Sam and Patsy kept saying, "Don't worry, everything will be okay!" I remember burying my head into Sam's shirt to cry. His shirt was wet. I remember that.

Then, one day, Sam and Patsy adopted us. I got a new last name, Kaminsky, and Ruby became my sister. I liked that best of all! I love them. After they adopted us, they have been Mom and Dad to me ever since. I remember that day they adopted us so well. But why can't I remember my parents? I can't see their faces.

CHAPTER FIVE
RESCUE
June 10, 1958

I come down in the morning to Mom and Dad talking in the kitchen. It sounds serious. "What's up?" I ask.

Dad pours his coffee. "Mom and I were just talking about Kiser Wilson. He didn't have much family. He had a sister who is in a nursing home, and a brother, Fred, who has a problem with alcohol. That's the brother the girl belonged to. There was another brother, Robert. He was killed in the Korean War in 1950. He was Fred's twin."

"So, Kiser's niece wanted to go back to live with a drunken father, instead of Kiser?"

"Seems so. They say Fred was a good man at one time. He took to the bottle after losing his twin brother."

"Well, couldn't someone help her dad to quit drinking and be better?"

"Sophie, everyone handles grief differently. He was really close with his twin brother I hear. The thing is, Sophie, it seems that the girl never went home. Kiser apparently didn't get around to checking on her before he was killed. Fred told the police that she never showed up."

"Well, where would she be?" I'm puzzled.

"That's the million-dollar question. The police are on it though."

My mind is spinning and turning. I am looking at my cereal but I'm not lifting my spoon. I want to tell Dad about the note I found in the Cassidy School, but I don't dare. I'd be in big trouble for walking that far.

"What's up, Sophie? You aren't eating!"

"Just thinkin'. That's all."

"What are you thinking about?"

"Thinkin' what could have happened to her. Dad, do you think someone could have taken her?"

"That is a possibility. Though, nothing like that ever happened around here. It would sure be odd. Maybe she simply ran away."

"Can you take me to Numine after breakfast, Dad? Jax is home today."

"Sure. But I can't say it enough. You MUST behave yourself. I don't want anything happening to you. You know, you are my cat's meow!"

"Your cat's meow? Really, Dad! Do you ever run out of sayings?"

"Hope not!" He laughs

By mid-morning I am there. She is on her porch when I arrive. "Jax, did you hear about that niece of Kiser Wilson's?"

"What about her?"

"She never showed up at her dad's place. They don't know where she is! Now, I'm thinking she is the one that wrote that note that said HELP. Maybe she was kidnapped!"

"That's kind of crazy, Sophie. That kind of stuff doesn't happen around here!"

"And what if it did. WHAT IF IT DID? Where's that guy, Twigs, that you talked to at the post office? Where does he live? He knows about that guy, Boofer. What if it is Boofer who has her? He could have had her in the school building when she wrote the note."

"Your mind is weaving crazy stories, but if it makes you happy, we'll go ask Twigs. He just lives up there by the church."

As we arrive at his house, he is outside working on a mower. He looks like he is maybe a junior in high school. He is tall and skinny, which is maybe why he got the nickname Twigs.

"Hey, Twigs!" Jax begins. "You told me at the post office that you saw that guy, Boofer, in the Cassidy School that day he chased you out of the yard. What do you suppose he was doing in there?"

"Who knows! Maybe just takin' a break? Or takin' up residence there? Don't know. Why?"

"Where does he live, Twigs?"

"He's just an old hermit who lives in a beaten down trailer in the woods up there at Smeltzer Hollow. He's not all there, if you know what I mean. He's crazier than a three-eyed cat!"

That scares me. "Can you describe how to get to his trailer?"

"What are you girls up to?"

We told him about the note in the school desk, and Kiser's niece being missing. He doesn't call us crazy. He looks concerned.

"Give me a minute. I'll go with you." He pushes the mower into the shed and goes into his house. When he comes out, I see him sticking a knife in his belt.

"You think we are going to need that?"

"I told you, he is not all there. He's always been nice to me, but he's only got one oar in the water. Who knows? He could be dangerous!"

We walk up through Numine and up the slight hill towards Smeltzer Hollow. At the edge of a field beside a white wooden house, we enter a skinny lane. We stay on the lane until we reach a small clearing. There is a camping trailer on wheels, and the hitch is sitting on cement blocks. It looks filthy. There are blankets on the windows and chickens running around in the high grass. I wouldn't let my dog live in a place like this!

Twigs knocks on the door. Knock. Knock. Knock. Boofer opens the door. "What do you want?"

He is a scrawny guy, and short. He is bald on the top with wild hair around his ears. He needs a shave. His white tee shirt is gray instead of white, and it has holes in it.

Twigs tries to look around him. "Had a question for you, Boofer. What were you doing in the Cassidy School that day I saw you? You know, when you hollered at me to get out of there."

Just then, we hear a whimper from inside. Twigs grabs Boofer by his arm and yanks him outside onto the grass, holding the knife to his throat.

Boofer is fighting to loosen Twig's grip. "I was jist lonely! That's all. Jist lonely! I ain't hurt her or nuthin'!"

Jax and I run into the camper. Sitting on the floor by a make-shift bed is a teenage girl. There is a bandana tied around her mouth and her eyes are wide with terror. Her hair is long and greasy and her hands are in front of her tied together with rope. There is a chain around her ankle that connects her to the leg of the bed. I rip the cloth from her mouth as Jax works on the ropes. She is crying. "What's your name?" I ask.

She talks in a whimper. "Helen. Helen Wilson."

"Don't worry, Helen, you are safe now," I tell her. Jax runs to Twigs. Together they get the key to the chain padlock out of Boofer's pocket. We open the padlock and release the chain. We stand her up. She is weak.

Outside, by now, Boofer is not fighting. He is crying. "I was jist lonely. That's all. Jist lonely."

Twigs hollers to us. "Walk her down the hill, I'll be right behind you with Boofer. Get going!"

We start to walk as we talk to her. "How did you get here, Helen?"

"I was mad at my Uncle Kiser, 'cause he made me help with hay. I screamed at him I was goin' home. I just started walkin', and when I got in front of the Cassidy School, this guy grabbed me. We were in that school for hours. When night came, we left 'cause someone had come 'round during the day. I left a note in a desk there, hopin' someone would see it."

"I saw it, Helen. That was smart of you to do that. Did he hurt you?"

"He kept me tied up, and kept talkin' to me, tellin' me how lonely he was. He fed me and didn't hit me or nothin'. He just kept talkin' 'bout bein' lonely and stuff. I was so scared. SO SCARED!" She starts to sob.

"You're safe now, Helen. It will be okay."

As we reach the white house we had passed, the owner is in his yard. As we approach him, he sees something is badly wrong. After explaining, he hurries us into his house and calls the police.

"We need to help Twigs!" I tell him. "He's bringing Boofer down!"

"You girls stay right here." He said, as he runs out the door and up the lane to Boofer's.

In just minutes, I hear the sirens. Two police cars pull in. They talked to us briefly, then started up the path. They aren't gone but two minutes when we hear a gunshot.

"Oh my God!" I scream and run out the door.

Jax grabs me. "Stay here on the porch, Sophie. We have to wait!"

Shortly, the two cops come down the lane with Twigs between them. One cop has his arm over Twigs shoulder. The guy from the house is behind them.

As they reach the porch, I can see Twigs is troubled. "What happened?" I ask.

One cop does the talking. "When we got up there, we saw them sitting by a tree talking. When we started to approach, Boofer grabbed the knife out of Twigs' hand, and lunged at us. We had to shoot."

"Is he dead?" I ask.

"Yes, unfortunately. It didn't have to be that way but we had to stop him. Twigs here is having a hard time with it."

"Sit down, Twigs." I tell him. He does. I sit beside him and take his hand. "It's okay Twigs. It's over now."

"Won't ever be over for me. He was just an old lonely soul. He was telling me about his loneliness and the crap of a life he has lived. I don't think he even knew what he had done. He was kind of dumb, you know."

The cop pats him on the back. "You didn't kill him, son. He did that to himself."

Twigs took a deep breath. "A man killed in front of me. I don't know if I can ever unsee that."

I throw my arms around him. "You saved her, Twigs. You are a hero!"

Twigs begins to cry. "I ain't no hero. A man is dead!"

The man from the house tries to comfort him. "It's not your fault he is dead, Twigs. Boofer's been up there in the woods in that trailer long as I can remember. His mind wasn't right. I never knew him to do something stupid like this but let's face it, this could have been much worse. And, he could have kept doing it, since he didn't know right from wrong n' all. You might have saved more than just Helen. Boofer is in a better place now, where he can't hurt no one."

Twigs seems to settle down. The ambulance and coroner arrive shortly after to take the body. Once they are gone, the cop asks us for our phone numbers and he calls our parents to come to the firehall. They tell us to get into the police car to go there. My dad is going to kill me!

37

When we arrive, our parents are already there. Mom grabs me, "Thank God you are okay."

Dad hugs me and whispers in my ear. "We'll talk about this later."

Helen's dad rushes up to her and throws his arms around her. "I'm sorry, Dad!" she sobs. "Can I come home?"

"Of course, you can. I'm gonna be better, Helen. You'll see! I'm gonna throw the damn bottle away!"

"Where's Uncle Kiser?" she asks, looking around.

"Your Uncle Kiser done got himself murdered, honey. Someone was mad at him about something I suppose."

Helen starts to cry. "Murdered? Poor Uncle Kiser." Her dad rubs her back as she cries into his shoulder.

We are all asked to sit down at a long table.

Twigs sits down. He is quiet. He has his hands on the table as if he is praying. His mother caresses his arm. Jax sits between her parents, and lays her head on her mother's shoulder. She looks exhausted. We all are.

The cops sit down to describe what happened. I feel my dad glaring at me. Oh Lord, I'm in trouble!

It was a short ride home in silence. As we enter the house Dad orders me, "Get ready for bed."

I was glad to run up the stairs out of his sight. Ten minutes later he is sitting on my bed, staring at me. Mom is with him. "Do you know what danger you put yourself in today, Sophie?"

I'm playing with the silky edge of my blanket and I keep my head down. "I know."

Dad leans on my bed and gets his face in front of mine. "I don't know what to do with you!"

I start to cry. He puts his arms around me. "It's okay, honey. I know you meant well. But, you don't seem to understand dangerous situations. That is what scares me. I can't bear to think of something happening to you!"

"I'll try to be better, Dad. Really I will!"

"You saved a girl today and I am proud of you. But, if you had come to me first, I would have been there with you. You must promise me you will not disobey me again, or you cannot go to Numine."

Not go to Numine? Oh no! "I won't ever disobey you again, Dad. I promise!"

I cuddle into a threesome hug with him and Mom.

Now I must hope that little voice in my head that makes me do things will shut-up.

CHAPTER SIX
NONNA
December 1958

Summer passed into fall and fall into winter.

Helen's dad got sober and he and Helen moved into Kiser's farm.

Everyone in town called Twigs, Jax and me heroes, but we didn't feel like we were heroes.

I can't quit thinking about Kiser. "Dad, how can it be they can't find the man who killed that Mr. Wilson?"

"Murders are hard to solve, Sophie. They might have some ideas, but they can't arrest anyone without hard evidence. I hear all they've got so far is a boot print in the blood. Size ten they think, with one of the treads missing."

"That doesn't seem right to me. Go to every guy in town with a size ten boot and see if it fits! Just like they did in Cinderella. Why not?"

"This isn't Cinderella, Sophie. There's lots of people working on it. We are all just spokes on a wheel. Just spokes on a wheel. Quit worrying!"

"Spokes on a wheel means what, Dad?"

He laughs and walks away.

It is a cold winter day today. I like winter. Most people tell me that is odd. I'm odd, I guess. I love the feel of my feet in warm boots and a hat on my head snuggled under the tight hood of my coat. I love my hands sliding into warm mittens. Mom calls it my cocoon.

Today we are going to visit Nonna. She lives above the car garage, that Zio Dom owns. Dad used to work at the car garage when we were small, but he quit there for a better job at a carbide company.

Dutch, Julia and I are invited for supper. We head out the door and down the steps. It is cold, but I am warm in my little cocoon of clothing. We cut down through the Stefancik yard, then across Boggio's sidewalk. Mr. Boggio is getting into his car. "Hey, girls!" He chimes. The kind of chime that needs only a hand wave. The next house is Plazarin's and looking across the yard, I can see Mrs. Bell at her kitchen sink through the window. She doesn't see us. We cross the street, just as Mrs. Krecota reaches out her door for the newspaper lying on her step. "Where you going, girls?"

"To see Nonna!" This is life, living in a small town. Everyone wants to know what you are doing.

On Main Street, at Jack Boyer's place, we cross over the road. To our right is the Pennsylvania State Liquor Store. Bottles of alcohol line every shelf. On the top shelf are cool decanters. The business they get from this town is amazing, for a small town. Lots of people drink. Maybe people drink in every town, but I wouldn't know. I've never been further than Numine.

The guy who works in the State Store is a small fellow with a limp and a handlebar mustache. He isn't very friendly, but today he waves at us through the big window as we pass. Mr. Kulick is just getting in his car. "Hey, girls! Going to visit your Nonna?"

"Yep!" I holler and wave a quick goodbye, putting a skip into my step. Nonna's place is next. She is an old Italian woman with broken English. She is very short. Her face is wrinkled and she has crooked fingers.

It is mid-afternoon as we enter the beaten wooden door to the narrow stairs going straight up. We can smell the garlic cooking. The aroma drifts into my nostrils as my tastebuds stand at attention.

We kick off our boots inside the door and hang our coats on the hook. Up the stairs we go, me in the lead. I always count the steps as I go up. One, two, three, all the way to twelve, and I am there. The linoleum in front of me is black with a diamond shape here and there. I like to make the diamonds my stepping stones as I turn right into her kitchen. Her back is to us as she stirs a pot on the stove. Her stained white apron is tied around her waist. Her thin gray hair is tied neatly in a bun. Her cotton socks are rolled down to her old lady shoes. She didn't hear us coming. "Hi, Nonna!" I am hoping I don't scare her, but I kind of did.

"Ah, mama mia!" She exclaims as she throws her arms around us. "Mio Bambinos!" She hugs us as she always does, stroking our cheeks and running her hand across our hair. She secretes love like the steam rolling out of a locomotive.

"Ciao, bambinos?"

Dutch corrects her. "You say 'hello' Nonna! Use your English!"

She laughs, "Hello, my-eh babies!" She tries so hard, but her English is not very good.

Julia smells the pot. "Whatcha cooking?" Everything she cooks smells good.

"Risotta, tesoro!" She smiles and pauses. "Excuse-eh me. Risotta, darling!"

"Good job, Nonna!" I grab a spoon and I taste the gravy she has made from tiny chunks of veal. "Ummm, delicious!" She grins. She is very proud of her good cooking.

"Where's Nonno?" Dutch asks.

"In-eh da wine-eh cellar makin' his-eh wine-eh."

Our Nonno, Giuseppe, is a wine maker. He is an odd fellow, with a purplish red nose. The skin on his nose is funny looking too. It has craters like on the moon. He always wears a stained white shirt and dark green pants held up with thick suspenders. His big belly hangs over the front of his pants. He isn't warm and cuddly like Nonna is. He doesn't talk much. He just mostly grunts. Many times, when we come here, there are people sitting around his table drinking his wine. There is always money on the table. I asked Dad about that once. He said they call that a Speakeasy. Dad said that during the prohibition in the twenties, that the sale of liquor was prohibited, so people sold their liquor illegally out of their homes. He said they called them either a Speakeasy or a Blind Pig or Blind Tiger. I don't like to think that Nonno is doing something illegal. But it is 1958 now, so I suppose it is not illegal anymore since the prohibition is long over.

Nonna has a picture of my mother hanging on her wall. My mother is a baby in the picture. Zio Dom is beside her. He is only two. This is the only picture she has. There was never even a wedding picture, since they had run off to get married. So, I only know my mother as a baby. I always kiss my fingers, then touch the picture, giving my mother a kiss. It is the least I can do, since I don't remember her.

"Do you like my braids, Nonna?" As I turn them both up to display the ribbons at the ends. Nonna smiles and nods yes, then walks over the drawer of her trendle sewing machine. She comes out with bows that she made us out of her ribbons. She gives them to us with that big smile that her eyes wrinkle at the corners and her wrinkled cheeks rise-up to meet her eyes. Her skin is like onion skin paper, but it is soft. Very soft.

Her long crooked fingers hold the bows up to my braids. "You like?"

"Yes, Nonna. Thank you!" She is always giving us something. Never a big thing, just little things she has around. She doesn't go out much. She is one of those elderly Italian women who let their man run their life for them. Yet she loves her simple life living above the car garage.

Nonna does a puzzle with us before supper and we heartily eat the delicious risotto she has made.

Nonno never did come up out of the wine cellar. "Give Nonno a hug from us." Dutch tells her.

Nonna, as always, puts her hands on our cheeks and kisses each of us. "*Ti voglio bene.*" We don't correct her this time. We know that means *I LOVE YOU.*

We give her the everlasting hug that she loves, and we head down the stairs. When we reach the bottom, Zio Dom jumps out from behind a wall to scare us. I push him. "Stop that, Zio! You scared me!"

He picks me up and swings me around, as he starts to sing, "O sole mio, Sta 'nfronte a te, "O sole Mio..." and I wiggle out of his grasp.

"Gotta get home!" I scold him, but he just laughs. Dutch and Julia are already out the door. He is always singing, in his nasal voice with the smell of whiskey on his breath, but I like Zio Dom. He grabs my coat from the hook and helps me put it on, then hat, gloves and boots last. Back into my cocoon. Off I go, home to Yatesboro with my belly full and my bows in my pocket.

CHAPTER SEVEN
GOOD NEWS AND BAD
January 1959

The school bus brings us right to our front door. I am in fourth grade already.

Today, as we arrive home, Mom and Dad are dancing together in the kitchen. Dad is singing to her. "In The Still of the Night, I held you, held you tight." They are often dancing or kissing when we arrive home. They stop as they see us enter. Dad's grin is a mile wide. "Did you all have a good day?"

Ruby throws her books onto the kitchen table. "I got an A plus on that Science project I did."

Dad laughs. "Like that surprises us!" Ruby gets all A's, all the time. Ruby will graduate in May. She is the smartest in her class.

Mom stands up. "Come on in, we want to talk to you."

We all grab a chair at the table. Sammy jumps onto Ruby's lap.

Dad takes Mom's hands. "We have a big surprise for you. Are you ready?"

They play such silly games. "We're ready!" I say, playing along.

Dad's grin I think will break his face. "You are going to have a little brother or sister in a few months."

Ruby looks shocked. "A baby?"

Mom answers. "Yep, a baby!"

"That will be a lot of kids!" I'm sorry as soon as I say it. I don't know why I did.

"Shut-up, Sophie!" Dutch scolds me.

Dutch, Julia and I share a room and I had always hoped to get my own room. That won't happen now.

"I always wanted a big family." Mom chimes, as Dad hugs her as she cuddles into his chest.

We chat about the new baby through supper and Ruby talks about getting the basinett out of storage. Mom and Dad are beaming and I suppose that is what is important. It is obviously not too many kids for them.

The sun is beginning its slow descent and the sky is a swirl of muted colors. "Can I go to Debra's to tell her about the baby?"

"You can go, but come right back, Sophie!" Dad gives me that eye of mistrust.

"Okay!" I laugh as I get my cocoon on and run out the door. I run down the street and pass the Kuchar house. Mr. Whitacre across the street is shoveling his walk. "Hey, Sophie!"

"Hey, Mr. Whitacre!" When I see Mr. Whitacre, I always get sad, because he lost a son, Arthur. His boy was just young, probably around my age now, when he fell off the Yatesboro baseball stadium roof and died years ago. His boy would be probably close to thirty-years-old now, had he lived. Mom told me about it. She was there. She said it is something she will never forget. I feel so bad for Mr. Whitacre, but I try to push it out of my head and keep moving. If I don't, I'll be too sad to go to Debra's.

Passing the Wisilko house, I cross the road to the Dodds house. I am there.

Debra is a good friend. She is taller than me and one year younger. I am jealous of her hair. It is brown and thick. She usually wears it in a ponytail and she always looks pretty. I told Dad just last week that I was jealous of her hair. His answer was, "A rising tide lifts all boats." I asked him what that meant. He just said "No room for envy! Be envious of none!"

I skip up the back wooden stairs to the old screen door. Knock, Knock, Knock. "Debra, you there?"

She comes from the living room. "Hey Sophie! Come on in!"

Krissy is here with Susie Carenini. Krissy lives next to Susie in Rose Valley. She is twelve, and she often walks up the hill with Susie when she comes here. Susie is an older Italian woman, and is a good friend to Mrs. Dodds. Susie is in the kitchen helping Mrs. Dodds with dishes. From the living room record player Paul Anka is singing Put your head on my shoulder, hold me in your arms, baby, squeeze me oh-so-tight. Debra picks up the arm on the record player to stop the music. "What's up, Sophie?"

"Mom's having another baby!" I cheerfully spout.

"That is wonderful, Sophie! And you'll be able to help now that you are older."

I hadn't thought about that. I don't really want to help. I like being with my friends. Julia and Dutch can help. But I answer. "I guess so."

Just then we hear "Oh my God!" We look towards the kitchen. A water glass is attached to Susie's hand, with a dishcloth inside the glass surrounding her hand. She was cleaning the glass with the dishcloth and her hand got stuck in the glass. "Mama Mia!!" She is trying to laugh but I think she is scared. Debra's mom takes her to the sink and squirts dish soap all over. With the soapy water she tries to release the glass. No luck. She takes a tiny hammer out of the drawer. She lays Susie's hand on the counter with the glass on her hand and tap, tap, tap. The glass breaks, no harm done to Susie. It all happened so fast. There was no time to be scared. Susie laughed when it was all over. "Oh, mama mia! I thought the dish soap would work, but not to be!"

I am still rather amazed at what just happened. "Dish soap is good for everything! Mom lets me put it in my bath water."

Susie looks at me with wide eyes. "Oh no! No, bambino! Don't put it in the bath! The soap will get in your vagina!"

Deb and Krissy start laughing and Krissy is holding her legs close together like she is peeing her pants. I am not laughing. Does she mean my hoo-chee? It will get in my hoo-chee? I am worried. I used dish soap last night in my bath! I am scared. I start to run out the door.

I hear Debra holler, "Sophie, where you going?"

I am near tears as I holler back, "Gotta get home and tell Mom there's dish soap in my hoo-chee!"

CHAPTER EIGHT
AUNT INA
April and May 1959

I never put dish soap in my bath water again, even though Mom assured me it didn't get into my hoo-chee. When we visit Nonna the next day, I tell her about what Susie Carenini said. Since Nonna is Italian like Susie, maybe there IS something about dish soap we *mixed breeds* don't know. Nonna will know.

Nonna just laughs. "Dat Susie is just-eh foolin' you-eh, bambino. She always'eh talk'eh like'eh dat." I felt better knowing that. I kiss my fingers and touched my mother's picture. "Your mama was-eh pretty baby, no?" Nonna has tears in her eyes.

"As pretty as YOU, Nonna!" That made her laugh.

She lets us help mix up a cake and put it in the oven. "Dis-a for you!"

She makes me smile. "We'll be back tomorrow to eat some. Okay, Nonna?"

Nonna nods yes and opens a kitchen drawer, and after a little digging, she gives Dutch, Julia and me three quarters each.

"Thank you, Nonna!" I kiss her, then Dutch and Julia do. She loves her kisses.

She grabs each of our cheeks as she always does. "Ti voglio bene!"

My quarters go into my pink piggy bank before I crawl into bed. I say my prayers out loud as I lay in my bed. "God, please take care of me. Thank you. Amen."

Julia and Dutch sleep in the double bed beside me. "That's pitiful!" Julia says.

Dutch nudges her. "Let it go, Julia!"

"What's wrong with it? What do you want me to ask for, Julia!"

"You're supposed to ask him to take care of ALL of us, not just you! The food you eat, your health, your warm house, just whatever! And you don't end with THANK YOU! REALLY!"

I jump across my bed onto hers and start pulling her hair. She squeals like a baby.

Dad comes rushing in. "What's going on?"

I tell him what Julia said, and he chuckles. "We all have our own way of praying, Julia. Not one way is any more correct than the other. Now go to sleep!" We quickly crawl under our blankets and do as he said.

******

In the morning, it is a beautiful spring day and the birds are singing. It is easy to get ready for school with music in the air, if I can get past wanting to hit Julia. Surprisingly enough, before we head out the door, she mutters, "I'm sorry."

"Forget about it." I grab my lunch box and brush past her. "I'm walking to school today!"

51

She quickly catches up with me. As we pass our church on Main Street, Yatesboro Presbyterian, she asks me if I knew that the church had burned down in 1943 and this was a new one.

"No, I didn't know. So what?"

She is chirping a mile a minute trying to make up for last night I suppose. "Well, Mom told me all about it. Rev. Homer Becker was our preacher then. Him and his wife, Magdalena, lived in the house right next to it, where Freda lives now. The day it burned, Rev. Becker was in the office running the mimeograph machine and he smelled the smoke. They figured the coal furnace caused it."

I answer politely. "Don't suppose they could have saved it. It would have been awfully old wood."

"'Suppose so." Julia jumps over each crack in the sidewalk. "Step on a crack, break your mother's back. Step on a nail, put our dad in jail! Hey, Sophie, you know how Catholic kids are always telling us *'this is a sin'* and *'that is a sin'* and that only Catholics are going to heaven?"

I look at her puzzled. "So, we're not going to heaven? I never knew that!"

"It's just them that says that. Don't worry. We are going to heaven! But last Saturday I took my Catholic friend, Rita, into our church while Mom was packing something up from the Sunday School room. Rita asked me where the kneelers were. I told her we didn't kneel, and she quickly told me that is why Protestants aren't going to heaven."

"That's a mean thing to say!"

Just then a group of kids join us on our walk up the street. Most are Catholics. The oldest boy is three years older than Julia, so he is thirteen.

In front of Kathy Samson's house, a frog jumps across the sidewalk in front of us and Julia goes after it. She picks it up, looks at its face, and lets it go, as she starts to read writing on the sidewalk that it has just hopped across. The first letter is an F. The next letter is a U, then a C, and the last letter is hard to read, but it looks like a K. Julia looks at me. "What does that mean?"

The oldest Catholic boy in front of us stops walking and turns around. "That word is a sin! If you say it, you will go to hell!"

Julia leans over to me. "Here we go again." She looks back at him. "Well, it says F***! Then she proceeds to holler. "F***, F***, F***, F***! You SEE? I said it five times and I didn't go to hell!"

The other kids put their hands over their mouths and ran the rest of the way.

The oldest boy stays his same pace but curtly tells Julia, "Wait 'til your mom finds out about this!"

It was after dinner that Mom got the call, from his mom. "Your daughter has a dirty mouth. She used a nasty word in front of a bunch of kids!"

"What was the word?" Mom asks.

"It has four letters and begins with an 'f' and ends with a 'k'."

"Thanks for calling. I will deal with this." Mom hangs up.

Mom puts her hands on the table glaring at Julia. "Do you have something to tell me, Julia? About a dirty word?"

"Oh, for heaven's sake, Mom. I only said it because those Catholic kids told me I'd go to hell if I said it. I was just proving a point. Do you think I'll go to hell?"

"No, you won't go to hell, Julia. But I don't want you using that word. You will apologize to the kids you were with! Do you understand?"

"Apologize, Mom? That's not fair! They shouldn't be telling us we aren't going to heaven!"

"I know that bothers you honey, but trust me. You are going to heaven. We all are!" she returns to the sink.

Julia leans over to me and whispers. "You see, those Catholic kids don't know what the f*** they are talking about!"

Oh Lord!

******

In the evenings, sometimes, we visit Aunt Ina, Mom's sister. She lives across the street. Mom's other sister, Aunt Dee, used to live there too, but moved to Erie when she got married four years ago. Aunt Dee has three kids already. BANG, BANG, BANG! Three kids! That's a lot of kids in four years!

I've got two uncles. Uncle Doug lives here with his daughter, Red. I never knew his wife, she left long ago. Red is seven now. Her name is Melissa. She has red hair and freckles, so we call her Red. My Uncle Sid lives on this street too with his wife, Annabelle. They had only one daughter, Annie. She is the same age as Red. My Aunt Bella lives across the street, with her husband and three kids. Aunt Bella is funny. She teaches us naughty songs. Aunt Ina hollers at her for it, but luckily Aunt Bella doesn't listen. We like learning her songs.

As we walk into Aunt Ina's we know to be quiet, as she is watching The Lawrence Welk Show. Red, Julia, Annie and I play Buttony Button on the upstairs. "Buttony, Button, who's got the button?"

Mom enjoys watching Lawrence Welk with her. As soon as it is over, and the bubbles fly, the chatter begins.

Aunt Bella just came in the door. She brought her famous German Chocolate cake. Aunt Bella is so darn skinny, she needs to eat some of that cake! She smokes too. She has a funny way about her. I just laugh at her when she talks. She looks serious tonight. "You know they still didn't catch that S-O-B that killed that guy in Numine yet?"

"It's been more than a year now. Doubt they'll find him at this point," Aunt Ina replies.

"Oh, I don't know about that. I've heard of them catching a criminal years later," Mom said. "I heard they had a boot print, and some other clues, but I don't know what."

That intrigues me. What could the clues be? Did Kiser make somebody mad?

"Did you hear that Buddy Holly was killed today in a plane crash?" Aunt Bella asks.

55

"Who's that?" Aunt Ina asks.

"You don't know his music? *Well, that'll be the day, when you say goodbye, Yes, that'll be the day, when you make me cry........,*"

"Guess I'm getting old," Aunt Ina replies.

Aunt Bella is a wealth of information. "Ina, do you watch the news? Do you even know that Alaska was admitted as our 49th state not long ago?" Aunt Bella is rather smart.

"I'm not stupid, Bella!" Aunt Ina replies sternly.

That seems like boring unimportant information to me. "I'm not real interested in that stuff." I admit proudly.

Dutch doesn't like that I said that. "Sophie, you need to GET interested in what is going on in the world. Do you know that there is a war in Vietnam? You better pay attention. Someday Uncle Sam will hand you a gun and tell you to fight!"

That scares me. A war? Me fight? That war would never affect me. Why would she say that?

Aunt Ina seems worried as she stares at Mom. "You okay, Patsy?"

Mom is suddenly bent over. "That depends on what you mean by 'okay'. I think the baby is knocking at my door!"

"GO GET YOUR DAD!" Aunt Ina hollers.

I never saw Dad run so fast once we told him. He runs out the door and we follow. He falls at Mom's knees. "Relax, Sam," Mom tells him. "It will be okay, it is just TIME, that's all."

Aunt Ina gets her keys and purse and we all pile into her car to go to the hospital. Dad takes Mom in his own car. Mom is whisked away in a wheelchair and Dad goes with her. We are all so nervous and Ruby won't sit down. She paces the floor as we three girls and Sammy cuddle ourselves into chairs in the waiting room and fall asleep.

Theo came into the world near midnight. We were all sleeping when Dad woke us up to tell us.

"How big is he? What did he weigh? Does he have hair?" Dutch and Julia are firing questions at him.

Dad is beaming and half crying. "He was 7 lb. 1 oz. and just a bit of hair. We named him Theodore James, but we will call him Theo. Mom is good. She was a champ!"

Dad brought Mom and Theo home three days later. Ruby and Aunt Ina took care of us until they got home. We finished getting Theo's bassinet ready and Aunt Ina helped us make a cake to celebrate Theo's arrival.

We swarmed him like a hoard of bees when they got home. Mom and Dad had to pull him away from us at dinnertime.

A knock just came to the door. When I open it, there are four men standing there. Al Passerini, Sonny Avi, Gene Hockenberry, and J. J. Maffei. They are the quartet that sings at Avi's and at the Community Building. They do Minstrel shows, Gay Nineties, and Roaring Twenties. Dad went along with them once when they sang at Deshaun Hospital for the wounded veterans. Elaine Updyke directs them.

Sonny speaks up, "Hi Sophie. Will you please tell your dad we are here to serenade you all. We owe him one!"

I know why. Not long ago these men were on their way home from singing somewhere and stopped at a bar where there was a band. At intermission they got up and sang. The people there liked them so much, that they started buying them drinks. After an hour of that, none of them could drive home. They called Dad to come get them. It was an hour drive, but he did it.

They begin to sing to us as we gather to listen. First, they sing *Till The End of Time,* then *Sentimental Journey.* Their last song is *I Only Have Eyes for You.*

When they are done, they hand Dad a fifth of whiskey. "Here, you are going to need this." Dad just laughed.

I think to myself, *Yep, you are going to need it. You've got a lot of kids!*

******

A month later Ruby graduates. The graduation ceremony is in the Community Building and Mom cradles Theo as I try to keep Sammy entertained.

Ruby is valedictorian of her class. The Community Building is decorated in maroon and white. Under her maroon graduation gown, she is wearing a white dress she bought just for graduation. Dad and Mom are proud as punch as she does her speech. She then walks across the stage for her diploma. I look at Dad and Mom. They are both crying.

Ruby's old boyfriend, Michael is here. He went off to college last year and broke up with her. He told her he wanted his freedom. She cried a long time but got over it. She is interested now in what other *fish are in the sea*.

Michael congratulated her afterwards and left with his friends. She didn't care.

Dad gave Ruby a bracelet with a little heart attached. He told her that he gave the same bracelet to Mom on her graduation day. Ruby loved it. She got a scholarship for college and will be leaving us. I don't like to think about that. I will really miss Ruby.

******

Three days later, we are at the Memorial Day Parade in Rural Valley. I decorated my bike to ride in the parade. So did Julia. I love the parade. The high school band leads the parade and I especially like hearing the drums. Even when the band isn't belting out music, the drums still do their rat-a-tat-tat, rat-a-tat-tat.

We end up at the American Legion for a program. Everyone goes there, and listens to a speech that is usually too long but no one cares that it is. A wreath is placed in honor of all who died in war, by a gold star mother. She is a mother who lost her son in war. People are quiet. It is important.

When it is over, everyone buys barbequed chicken to eat that the Legion is making. We kids get a pop and chips, for taking part in the parade. I love patriotism. I think I will be a patriot someday. Yes, while Julia is off saving people somewhere, I'll be a patriot!

Memorial Day Parade at Legion in 1965

A SVHS Graduating class entering the Community Building (Gym)

CHAPTER NINE
FRIGID COLD
January 1960

Christmas was a little frantic this year because of some of Mom's old friends. They've all got odd names, Slick, Husker, Tubby and Utz. On Christmas Eve, they were out drinking all night and came into our house at 2 a.m. ringing bells. They dragged us out of bed to see what Santa brought. They woke the baby too. Dad laughed, but Mom didn't. She scolded all of them, but they just laughed. Tubby could hardly stand up. "Ah, come on, Patsy, have some fun!"

I think Mom wanted to hit them, but she didn't. She was mad at Dad for laughing at them. They kept tickling us and finding packages for us to open. I thought they were funny. We didn't mind, only Mom did.

Dad spent Christmas Day making it up to her. He made her take a nap, like the rest of us. I think Mom was glad when Christmas was over. By New Year's Eve she took all the decorations down.

******

January came in like a lion. The coal furnace is constantly at work. We all take turns shoveling coal but Dad does most of it. Last night he had popsicle sticks taped to his fingers, because they were all cracked from shoveling so much coal.

The walk to Nonna's house seems long when it is so cold outside, but we try to go once a week. It makes her happy. Today, Nonno has five men around the table playing poker and drinking his wine, that they pay for. We give Nonno a kiss. He simply leans down for us to kiss him and grunts. It is a loving grunt, though. That is what he does. We know he loves us. We don't stay long. Just long enough to hug Nonna, eat a piece of cake with her, and kiss my mother's picture

Once home, Julia gets knee deep into listening to news about *The Freedom Riders* in North Carolina. They took a lot of crap when they tried to use whites' only restrooms and lunch counters at bus stations in the southern states, but they drew international attention to the civil rights movement. She is real sensitive about the rights of others and hates how some are so mistreated. She is always obsessing about something.

"Read this book, Sophie!" She hands me a small book with kids and a train car on the cover. On the front it says THE BOXCAR CHILDREN in yellow letters.

"Why? I don't like to read!"

"Oh, for heaven's sake! Are you going to be stupid ALL your life? Read it! It's about these poor orphaned kids that stick together, living in a boxcar."

Now I know why she likes it. She is always drawn to the disadvantaged. I'll read it, but I'll never let her know if I liked it or not.

Last March, Hawaii became our 50th state, and the Salk polio vaccine came out. It is better than the first one they say. I'm trying to listen to the news more, so Julia doesn't call me stupid.

THE BOXCAR CHILDREN by Gertude Chandler Warner

Monday comes, and I walk to the elementary school under a heavy coat and snow pants. It is ten degrees this morning. On my head is a white furry hat Mom bought me with tassels hanging down both sides. Mom made me gray mittens for my hands. The snow crunches under my feet as I walk. Crunch, crunch, crunch.

My teacher, Mrs. Iker, greets us as we enter. She is a roly poly older lady with thinning hair. If she likes you, she does. If she doesn't, she doesn't. Some of the kids sing a song behind her back, "Iker, Iker, we don't like 'er." Dad told me he better never hear me singing that!

Otto Black came in off the bus from out in the country. I hate to stare at him, but I can't help it. He is skinny as a tick on a broom handle, and his eyes are always sad. His hair is chopped short like it was cut with garden scissors. He wears the same dirty white t-shirt with a flannel shirt over the top. It is so badly worn, there are holes on the elbows and the plaid is faint. He has on the same pants every day and they are never clean. He never smiles. He isn't even wearing a coat! I don't think he owns one. I look down at his shoes, they have holes in them, and no socks! I feel sorry for him. His family is so very poor.

"Where's your coat, Otto?" I ask.

He doesn't answer. He rarely talks much. He is puzzling!

At recess he goes out with the rest of us, no coat, and no socks. I didn't pay attention to him on the playground, but when we enter the school, I see everyone gathered around him, staring at him. He is slumped in the corner, on the floor, hugging his knees. He is crying. His skin is beet red and he is breathing hard. He is shivering.

Mrs. Iker starts pushing our desks together. "Come here, Otto." She helps him up. She lays him down on our desks. "Students, go get me all your coats!" She took all our coats and piled them on top of Otto. With her hanky she wipes the tears from his face.

As her hanky glides over his cheek, Otto hollers. "Ouch!"

She picks up her hanky. His cheek is black and blue. "Did you hurt yourself, Otto?"

"I fell," he whispers.

She removes his shoes and puts my mittens on his feet. On his head she puts my white furry hat. I'm not sure I like that she did that, but I look at poor Otto lying there, so very cold. My heart breaks for him. He will be okay now. He drifts off to sleep, as we do our spelling on the blackboard. The bell rings for dismissal. Mrs. Iker put her own woolen coat sweater on him to go home. For socks, she took off her own socks to put onto his feet under his worn-out shoes. Maybe now kids will start singing, *Iker, Iker, we really like'er.* They should.

Otto hands me my mittens. I push them back. "No, Otto, you wear those home."

He looks at me with his sad eyes, and takes them. Ray gave him his knit cap. I watch him go to his bus and slowly climb the stairs. I am so sad for him.

I run in my door from school. "Mom, Otto was so cold today. He had no coat, no socks, and no hat! He had nothing. I felt so bad. He cried! He was THAT cold!"

Mom stares at me? "Otto Black, you mean?"

"Yes, Mom. Do you know him? He was so cold! It was awful!"

"I know who you mean, honey."

"Can we do something to help him, Mom?"

I can see her thinking. "Dutch has an extra coat she doesn't like because it is black. Go get it in the upstairs closet. We'll take it to him tonight. I think I can find his place. They live out there in Owl Hollow."

Mom went through our sock drawers to take what we didn't need. We pitched in mittens, a scarf, and a knit cap. After dinner, I got in the car with Mom to take them to Otto. Dad is working late tonight.

Four miles up Route 85, we pass Shannock Bar and take a right into the country. "I'm pretty sure I know where it is." She whispers as we pass the Patterson house on the left, then Bohan's, and start up a narrow lane. On the right we pass a big barn with a farmhouse beside. "This is Kiser

65

Wilson's place. You know that his brother and Helen moved into it, don't you?"

"Yes, I knew they did. The kids said Helen is going to beauty school now."

"Good for her! I'm so glad her dad got himself straightened out."

I look at the big house. A shovel leans against the barn and an old tractor sits, covered with snow. Kiser was just a farmer. An innocent old farmer. How could someone kill him? What could he have done to make someone that angry?

Mom keeps driving straight on the narrow dirt lane. It winds slightly up a hill. Her eyes are squinting trying to see out the windshield. The snow is coming down hard and the wipers are swooshing back and forth. The moon is full. Full moons scare me. They are an omen. They can foretell the future.

She leans towards the windshield. "There used to be a farm here where we got milk when we were kids, Sophie. We'll find it."

Slowly we go, sliding now and then on the slippery lane, wipers back and forth, back, and forth. Suddenly, we can faintly see through the white snow a wooden shack. We stop. We are in the middle of nowhere, looking at hell. The roof of the shack is covered with moss. It is two stories, and I see only two windows, one up and one down. A dim light glows in the upstairs window. The porch steps are rotting as well as the porch floor. A wooden fence crosses the yard, tilted and in disrepair. There is an old shed, or more of a lean-to. Wood is stacked under it. Smoke is coming from a chimney that is crumbling. There are old vehicles sitting around with no wheels on. Beside the shack, under some pine trees, there is a school bus. Kind of, but it is blue instead of yellow. The blue paint is chipping off and weeds are grown over the wheels. A refrigerator sits in the snow. Across the yard to the left is an old barn. There are chicken feet attached to the barn doors, and deer horns all over the front. It's creepy looking. A well with a bucket attached is several feet in front of us. I can hear a dog barking.

Mom and I are staring. Her hands fasten tightly around the steering wheel. I look over at her. Her knuckles are white and her eyes are wide. As she looks back at me, I can see beyond her out her side window, a man coming towards her carrying a pipe wrench. I scream. At the same time, TAP, TAP, TAP. He hits her window with the wrench. Mom jumps a mile. She opens her window only an inch.

He is dirty. His teeth are yellow as an old dog's teeth. His denim jacket is filthy, and torn in several places. His brown coveralls are dirty and ragged. I recognize him. He works at Doc Crawford's garage in Numine. His name is Dastard Black. We passed there once and he was under a car. When we passed and he saw us, he came out from under the car. He glared at us. He scared me. We asked Doc Crawford about him. "His name is Dastard Black, and you pay no mind to him. He's not a nice fella. He lives out in the woods yonder with that boy of his."

Doc Crawford's Garage in Numine

Dastard is glaring at Mom. "What you are you doing here?" He asks sternly through the window.

Mom opens her window only slightly. "We brought some winter clothes for Otto. Would you take them to him please?" I can tell by her voice she is scared. The hair on my arms is standing on end. I can't breathe.

"Give them here!" He says abruptly and unappreciatively.

Mom reaches to the back seat for the bags, opens the door, drops them, and shuts the door quickly. He bent over and picked them up.

He looks so mean. He doesn't say thank you. "Now you need to git outa here!" As he turns, I see the line down the side of his face. A scar. From a knife I suppose. I look over at the shack. An old man comes out the door. He is on a cane and he looks filthy. He spits over the side of the porch and glares at us.

Mom backs the car out of the lane. I watch Dastard staring at us, standing there like a ghoul, the snow falling around him. He has a firm grip on the wrench, that I'm sure wasn't meant for fixing something.

"I'm scared, Mom."

"It's okay, Sophie. We'll be okay."

"But what about Otto? He'll never be okay." I start to cry.

Mom is troubled too. "Don't cry, Sophie. Something is plumb out of kilter here. We know that for sure. Just pray for Otto. Just pray."

At home I go to my room and try to understand what I just saw. I look out my window and see a shooting star across the sky in a brilliant streak of white. Is that a good sign? Or is it an omen, like a full moon is?

I try hard to forget about what happened, but, I can't. I am so worried about Otto.

******

At school the next day, I look for him. He isn't here. I have a hard time concentrating. My teacher stops me as we are leaving our room for lunch. "Are you okay, Sophie? You seem troubled today."

"I'm worried about Otto, Mrs. Iker. He isn't here today."

"Don't worry, honey. I am sure Otto is okay."

I don't agree with that. How could he possibly be okay? I keep walking towards the cafeteria. It seems like a

long way today. I am walking around like everything's fine,
but deep down inside my shoe, my sock is sliding off.

CHAPTER TEN
A TROUBLED SOUL
March of 1960

Two days later, Otto showed up for school. He handed me my mittens. "Here. Thanks." Is all he said, with his head down.

"Anytime, Otto! Are you okay?"

He doesn't answer. I am glad that he wears the winter clothes we took him. At least he is warm now. I want to get to know him. I hand him a cookie that I took from our cookie jar at home. "Here, Otto. Mom made these. They are really good."

"Thanks." He reaches for it.

I see the bruise on his left eye. "What happened, Otto?"

"Nothing."

"When we brought those clothes out to your house, I saw your Grandpap. Does he live with you?"

"Yep. He isn't worth the whiskey he drinks."

"I heard a dog barking. You have a dog?"

"Yep, Thor. Just a pup."

"Where'd you get him?"

"Someone left him off out in the woods."

"They left him off? How do you mean?"

"It's what people do, when they don't want their dog."

"That's awful, Otto. I'm glad you found him."

"Yep. He's the only friend I got."

"That's not true, Otto. I'm your friend!"

A faint smile tried to emerge on his face. "Okay, then."

"Are you okay out there, Otto? I mean REALLY okay?"

"I'm no pansy!"

"Didn't say you were, Otto. I just need to know you are okay. You can talk to me. Share your troubles with me. My Dad always says that a trouble shared is a trouble halved."

He doesn't answer. He puts his head down and opens his book. Someday I am going to get through to him. I know I am. He is troubled. A troubled soul.

I asked Jax to come down to Rural Valley after school. Her dad brought her just after Numine school let out. It is a decent day, for March, so we walk to the school. There are teenagers hanging out on the steps. No room for us, so we move on.

Teens on the gym steps

As we walk up Main Street, I try to explain to her how it looked years ago. Passing the building across from the Rural Valley Elementary School, the sign still hangs on the door RURAL VALLEY ADVANCE, though closed now.

"This was our newspaper in Rural Valley. It closed down years ago."

"You had a newspaper?"

"Sure did. H.O. Peters and his wife, Alice, owned it." On the left window is: RURAL VALLEY ADVANCE and on the right window is JOB PRINTING & ADVERTISING. "Mom told me they had a Dalmatian dog named Sport, too."

"A newspaper in little Rural Valley, ain't that somethin'." Jax chuckles.

"Their daughter, Leota and her husband, Earl Whiteman, opened a printing shop up past where Kay Schrecengost lives. They did stuff like advertising, and printing stuff for Dayton Fair. It is torn down now."

"Too bad things don't stay the same way. Changes. Always changes," Jax says as she skips through someone's hopscotch.

To our right is an empty lot. "There used to be a *Five and Dime* right here."

"A *Five and Dime* in Rural Valley? That would be neat, Sophie."

"Long gone before I ever knew it."

She looks across the street at the *Broad Hotel*. "Does anybody stay in that hotel?" She asks.

"I suppose they do. It used to be the *St. James Hotel*. Mom said her parents used to work there when she was young. Mrs. Dean lives right there in that red brick house next to it."

We cross over the Main Street to Chuck Moore's Grocery Store. At the counter he keeps all his penny candy. We treat ourselves to two pieces each, and head back across Main Street passing the *Rural Valley Bank* and *Abe Cohen Clothing Store.*

We are at the Lias house. We can hear someone playing the piano as we pass. "Dale and Ruth Lias have a lot of kids. Used to be thirteen of them, but now twelve."

"Why twelve now? What happened?"

"They had a brother, Jimmy. He was the third child. His real name was James Carl. He was only three when he was killed running across the street, right in front of their house, years ago. A car hit him. He was coming home from Sunday School and saw his Uncle Jimmy on his front porch across the street. Poor little fella. I suppose he wasn't old enough to look first, and at three I suppose he ran like the wind away from his siblings. It was twelve years before I was born. He'd be in his twenties now, if he had lived I mean."

"Oh no!" Jax is troubled. She is like me; I soak in tragedies like I am a sponge. "How horrible!"

I get quiet. I feel a lump coming up into my throat just thinking about how horrible that would have been.

I need to change the subject for that lump to go back down my throat. "The rest of the street has changed somewhat. There used to be a shoe store here and the Post Office." When we reach the alley, we are at King's Rexall

Drug Store, then Carson's Funeral Home. "Used to be a grocery store fit in here called Beer's Market."

"Changes, changes, and more changes." Jax surmises.

"Yep. Dad says things seep away like water into sand." I hop over a colony of tiny ants.

"And do you remember I showed you where Cowanshannock Twp. High School used to be in Yatesboro, by the Catholic Church, right?" I ask her.

"I remember, what about it?"

"Well, I guess that when they changed its name to Shannock Valley High School in 1947, that kids from Plumville came down to high school there. Yatesboro colors were orange and black and the Plumville kids was green and white. So, they had to vote. They settled on Maroon and White for the colors. That's the colors we still have now in high school. I think this stuff is interesting, don't you?"

"I suppose." She answers politely but I know she is not as interested as I am.

Cownashannock High School (St. Mary's Church Hall now)

"And back in the day, there was coal and iron police here in Rural Valley and Yatesboro. They patrolled the streets for the coal and iron companies. Nobody could be on the streets after dark."

"Why?" she asks.

"To keep unions from forming. I guess they figured unions were a bad thing. Don't ask me!"

We came to the building on our right, *Valley Service and Supply.* "They sell Chrysler and Plymouths in here."

Darrell Rearick, one of the owners, is sweeping outside. "Hey girls!"

"Hey, Mr. Rearick!" I reply. I can see his wife Mildred through the window sitting at the cash register. She waves. We cross over the street to the next block.

"He's a nice man," I tell Jax. "His daughter, Carol, told me how she plays in there, going in and out of cars, pretending she is driving."

"You know a lot about a lot of stuff, Sophie."

Jax swirls around once and stops. "Hey, did you hear what Mrs. Hilliard's class in Numine did yesterday?"

"No. What happened?"

"Well, you know how we have to get under our desks when they blow the whistle? Well, Mrs. Hilliard had left the room and the whistle blew, but it was the whistle for school to end. She wasn't there to tell the kids, so they didn't know any better. That boy, Tom, hollered at all the kids to get under the desks. When Mrs. Hilliard walked back into her room, she found all the kids under their desks! They should have been on the school bus going home!"

"That's hilarious!" I laugh.

"Yeah, that Tom is funny. He lives right behind St. Gabriel's Catholic Church you know. Last Sunday, while the Catholics were having church, he kept bouncing a ball off the side of the church. He wasn't thinkin' about them in there havin' church, and all."

"What happened?"

"The Priest came out and rid him up one side and down the other. Tom was so scared; he ran in the house and told his mom he was sure he was going to hell!" She laughs. "I saw Tom just yesterday at Andy Beresnyak's Barbershop. I was a there with Dad. Anyways, Tom was tellin' Andy that he went with his dad to the Numine Hotel last week. His dad is a plasterer, you know."

"What did he go there for?" I ask.

They needed some plastering done. Well, anyways, this guy named Jim took Tom and his dad up to the room that needed the ceiling plastered. When they got there, Jim's boy was layin' right there in the bed sleepin'. Jim told them, "just do it, go ahead and plaster." so they did. Plastered that whole darn ceiling and that boy never woke up!"

I laugh. "That's funny. I don't think I know that boy, Tom."

"It was Tom that taught me how to drink Numine Water. You know that the water comes down over three rows of charcoal from a well at the top of that building sittin' over there before you get to the boney dump. Tom's been in there, watchin' it. He says when you drink the water, you drink, then exhale. Drink, then exhale."

"Good to know for when I'm in Numine, Jax!"

She laughs. "Tom's the one that told me to never go up Main Street when the rock fight was going on."

"Rock fight?"

"Yeah, there's three Bury Boys and four North boys and they are always in rock fights with each other!"

"Holy crap, Jax! Funny you never mentioned that!"

"Well, we ain't got hit with no rocks yet, did we?"

As we pass Rural Valley Bakery, we smell the aroma. It is a mixture of fresh dough, cinnamon, and brown sugar. I peek through the window. "You know, they say Mrs. Christoff stays up all night baking!"

"All night? That wouldn't be easy!"

Just then we see Mrs. Christoff motioning for us to come in. We walk inside. She hands us each a donut wrapped in a paper napkin. I smell it first. "Mmmmm, thank you, Mrs. Christoff!"

She just smiles. "You are very welcome!

Rural Valley Bakery

From there, we turn around and go all the way to Yatesboro, munching on our donuts. We go to Minnie Connell's candy and cigarette store. The big window on the front welcomes us with the array of colored candy stacked inside. As we enter, Hanni Swartz is at the counter. She is the *lady about town* Mom told me. I'm not sure what that means. Hanni wears the brightest red lipstick I've ever seen, and her hair is all piled on top of her head swirled into big curls. Her skirt is too short, and she smells of cheap cologne. She is here for cigarettes. We walk in and Hanni turns as she hears us. "Well, look at these two pretty girls!"

"Thank you." I reply. "You buying cigarettes?" Jax pushes me hard on my shoulder which means shut-up.

Hanni laughs, "Yes, darling. And for your information, you will probably smoke too someday!"

Minnie does NOT like her saying that to me. Minnie is a tiny woman with gray hair always covered with a hairnet. Right now, her face is red. She says rather sternly to me, "Sophie, If God wanted you to smoke, he would have put a smoke stack on your head!"

Hanni doesn't like that. "WHATEVER!" She turns on her heel and heads out the door.

She brushes shoulders with Mr. Beranti, who is coming in the door. "Excuuuuse me!" He says to her, seeing she is in a huff.

Minnie tells him what Hanni said to me and how she got mad. Mr. Beranti just laughs. "Don't worry about what that woman says or thinks. She lives right across the street from me you know. She thinks she is hot stuff! She stays out at night until stupid o'clock and she never bathes in the same lake twice!"

"What does that mean?" I ask. Minnie raises her eyebrows at Mr. Beranti. He doesn't answer.

Minnie laughs. "Well, girls, you might call Hanni a 'troubled soul' and that is all you need to know."

Once again, an adult conversation I am part of, but don't understand.

Rural Valley Advance Newspaper, Rural Valley

St. James Hotel Rural Valley   Later becoming the Broad Hotel

Rural Valley Bank on Main Street Rural Valley

Darrell Rearick at Valley Service & Supply, Rural Valley.

CHAPTER ELEVEN
BEST FRIENDS
April 1960

Mom sent me to the store for a loaf of bread. When I returned from Palilla's Market and put the bag on the table, Mom pulled out the bread, plus the Cracker Jacks I bought.

"Sophie, I sent you for just a loaf of bread, didn't I?"

"But, Mom, you have to know that the odds of going to the store for a loaf of bread and coming out with only a loaf of bread are three billion to one!"

Mom laughs, even though she is perturbed. She doesn't want me to eat sugar. Every day, Mom and Dad are insistent that I eat my vegetables too. I hate them. Mom works hard at convincing me. "You'll live longer if you eat right!"

"But, Mom, vegetables just don't smell as good as bacon!" She acts like she didn't like me saying that, but I could see her chuckle as she turns away. Dad is at the sink laughing as they kiss each other. They are always kissing! I really thought adults outgrow that stuff. I guess not.

I am going to Numine today after our visit to Nonna is done. Julia and Dutch are good about staying home helping Mom more than me. I'm afraid I might be lazy. Or maybe just too spirited, as Dad calls it. Sammy is seven now and Theo is one. I don't mind letting the girls entertain them, instead of me. I want to be with my friends.

Mom worries about my obsession with that.

"Sophie, you spend too much time worrying that you have lots of friends and that they all like you. You know, a friend to all is a friend to none." And that means what? Adults have the most unusual sayings.

There is a thin book on the table with the word SH-WAN-EE on the front. "What is that?" I ask.

"It's my yearbook from school. I graduated in 1948. Go ahead and look at it."

I pick it up and begin to go through it. "But I don't understand. Why does it say SH-WAN-EE on the front and not SHANNOCK VALLEY?"

"This is the Shwanee Valley, Sophie. Years and years ago, this area was inhabited by the Shwanee Indian Tribe. Now, I'm talking about a LONG time ago, centuries ago."

"Wow, that is interesting. What happened to them?"

"From what history I know, they farmed, fished, and hunted and lived in Wigwams, which were little round huts, not teepees like you would think. Legend has it that they left in the late 1700's."

"Why did they leave?"

"I suppose the white man chased them out, like they did all Native Americans. It is sad."

I am intrigued by this history. "Sad isn't a good enough word, Mom." She nods in agreement.

After lunch, Dad takes me to Numine, to Jax's house. Jax is on the porch waiting for me. "Let's go Sophie, I hear

Snuffy Smitt is with Shin today. They are sitting in front of the hotel. I want you to meet her."

Skipping down off her porch, it is a short trek to the hotel. There sits Shin and Snuffy. She is an odd-looking character. Very short, with a turned-up nose and rosy chubby cheeks. She has a babushka on her head. She is smoking and she has her own personal little brown paper bag with something in it. Jax goes right up to her. "Hey, Snuffy! This here is my friend, Sophie."

Snuffy looks me up and down. After a drag of her cigarette, she points towards Plumville way. "Fire in Beyer! Fire in Beyer!"

Jax had told me to expect odd conversation with Snuffy. "What do you mean?" I ask her.

"FIRE IN BEYER!" She says louder.

Shin grins. "She's just t-tryin' to t-tell ya there's a house on f-fire in B-Beyer. Ain't that r-right, honey?"

She nods her head up and down. "Fire in Beyer! Fire in Beyer!"

That was enough conversation for me. We head back to her house. Janet and Snooky are on the porch when we arrive. They are sisters. They are as funny as a barrel of monkeys rolling off an elephant's back. Snooky has black long hair and she never stops smiling. Janet is a year older than Snooky, and has brown short hair. She is an instigator. Janet was at the Numine show building last night for a movie. "Mr. Nagy showed his flashlight on me a hundred times in one movie!"

"That's funny!" I say, "Mr. Nagy in Rural Valley does the same thing!"

"You know we are talking about the same guy, don't you?"

I didn't know that but don't want to be stupid. "Of course, I know. He is a busy guy going between two show buildings!"

"Let's go to Oddi's Store!" Jax proposes. I hop down the porch steps with them and we skip up the street to Oddi's candy store. It is right beside Doc Crawford's service station.

The store smells of cinnamon as we enter. The two rows of shelves are loaded with sweet treats. Inside is a large man behind the counter with acne spotted skin and corn colored hair. There is a girl with him. She is young. Pretty, but poor looking. Her hair is unkempt and her slim build barely holds up the shift dress she is wearing. Probably a teenager who needed a job. She is at the cash register. Something about them doesn't feel right. Janet and Jax are busy searching the candy counter for sugary swirls. Snooky is at the bubblegum aisle. I am watching the man and the teenager. He says something to her. She turns away. He comes behind her whispering in her ear. She jerks her head away. I can see she is disgusted, and she is scared. He grabs her arm, then his other hand goes to her butt. She pulls away hard. I see her wince. He moves toward her again. The girl runs to the front of the counter where I am. I react to the man. "HEY, WHAT DO YOU THINK YOU ARE DOING!" Janet, Jax and Snooky are paying attention now.

He pauses momentarily. I am thinking hard how I can escape quickly. If he wants to hit me, he's got to get his big body over or around that counter and I could be out the door by then. But he doesn't come towards me. He stares with piercing eyes, "You better not mess with me, I'll have the Blackhands get you!"

I grab the teenager's hand. I holler, "RUN!" We run. I can hear him hollering at us, "You BETTER run!" We run a block or so, and fall onto the steps of the school house. The teenager is crying now. I feel so sorry for her. "You don't have to work with people like that, you know." I tell her.

She nods her head, "I know. I won't go back there. Thanks for saving me."

"What's your name?" I ask her. "Where do you live?"

"I live just over there." As she wipes her eyes and points. "I'm Chloe. Chloe Jensen."

Jax chimes in, "You are Alex Jensen's sister? I know him, he plays baseball."

"Yeah." She is calmer now. "Please don't tell my brother what happened. He'll get himself in trouble over it. I'm okay now. Gonna go home to mom. Thanks again." She leaves, and I watch her as she walks four doors over and enters a broken-down house. The wooden steps going up to it are tilted as the steps are at *The Bucket of Blood*. The porch is full of junk.

I am sad for her. She is a troubled soul, just like Otto.

I saw a bruise on Otto's face again yesterday. I asked him what happened. I got one word. "Nothin'." Mom tells me to just be his friend and not expect much in return. I am going to find a way to break through that wall he has up in front of him, even if it is brick by brick. I know I can!

CHAPTER TWELVE
LOSS BEYOND COMPREHENSION
May 2, 1960

A month goes by before I get back up to Jax's house. Snooky and Janet are here again. We sit on her big porch swing chatting, talking about the Beatles that we heard about from Liverpool, England.

"I saw their faces on the news. They are to die for! Especially Paul. And they are coming to the United States!" I tell them. "I heard them on the radio singing *I Want to Hold Your Hand*. I am obsessed with them!"

"From Liverpool, England? Wow!" Snooky is amazed.

"Yep, Liverpool! Let's go tell Peggy!" I propose.

Across from Jax lives the Doms family. They have lots of kids. Darla, Peggy, Paul, Debbie, and Butchie, the baby. When I go to Jax's, we all play together.

Darla, being the oldest at seventeen, looks after her siblings. She is short and blonde and she has that positive personality that you've got to love. She taught me how to crochet a chain stitch with yarn. Crocheting is her passion. I wish I had a passion for something, but I don't. A passion is the excitement between the tedious spaces, Dad says. Well, I do kind of have a passion to help Otto, but I don't call that excitement. I call it frustrating!

The next girl, Peggy, is fifteen. I idolize her. Her real name is Margaret but she likes to be called *Peggy*. She has a petite frame and her brown hair is always curled just perfectly. When she smiles, she lights up a room. She is so pretty, and she is a majorette at the high school. She often performs for us, twirling her baton.

I tell her about the Beatles. She had already heard. "Can I try your perfume, Peggy?" I ask.

She laughs. "Sure, Sophie. Go up to my room. It is on the dresser." Her perfume is called Ambush. It is in a pretty glass bottle.

I run up her stairs and find it sitting on her dresser, beside her jewelry box. I suppose I sprayed too much, because when I go back down the stairs, Paul waves his hands like I stink. "Holy crap, Sophie! She didn't tell you to take a bath in it!" Paul is thirteen, and always talks tough, but I know he isn't. I like him. He plays baseball too.

I stick my tongue out at him. He sticks his out at me. "You coming to my game tomorrow, Sophie? I'm on the Tiger Team you know, and we play the Yatesboro Miners tomorrow in Yatesboro."

"That depends. Can I wear my ambush?" I laugh and run out the door.

Peggy Doms, SVHS Majorette

Tiger Baseball Team. Paul Doms second from right front row

Debbie is carving her name into the old boards of her porch floor. "Do you wanna play with me and Butchie, Sophie?" At seven, she idolizes me, I think.

"Well, sure I do, Deb!"

Butchie, the baby of them all at four years old, is a roly poly bundle of love. His hair is light. His face is round like a pumpkin, and he has big dimples on both cheeks. He is always laughing.

Just then, Mrs. Maimone from next-door just came over with her *Monie* salad. She makes it all the time for the Doms and for Jax's family too. Darla gets us forks from the house. Three of us sit on the porch swing with our salads. Peggy and Deb sit on the steps while Paul, Butchie and Darla head for the kitchen.

When we are done eating, Jax, Deb and I kick a ball back and forth to Butchie and he squeals like a little girl. I like to pick him up and swing him around. He laughs so hard that I think his belly will burst. After I'm done swinging, we join in ring-around-the-rosey with Butchie. We let Butchie sing the words. "Ring-around-the-rosey, pocket-full-of-posey, ashes-ashes, we-all-falled-down!" He does a little hop and lands on his butt.

I want him to say it right so I tell him, "Butchie, it's we all FALL down, not falled down."

He looks at me angrily, "NO, SOPHIE!" He then grabs our hands to start going around again. He hollers it this time, glaring at me. "Ring-a-round-the-rosey, pocket-full-of-posey, ashes-ashes, WE-ALL-FALLED DOWN!" And he laughs, then does the little hop, landing on his butt.

Jax nudges me, laughing. "You better let it go, Sophie."

"I guess." I laugh with her. "I never got told off by a four-year-old-before!"

We finish the afternoon playing and Peggy shows me how to twirl a baton between my fingers. I'm just starting to get it when Jax's mom calls us for supper. Mrs. Doms calls her kids in too, but Butchie doesn't want us to leave. I laugh. "Go eat your supper, Butchie, we'll see you tomorrow!" I watch Peggy as she twirls her baton as she walks across her porch and into her house. "Bye, Peggy!" I holler.

She looks back with that pretty smile of hers. "Don't eat too much! Come over tomorrow, I'll do your nails!"

Jax's mom made us spaghetti for supper. After we eat, Snooky and Janet head home. Jax and I go upstairs to listen to records. We hang our heads out her window for a bit. Above us, a few wispy clouds are spread among the stars. The full moon hovers just over the horizon.

"Look at that, Jax. A full moon. I'm scared of full moons!"

"Why are you scared of a full moon, Sophie?"

"I think they are a bad omen."

"That's just plain silly, Sophie."

It is getting late. Before we know it, it is almost midnight. Jax plays *It's Now or Never* by Elvis, then *Cathy's Clown* by the Everly Brothers. When she plays *The Twist* by Chubby Checker, we twist like crazy in her bedroom. We sing at the top of our lungs, holding our hair brushes like

93

they are microphones. We swing our high ponytails, and we shout out the lyrics, swinging our hips left to right. "Come on, baby….Let's do the twist. Come on, baby…Let's do the twist. Take me by my little hand, ….And go like this!" Suddenly, we hear a loud BOOM! The house shakes. We stop. We stare at each other, frozen in fear. We run to her window which faces the Doms. THE DOMS HOUSE IS ON FIRE!!! We scream and run down the stairs and out onto the porch. People are everywhere. Men are trying to find a way to get into the house. They can't, it is engulfed in flames. The neighbors are here. Mrs. Maimone is just standing crying and Mr. Pnakovich is running around the burning house with the other men, all hollering to the family that is inside to get out. They are trying to find buckets and water hoses. I see Mr. Muir and Mr. Vallies frantically trying to get a garden hose working. I hear the fire trucks coming. I start to run towards the burning house. Jax's mom grabs me and we fall to the ground. NO….NO….NO!!! I scream. Jax is being restrained by Mrs. Kuhta. I look up at the burning house. A girl is hanging out of the upstairs bedroom window, hanging onto the window sill. Who is it? IT'S DARLA! She is crying. Mr. North and Mr. Honkus are hollering, "JUMP, DARLA! JUMP!"

My stomach is in my throat. I am sweating yet freezing. My terror wells up in my body and I feel like I am drowning in it. The firemen jump out of their trucks with their hoses. They spray water hard, trying to stay away from Darla. She is still hanging on.

Mr. Cosgrove is here. He is a fireman. He has a bellowing voice. "Everyone, BE QUIET!" He bellows. He then gets below Darla at the window. He talks to her calmly but very loudly. "Darla, honey, just jump. Just let go. I'll be here to catch you. Now you let go, Darla." The flames violently and without mercy shoot out the window above Darla's hands. He screams louder with panic. "LET GO, DARLA!" At that moment, Darla falls from the upstairs window to the ground. Mr. Cosgrove tries to catch her and they both go to the ground. His helmet falls off his head, but he holds on tight to Darla. He has broken her fall. People run to her. People are hollering to get damp towels. The plastic from the upstairs bedroom curtains is melted to Darla's nightgown. An ambulance is here now.   They rush her to the ambulance.

I look up at the window, at Peggy's bedroom. Where is she? "PEGGY!" I scream. "PEGGY!" The black smoke and red flames billow out Peggy's bedroom window.

"That's Peggy's bedroom!" I scream. "Where are the other kids? "HELP THEM!"

I see a woman in the grass through the smoke. People are surrounding her. It's Mrs. Doms! She is on the ground. She looks beaten, her skin dark from the smoke. She is gasping for air. They take her to the ambulance where Darla is. She seems to not know where she is, or what happened. Her blank eyes stare as if to say, "Help me!"

I turn back. Where are the kids? "WHERE ARE THEY???" I am screaming. "WHERE ARE THEY???"

95

The house is entirely engulfed in flames. Mr. Doms pulls in screeching his tires to a halt. They had called him at work. He runs towards the house, men stop him. "LET ME GO, LET ME GO!" He screams.

I can hear one man saying, "You can't save them, Red. It's too late."

He screams. He collapses. Men are trying to comfort him. I look around. It is devastation. The people standing around look like statues with blank faces that show shock, grief, and horror. The red blaze of the fire lights their faces. The tears run down their cheeks, leaving valleys of dark streaks from the smoke. It burns so hot it burns my nose and waters my eyes. It is shooting out every window, like long arms of the devil, saying COME! The sound of the crackling is deafening. The black thick smoke billowing into the air is the evil that came here today. As I look up to Peggy's window, I see the devil's face in the smoke. He is laughing. I scream. Someone grabs me. I feel blank, like all the blood left my body. I talk but my voice sounds like it is in a tunnel. "I don't understand. Where are the kids. WHERE ARE THEY?" Tears are streaming down my face. My stomach comes up through my throat as I vomit. My head is exploding.

Jax's mom pulls me into her and holds on tight. She is crying. "They are with Jesus, honey. Only Darla and her mom survived."

I fall to my knees. "NO!" Her dad picks me up and takes me into the house. I don't remember a lot. I remember my dad and mom showing up, leaning over me, telling me it was going to be okay. Dad scoops me into his arms and puts me on the back seat of his car. Mom sits with me stroking my hair as my head lays on her lap. I don't remember where Jax was or anything. It is all a fog. Mom and Dad put me to bed and sit with me.

Mom sings a song she used to sing to me when I was small. I hear her voice crack as she sings. "Hush little baby, don't say a word, Mama's gonna buy you a Mocking bird, and if that Mocking bird don't sing, Mama's gonna buy you a diamond ring, and if............ I don't remember more. I drifted off into an abyss. My dreams are dark and troubling.

******

When I awake in the morning, I stare at my ceiling hoping it had all been a nightmare. I know it wasn't.

Dutch is sitting on my bed. "How you feeling, Sophie?" she asks, seeing my confusion. She lays her hand on mine.

"I don't know what year it is." I start to weep again.

She strokes my hair. "It's 1960. You know what year it is, right?"

"Yesterday. What day was it?"

Dutch curls up beside me. "Yesterday was May 2nd. May 2nd, 1960. Why do you need to know that?"

I let out a wail and turn into my pillow. "I need to know what the day was, the day I want to forget forever!"

Dutch rubs my back. "Sophie, you have to be thankful Darla is okay. Her mom is okay too. Jax's house is still standing. You must be thankful for at least that. The kids are all in heaven now. Heaven is a wonderful place to be."

I don't know how to answer that. I can't be thankful for anything right now! The grief I feel is eating a hole through my body. I think of the full moon last night. A full moon is evil! I think of Peggy twirling her baton. I think of Butchie kicking his ball around the yard and how he said "falled down." Did he know? Why was he so insistent? Did he know they would all "falled" down? Debbie, just seven, and sweet. Even Paul, he always teased me, but I loved him. I loved them all. I don't know how I am going to go on. The only thing I can say to Dutch is "GO AWAY!"

******

I spent two days in bed. On the third day, there was a mass funeral held at Numine Presbyterian Church with Rev. Stull officiating. The entire Numine Grade School and all the teachers are standing outside the church. Most of the high school is here, huddled in groups crying. Paul's friends are here. They played baseball with him. Their heads are down. The majorette squad is here, sitting in silence, tears falling onto their laps. The high school band director is playing *Amazing Grace* on the trumpet, softly.

Dad holds my hand as we enter the church. Mom keeps her arms around me. There are just the three of us. The church feels cold. People look like statues. The sun streaks through the stained glass resting on the four coffins.

Rev. Stull says their names. "Margaret Ann Doms, Paul John Doms, Debra Lee Doms, Howard Dana Doms." (Little Butchie, sweet little Butchie). I didn't hear much more. I just keep hearing their names. Real kids. Happy kids, with smiles, laughs and voices. Gone in an instant. Gone!

Dad feels me shaking and puts both his arms around me as I cuddle into his chest. "It's okay Sophie, it will be okay." He says it but I don't feel it.

I don't feel like anything will ever be okay again. "God is mean!" I mutter.

Dad rubs my back. "No, Sophie. God just needed four angels. They are his angels now."

I look at him. "Dad, I saw the devil's face in the smoke coming out of Peggy's bedroom, and he was laughing."

He cuddles me close. "No, you didn't, honey. You just saw your grief in front of you. The devil did not take these children. God did."

******

Two days later Dad made me go back to school. He took me in his car and went in with me to the office. We talked with my Principal, Mr. Hall, and he and Dad discussed my state of mind. Mr. Hall makes a suggestion. "Sam, shall we take Sophie to the high school? The kids have set up somewhat of a memorial. It might do Sophie some good."

I feel like I am walking in a fog, but we go to the high school. We walk down the hallway towards the band room.

99

The hall seems so very long. My legs are moving but it is like I am walking through high water. I can see, as I approach, the flowers and pretty signs stuck to a locker. There is a picture of a bird. Someone wrote Fly Away Peggy, Fly to God. I see the name on the locker, PEGGY DOMS. I walk up to it, my fingers glide across the glitter on the signs that say LOVE YOU FOREVER, PEGGY. I touch her name on the locker, tracing each letter as I go. I smell the flowers. I look down. Leaning against the locker is her baton, burned, but still intact. I touch it. I cry. Dad cries with me. I needed this. Dad knew it.

I will grieve the Doms family forever. But somehow, I know Peggy, Paul, Debbie and Butchie would want me to go on. Dad said they are in a better place than we are! I sure hope so. I hope they never have to feel what I feel now. If nothing else, I find a little comfort in knowing they are happy, with no pain. No pain like what is in my gut at this moment. I like to think of them smiling, Paul playing baseball in heaven, Butchie and Debbie playing Ring-Around-The-Rosie, and Peggy twirling her baton.

Darla Doms: The only child that survived the fire

Mass Funeral Held for 4 Fire Victims

NU MINE — Funeral services for Margaret Ann, Paul John, Debra Lee and Howard Dana Doms, who died Monday, were held Thursday afternoon (May 5, 1960) in the NuMine Presbyterian church with Rev. T. R. R. Stull, church pastor, officiating.

The children lost their lives in a fire Monday night when flames destroyed their two-story frame home at NuMine.

Casket bearers were Carmon Eckman, Norman King, Brenton Rearick, Roy Wensel, Steve Feteti, Harold Krizmanich, Robert Caresani, Paul Stewart, Dennis Swanson, James Vallies, Richard Whiteman, Bruce Fisher.

Interment was made in the Manor cemetery.

Carson funeral home, Rural Valley, was in charge of arrangements.

CHAPTER THIRTEEN
FROLICS
Summer of 1960

Spring turned into summer and life went on. I didn't think it could, but it did.

It is hot as a pig's breath today! Dad said that winter was so cold that the milk cows gave icicles and now the summer is hotter than Dutch love in harvest.

We visit Nonna in the morning and are home by early afternoon. "Going to Deb's!" I holler as I walk out the door. It is already 3:00, hottest part of the day.

It is a hot walk. Deb is outside waiting for me. "Want to go to the dam?"

"Sure, I do!" Mom and Dad don't like the dam. Mom says she wishes it would dry up. They asked that we don't go there. But, I think if I don't get into the water, it will be okay.

As we approach the dam, we can see that Aunt Bella is here with her three kids. They are on a blanket getting ready to go swimming. We hear chatting as we look towards the cement wall. Coming out of the water are four naked teenage boys. Aunt Bella jumps off her blanket and runs to them. She pushes all four of them back in the water, one at a time. "You sons-o- bitches! If you wanna swim in this dam, you're gonna keep your damn swim suits on!"

I am embarrassed, mostly because I just saw boys naked. I just want to leave here. "Let's go, Deb!"

We sit on my porch until Mom has supper ready for us. Eating quickly, we head out the door again, heading up Main Street.

There is lots of chatter coming out of Avi's open door as we pass. At the End Zone, just as we cross the alley, a man comes flying out the door. We hear someone hollering to him to not come back. He is bald with tattoos down both arms. He stands up, brushes himself off, and walks down the alley.

"Gheez, Sophie. It could be dangerous walking by these places."

"It's not. People are just stupid when they drink." I laugh. "This here End Zone used to be Harvey Boyer's Meat Market when Mom was young. She said hamburger was ten cents a pound then. Too bad it didn't stay a meat market!" We walk briskly up the street greeting Mr. Arduini sitting on a chair outside his candy store. Moving on up through town, around the S curve and up the straight-away, Mary Louise Infanta comes zooming down the alley on her bike. I wave and wonder why Julia isn't with her. She plays often with Mary Louise. Julia is probably somewhere obsessing about something.

We keep going and pass Mr. Smith's building. It is just across the street catty-corner from Rural Valley Elementary. I hold my hands at the side of my face and peer through the glass.

"What you looking for, Sophie?"

"Nothing, really. Just nosey. It's closed. You know that fifty years ago this here was H. W. Smith Furniture

103

Company? It had the first Atlantic gasoline pump and he sold tires too. Then Beryl Smith sold appliances in here. It is empty now. I hear it's going be a laundromat!"

"How do you know all this stuff, Sophie?"

"Dad and Mom are real interested in telling us what was here long ago. They talk about it so much, if it didn't soak into my head, you'd have to call me a true idiot!"

She laughs. "You ain't no idiot, that's for sure!"

Up a little hill we go, passing the drug store and the funeral home. When we reach Bart's Bar across from the Liberty Theater, I'm wondering if my classmate, Mary Ann, is home. I pop my head in. "Is Mary Ann home?"

"No, Sophie. She's at her grandma's house."

We continue, crossing the street at the bake shop. After the alley and four more houses, the hill starts down. Right there to my left is a big house, at the alley. "This here used to be Kirkpatrick Inn. Did you know that?"

"An Inn? It looks like just a big house."

"Yep, and Mom told me that she found an old advertisement from there that said rooms were $1.00 a day and they had a very nice stable for your horse and the best carriage house in town!"

"Wow, that would have been a long, long time ago, Sophie!"

"It was. We weren't born yet, that's for sure. Maybe not my mom either!"

We venture down the hill and cross the road again, to the Schrecengost garage. "Merill Schrecengost bought this as a blacksmith shop years ago, but then it became a car garage. His son, Frank owns it now. A few years back, on Halloween, Frank got shot in his head out Bryan Road with a BB gun. He was just turning around in someone's driveway and the man thought he was coming to Halloween at his place. He shot him more than once. Frank lives with some of them still in his head. Doctors couldn't remove them all. It doesn't seem to affect him, though!"

"BBs in his head? That would be awful! Did the guy go to jail?"

"Guess not. He claimed he was defending himself. But Mom said everyone knew Frank wasn't out there for Halloween devilment. He wasn't that kind of a guy. Frank works hard here at his garage. I like the penny candy he sells." We pop in his door. "Hey, Mr. Schrecengost!" As I pick two cherry lollipops out of his big glass jar.

"Hey there, girls! Walking through Rural Valley today, are you?"

"Yep. I'm showing Jax the town. Heading up to where the Print Shop used to be. Someone told me they found the remains of a baby when they tore it down, and you can hear it crying!"

Mr. Schrecengost looks down at us over the glasses that sit at the end of his nose. "Better watch out there, girls! They say that the ghost baby will haunt you if you bother it!"

I must admit I'm a little scared. "Did you ever see it?"

He goes back to putting a nut onto a bolt. "No, but I hear it crying. Especially in the evenings!"

I don't know what to think as we head out the door.

"Maybe let's go another time, Deb."

She laughs. "Sophie, he is kidding you! He is just trying to scare you!" So, we meander up the hill past Mr. Schrecengost's house, waving to his wife, Kay, in the garden. The foundation is all that remains of the print shop. Nothing but dirt and block piled up. We sit in the grass staring at it, as we lick our lollipops.

An hour passes, as we talk. Deb is wondering if I am being bullied in school by the same bully she has. "Iggy Baliski won't let me alone. He's always telling me my hair is ugly. Yesterday he said my dress looked like it was my grandma's. He even makes fun of the way I talk. I hate him!"

"Don't let him bother you, Deb. He is an idiot! If you can just ignore him, he will stop."

Deb is like me. She wants everyone to like her. She smiles and goes back to licking her lollipop.

"What do ya' think, Sophie?" You think there's a ghost baby in there?"

"Listen carefully," I whisper. We stop licking our candy and sit very still. The quiet is deafening. It is early evening. There is only the sound of crickets as a rabbit hops across the grass. "Stay very quiet." I listen carefully, turning my ear towards the torn down building.

Suddenly, "BOO!" Debra hollers as she pushes me over. I almost pee my pants.

"That's just mean, Deb!"

She won't stop laughing. "You are so gullible, Sophie! There's no baby in there!"

I was scared, but disappointed I didn't hear a baby cry. Just then bats began to swoop near our heads. "RUN, JAX!"

I scared her good and she started to run and squeal. Good for her! We head down Main Street.

Lenny and Gene are sitting on the steps in front of Cogley's Restaurant. We talk to them often when we see them. They LOVE telling us stories of things they did when they were younger. Lenny is blonde with a thin mustache and Gene is tall with dark hair and brown eyes. They both work in the coal mines. They are in their mid-to-late twenties I suppose.

We plop ourselves down beside them. "Hey Lenny and Gene! Why aren't you working?" I ask.

Gene answers, "Midnight shift tonight. Slept all day, just got up. Where you goin'?"

"Thought we'd walk up to the school. Just somethin' to do."

Lenny takes a drag of his cigarette. He swirls the butt of his cigarette into the cement. "Gonna be dark in an hour or so. Did you know that where the new high school sits, that was called Gourley's Grove back in the day? It had a baseball field. Gene here was a darn good baseball player!"

"Gourley's Grove? No, I never knew that. What else was there?"

"Just picnic tables and stuff. People was just always there, playin' baseball or havin' a picnic." He points to the front of Cogley's. "Did you know that right here in front of this big window that Louise has, was once a big Frosty Bear sign?"

"Didn't know it, but what happened to it?"

Lenny laughs. "We had to give it back. Me and Gene stole it from that little restaurant down in Rose Valley when we were seniors. We just wanted Louise to have to guess where it came from. She figured it out right quick, and made us return it."

"Did you get in trouble?" I ask.

"Not really." Gene answers. "Everyone was kind enough not to tell our dads. Both would have knocked our blocks off!" We all laugh.

"Yeah," Gene continues. "Like that time that Charlie Ramer came around Yatesboro with his truck selling chickens from a cage. He sold eggs too. We called him 'Charlie the egg man'. Dad made me pick the chicken I wanted then told me to hold the feet tight, so he could chop the head off. I was holding the feet tight, like he told me, and he brought his axe down on the neck. It was sickening. The head was off, but that chicken kept flailing around like nobody's business with blood spewing all over the place including on me. I was screaming like a girl. Dad kept hollered at me, "LET GO OF IT!! LET GO OF THE DAMN CHICKEN FOR GOD'S SAKE!"

"Did you let go?" I ask.

"Hell, I THREW it at him! I was so mad by then I didn't care if I got in trouble for it. He knocked my block off that day. Sure did! But then he tried to make-up for his rage. He took me to the Company Store to buy me a bike. I got on it right away and rode it down the front steps of the company store, breaking the front wheel and fender. A near death experience for me, a moment of frenzied rage for my dad."

"What did you do about the bike?" I ask.

"I went all over town until I found an old wheel for the bike. It looked awful, but it worked."

He put his head down. "Too bad the Company Store burned down in '53. I loved that place. Do you know that the night it burned it was late at night? There must a' been a hundred people standing there watching it. We were all in our pajamas. I used to always go in there singing 'I owe my soul to the company store' and everyone would laugh. While it was burning, I started to sing that again. All the people standing in their pajamas joined me. Even Roscoe Morgan sang, he was the delivery driver for the store. Fred Dantonio, the Company Store Manager, was standing there crying, but when we started to sing, he sang too. Want to hear it?"

"Sure, Gene."

He began to sing.

> *"Some people say a man is made outta mud*
> *A poor man's made outta muscle and blood*
> *Muscle and blood and skin and bones*

A mind that's a-weak and a
back that's strong
    You load sixteen tons, what do
you get?
    Another day older and deeper
in debt.
    Saint Peter, don't you call me
'cause I can't go
    I owe my soul to the company
store."

"I didn't know you were a good singer, Gene. That's a sad song."

"Was the truth, Sophie, that's all. Everyone owed their soul to the Company Store." He laughed. "You know, Sophie, back in the day, we used to dance in the basement of the drugstore."

"Really? I wonder why they don't have dances now. Did you dance with anyone, Gene?"

"One time, and only because this girl grabbed me by my hair and dragged me out to dance." He shakes head. "It was SO embarrassing!" He pauses then looks up. "You ain't Catholic, are you, Sophie?

"Nope!"

I can see another story coming. "You know Father Philip? Well, the Catholic Church is across from my Grandma Hockenberry's. She wasn't Catholic either. Anyways, Grandma would always bake Father Philip bread every Friday and send it for him and Mary, the cook. Then one day, Father Philip knocked on my grandma's door and asked her if he could pray for her, because she wasn't Catholic. Grandma slammed the door on him. She was THAT mad! I told Grandma, "I'll get him!" So, I went and stole his grapes from his vines. He caught me, and took me into the kitchen and made me eat grapes until I puked."

"That's awful, Gene."

"It was a lesson learned, that's for sure. He was mad as a mule chewin' bumblebees. The cook, Mary, always liked me though. I thought she was a timid lady. She was sent one day to pick up a priest from Seminary in Pittsburgh and asked me to go along. She stopped at a red light and a guy whistled at her. She up and got out of that car and chewed that guy out big time! She was swearin' and cursin'! All those cars behind us were honkin' their horns. I never saw that coming!"

He takes a drag of his cigarette. "That Father Philip was somethin' else. We liked to pick on him. One time, some boys hooked a long wire onto the bell on the Yatesboro school tower. It was right across from the Catholic Church, you know. They strung the wire across the yard to a big tree. Then, at night, they'd sit in that tree and ring the bell, pullin' that wire. Nearly drove Father Philip nuts trying to figure out why the bell was ringin'."

We laugh. The things they did when they were young were really funny.

He is scratching the cement below him with some sort of old gun casing. "What is that?" I want to know. "Looks like something from a gun."

"Just junk." He answers. "You're too young to remember, but after WWII ended, the army put a scrap pile of metal in the school yard. I was just a kid then. We could take whatever we wanted. I got a bunch of things there, this bein' one of them. There were lots of cans. They asked us to pick up the cans, and we were given ranks by the number of tin cans we collected, like Private, Corporal, Sergeant, etc."

"What rank did you get?" I ask him.

"Private is all. That darn Joe Kitka lived right by the dump, so he was able to collect the most. Heck, they made him a General!"

He loves talking about the past. "I had some war bonds, you know. In grade school we bought savings stamps and put them in books. When we got enough, we turned them in for twenty-five-dollar bonds."

"What you do with them?"

He stares at the ground, "Used them for my mama's funeral." He pulls his wallet out and opens wide the long slit that holds money. There is only a picture in there. It is her. He hands it to me.

"She was beautiful, Gene." I smile at him. "And you know, they say a sign of a good son is someone who carries his mama's picture in his wallet where his money should be."

He laughs. "I gave my mama a hard time. I feel bad about that. Especially at Christmas time. Us guys did this every year. One guy would visit me, then I'd join him and we'd visit the next one, then the three of us would go to another, then the four of us would go to the fifth guy's house. You get the picture?"

"Sure do, Gene. When did it ever end?"

"Not sure, but all I can say is that as the night went on and the more drunk we got, Lord help the man who refused us entry!" He does a hearty belly laugh. "God bless my mama, she sure put up with a lot from me!"

He takes a drink from the glass coca cola bottle he is sipping from. "But we never got shut out by anyone. There are good people in Yatesboro. I used to shovel snow on the hill when the snow was so deep you couldn't walk in it and it was so cold my nose would nearly freeze off. Mrs. Francheschi would always give me her homemade red wine. That kept me warm. Mrs. Marken would bring me out cookies, and Mrs. McLaughlin always gave me the caramel popcorn she made. That Mrs. McLaughlin told me she never missed a day of school in her entire life! Ain't that something?"

"Sure is. Sounds like you were a devil sometimes, Gene."

"You are right. Mr. Vicini hates me to this day. I tipped his outhouse over!"

"I'd be mad at you too!" Gene doesn't care. He just laughs. "Gene, have you heard if they caught the murderer yet of that Kiser Wilson, they found in Numine two years ago?

"Nope, heard nothing. People have pretty much forgotten about that."

"Well, I haven't. It isn't right that a murderer is walking among us."

Darkness is falling. No time to go to the school. We meander home. I think of all the devilment Gene and Lenny got themselves into in their lives. If Gene has a little voice like me, his little voice was sure busy! Maybe that little voice in my head isn't so bad after all. That little voice hasn't gotten me into too much trouble........not yet anyways.

Teens hanging out at Cogley's Restaurant, Main Street RV

CHAPTER FOURTEEN
SCHOOLGIRL CHATS
September 1961

On May 5th of this year, Alan Shepard was the first American in space. Julia listened to the broadcast in Beryl Smith's sixth grade class and she was sure he was going to die. She came home from school that day near tears and when Mom asked why she was so upset she said, "Because he has two girls around my age, and he's going to die! They are not going to have their father!"

Mom had to sit her down and talk to her. Julia worries about stuff she doesn't need to worry about!

Last March, JFK established the Peace Corps. Julia is obsessed with it. "I'm going to do that someday. You will see. I'll go to other countries and help people!" she claims. I hope it happens for her, but sounds kind of crazy to me.

Before we know it, school starts again. Sixth grade for me. It is my last year at Rural Valley Elementary. They are building a new elementary school in the alley, right behind this old elementary. It will open next year and they will tear this one down. I won't get to go to the new one, I'll be in high school.

In class, I turn around to Otto. "We won't get to go to the new grade school, Otto."

He is disinterested. "Guess not."

"Are you excited to go to high school next year, Otto?"

"I don't get excited about much."

"Well, honestly, Otto. You need to get excited about something! Don't you think?"

He stares at me. "For what and why?" He puts his head down and starts reading.

"I'm going to buy you a hammer, Otto!"

"For what?" He asks.

"TO BREAK THAT WALL DOWN!"

I give up. Some days he is just hard to talk to. I heard two of the teachers talking about him yesterday in the hall. Mr. Heck had tried to talk to Otto and Otto didn't answer. When Otto walked away, I heard Mr. Heck telling Mrs. Smith, "The cheese done slid off that boy's cracker." I thought that was a horribly mean thing to say. I know very well what it meant. I don't think Otto is the nut. I think Mr. Heck is. You don't have to be hanging from a tree to be a nut. I wish I could tell Mr. Heck so, but I don't dare.

At the end of the school day, Jax came home with me. We sit on our front porch on the old swing that Mom and Dad won't give up for some reason, nor the three-legged stool that sits beside it. Debra came over, claiming the stool that swivels. Theo will sit in my lap forever as I swing him. He will soon be two. I tell him he is turning into a little person already.

Jax tells me about Numine Elementary. "We go to the basement to get our lunch, and they make me eat what I don't want!"

"They MAKE you eat? Really?" I ask. "The cafeteria ladies don't do that at our school."

"Not the cafeteria ladies, the teachers. Thelma, the cafeteria lady, feels sorry for us. But she must put the same on everyone's plate. Last week, it was fish sticks. I hate those things! If we don't eat everything, we don't get to go out to recess. So, I put my fish sticks in my pocket, and I went out to recess. When I got home and changed my clothes, my mom found them. Or maybe she smelled them! Mom wasn't mad at me; she was mad at the school. She called the principal."

"Then what happened?"

"I didn't have to eat everything on my plate after that."

"Well, they don't make us eat everything in my school. Good thing too, because I'd be putting slimy prunes in my pocket!" I chuckle, thinking of the slimy things.

Jax plants her feet on the floor to stop the swing from moving, "And listen to this. You know the big slide that is used as the fire escape at my school? Well, there was to be a fire drill today. Something horrible happened! You know that kid, Lee, in fifth grade who lives in that funny blue colored house? He doesn't like school or anything about it. Well, he knew the fire drill was coming. So, at recess, he snuck onto the top of the slide and took a crap."

"WHAT?" I am appalled.

Jax is laughing. "Oh Sophie, it was so funny! The siren rang for the fire drill and Mrs. Hilliard's second grade class went first. A little girl went up there and stepped right in it. She squealed and cried. They couldn't control her.

Meanwhile, Lee was at the back of the line laughing. He is in big trouble! He was dumb enough to admit it!"

"That's sickening!" I declare. "I would never go down that fire escape slide again!"

"Oh yes you would, Sophie! Especially with Mrs. Hilliard behind you! Anyways, Sophie, it's just poop! We all poop!"

View of the back of Numine Elementary School, fire escape slide in view

CHAPTER FIFTEEN
HALLOWEEN
October 1961

It has been three years since the murder at *The Bucket of Blood*. I can't forget about it. I still feel nervous. The murderer lives somewhere between Yatesboro and Numine, I'm sure of it!

It is a cold October night. There is a full moon. Mom and Dad tell me I am wrong about full moons being bad omens, but I don't think I am. I think of the night the Doms house burned down. There was a full moon that night. A moment of sadness overtakes me and that lump comes up my throat.

Mom has allowed me to have Jax, Janet and Snooky down for overnight. "Can we go out for a bit?" I ask.

Dad puts down his newspaper. "If you behave yourself, you can." Little does he know.

It is Halloween in two days. "Let's go pick up Debra." I run upstairs first and steal a cake of soap from the shower.

It is a chilly walk to Debra's. The oak trees along the street have shed their leaves. We love to rustle through them. The houses are decorated with orange lights, corn stalks, scarecrows, and spider webs. Mrs. Wisilko has tombstones in her yard, with hands coming up out of the ground. I love Halloween, though I keep looking up at that full moon, frightened.

Janet, the instigator, is telling us what she did last night. "There's a lady that lives on the front street of

Numine. Her name is Iona. She sits and sleeps all evening, every evening, in front of a blank television." Janet laughs. "Last night, I crept up her back steps, opened the door quietly, and went in. It was easy. She was sleeping in her chair, as always, in front of that blank television. I went behind her and strung toilet paper everywhere, on her ceiling light, on all her pictures, on her piano. Everywhere. She never woke up! It was so funny!"

"You did what?" I can't believe the things she does. "My Dad would kill me if I did that!"

Janet just laughs. "Well, you don't get caught, silly!"

My wheels are turning. Debra has a teacher she doesn't like. Mrs. McBrighton. Kids call her Mrs. McBitch. She is old and needs to retire. She even falls asleep at her desk. Her gray hair is like wire and her glasses are always half way down her nose. She scolded Debra's friend Joanne today because she was in the bathroom too long. Then she told the principal that Joanne was standing on the toilet, which she wasn't because Debra was with her and knew that she didn't do that. We have a substitute Principal, Mr. Isenhooth. We call him Mr. Eyestooclose, because they are. Mr. Eyestooclose stood on the landing of the stairs where Joanne had to go up to get to class from lunch. He hollered to her, "You git up here, now!" Joanne started to run but wasn't fast enough to get by him. He whacked her with a big paddle. Once she got hit, she sure found her speed! She ran up those stairs like a roadrunner. He was still trying to swing a second time. He missed, lost his balance, and almost fell. Everyone was laughing, which made him mad.

He didn't go after her, but decided no one in the entire school would get to go out for recess. This is all because of her mean teacher Mrs. McBitch. She lives in a white house on Main Street, by herself. We're gonna git'r.

We sneak around the back, no movement. Her car sits in the gravel leading to the back porch.

Debra is excited, "We'll get her for what she did! Give me that soap, Sophie!"

"You kidding? You are going to get me in trouble!"

"Not today!" Debra laughs. "Not today!" With the soap she goes to our teacher's car and soaps the windshield solid. There is no way Mrs. McBitch can drive it, at least not until she spends hours scraping it off. When Debra is getting almost to done, we hear the back door open. "RUN!" We run like the wind through the yards and into the alley, laughing. I'm laughing now, but if Mom and Dad know we did this, it will be lights out at 8:00 forever for me!

I try not to think about it. We walk arm in arm down the street, singing, *'Who put the bomp in the bomp-bah bomp-bah bomp, who put the ram in the ram-lama-ding-dong, who put the bop in the bop-shoo bop-shoo bog, who put the dip in the dip-da-dip-da-dip.'*

As we near my house I see Dad on the front porch waving for us to come. "What's wrong, Dad?"

He looks annoyed. "Janet's mom is on the phone. Something about a neighbor lady there telling her what Janet did last night. Seems as though the woman watched Janet stringing toilet paper in her house from the reflection of her tv! Your dad is on his way to pick you up, Janet!"

Holy crap! I hope she doesn't get in too much trouble. That is not too horrible a thing, is it? Kids do all kinds of stuff at Halloween! A boy named Francis told me he threw tomatoes at the girls practicing choir at the Catholic Church. He crossed the *BLACK ROAD* in Yatesboro with his buddies and waited for them to come out. Now that's bad!

It doesn't even have to be Halloween for bad stuff going on. Gene told me that years ago, the coal miners did bad things, because they hated the strip mines. Coal miners were all hunters, so they sat in the woods above the strip mines and shot high powered rifles at the dump trucks. When the policemen came, they shot off the flashing gumball lights on the police car. Now that is bad!

Gene told me himself that he used to throw mudballs at the bulldozers. The bulldozer drivers would then go after him and drive him into the woods. He said he did this all within sight of his girlfriend, Rosie's house. Her grandmother who lived there, was always on the porch. She saw it all. She told the family about it and they all said she was bonkers. He was dumb enough to tell Rosie, "No, she's not bonkers. I did it." He then told me, "When Rosie and I got engaged, her mother tried to run over me!"

I asked him what he did. He laughed. "I simply asked her what her problem was. And, you know what she said?"

"No."

"You are a brawler booze hound, and just another no-good."

"What did you say to that, Gene?"

I asked her, "Other than that, have you got anything against me?"   We all laugh at Gene.

Now that's bad!

Gene said that women back then were tough. They'd strike right with their coal miner husbands when there was a strike, walking the picket line and chewing snuff and everything! Now that's bad!

What Janet did wasn't so bad, was it?

CHAPTER SIXTEEN
SHENANIGANS
November 1961

November is a month that I like because Thanksgiving is coming and so is Christmas. There is never a day, though, that I don't look at Otto and feel sad for him. I'll bet he gets no turkey with mashed potatoes like I do, and I'll bet he gets no Christmas gifts. I brought him an apple today and try again to talk to him at the end of school as we walk down the hallway. "Hey, Otto. Want an apple?" He just takes it. It looks like Dutch's coat is getting small on him. I need to talk to Mom about that. I look at where the sleeves are halfway up his arms, and I see slices on his arm that are scabbed over. "What happened there, Otto?"

"Nothing," he answers curtly. I know to back off that subject.

"How's your grandpap, Otto?"

He stares at me with his unhappy eyes, "Old and hateful!"

I fear he has two men who are mean to him, not just one.

"Is Thor doing okay?"

"He's good."

"Otto, where is your mom?" It was out of my mouth before I thought about it. Maybe I shouldn't ask that.

His head goes down. When he looks up, his eyes are sad. "She left me. I was only one."

"I'm so sorry, Otto. You were just a baby!"

"Yep. She didn't care."

"Sure, she cared. I'm sure it was something she had to do, Otto. Sometimes there is just no other way out. What was her name?"

"Rosalie."

"Do you know where she went?"

"Nope. She never came back for me. Anyways, I wouldn't know her if she was standing in front of me. Never even saw a picture of her."

"Things happen for a reason, Otto. Someday you will know the reason."

"The reason lives at my house."

I know very well what he means. "My real mom is gone too, Otto. A drunk driver killed her and my dad when I was only four. I'm lucky that Sam and Patsy adopted us. They are my parents now. They are all I've known. I was too young to remember my mom and dad. I don't even know what they looked like."

"Who was the drunk?" He wants to know.

"Never found out. He was in a stolen car and he took off on foot. He took enough time to grab my mother's purse though. I can't remember my parents' faces, just like you don't remember. We have that in common. I know it's hard, to not remember faces. What are you doing tonight, Otto?"

"Nothing."

"Why don't you come home with me for supper. Mom and Dad would love that."

"I don't do suppers."

He turns and walks towards the door, passing Mrs. Feracioly. She smiles at him. "Have a good evening, Otto." Otto doesn't respond, as he walks out the double doors to his bus.

Mrs. Feracioly sees me staring at Otto. "Maybe tomorrow will be better, Sophie."

I just smile and nod and walk away. Oh my, Otto is frustrating!

I head up the street to the funeral home where Dad is. He started helping at the Carson Funeral Home by the drug store when he has a day off, for extra money. He said he'd take me home today.

As I walk in the door, he is adjusting funeral cards. "Hey, Sophie!"

"Hey, Dad. I'm glad you didn't forget you were taking me home today. I got Otto to talk a little today."

"What did you talk about?"

"I asked him about his mother. He said she left him when he was only one."

"That so?" Dad seems to not want to look at me. I'll bet he knew that already.

Dad gets the cards in place and turns to me. "You can't change him, Sophie. We'll all just keep trying to help him as best we can, with clothes and food, or whatever. You need to stop expecting more of him. He is stuck like a fly, caught in a spiderweb. You know that when cobwebs are plenty, kisses are few."

"What does that mean?" I ask.

"Well, when I was young, we had a girl lived near us that was poor as a church mouse. She only had a mom, and her mom was mean to her. The girl's name was Hazel. She never smiled. Never. My mother always used that saying. She said cobwebs represent her life. Her life wasn't good, so her cobwebs were plenty. Kisses represent any happiness she may have had. She had little or no happiness. So, her kisses were few. My mother always tried to make Hazel smile. She'd give her things and try to talk with her. Kind of like what you do with Otto."

"That's awful. What happened to Hazel?"

"They moved away one day. An aunt came from out of state and took them with her. Hopefully, her life got better."

I hate to think Otto has no happiness in his life. "You think Otto has no happiness at all, Dad?"

"Doubt it, honey. His Dad and Grandpap are a real piece of work."

"I know. His dad doesn't seem to care about him at all! I know that for sure!"

"Cat's in the Cradle, baby. Cat's in the Cradle."

He can see my confusion as to what that means. He changes the subject. "Did you know this was the Croyle Funeral Home until 1951?"

"Nope, didn't know that."

The Croyle Funeral Home on Main Street Rural Valley

"Do you want to hear what Mr. Croyle's son, Barney did a few years ago?"

"Yeah, I guess."

Dad starts laughing. "Barney picked a dead body up at Kittanning Hospital. It was a bitter cold day. On the way back here to the funeral home from Kittanning, he stopped at Maffei's Bar in Rose Valley for a beer. He walked in for a drink, and left the body sitting up in his car. Stan and his wife, Emma, owned the bar. Well, Emma looked out at Barney's car and saw the guy. She questioned Barney about the guy in his car, telling Barney to bring him in out of the cold. Barney replied, "Don't worry about it, the cold won't bother him.""

Emma, not satisfied, replied, "Well, I'll go get him. It isn't right to leave someone out in the cold like that!" She went out the door to the car, opened the car door. She nudged the man and he fell over. Emma screamed. She came back into the bar, furious at Barney. Barney had a grin from ear to ear and told her, "I TOLD you the cold wouldn't bother him!"

Dad is laughing. "Emma didn't allow Barney in her bar anymore."

"I wouldn't either!" I laugh, as Dad goes back to sorting cards for the podium.

"I need another hour here, Sophie. Can you wait?"

"Sure, I'm in no hurry." I sneak back the hall to where the extra coffins are, and climb in one. Such a cozy little bed for an after-school nap. I nod off.

Next thing I know, Dad is standing over me scolding me. "Sophie! GET OUT OF THERE! What's wrong with you? These are for dead people. Do you even know that?"

I must admit I didn't think about what they were. Strange how knowledge changes perception! NOT a good place for a nap.

We head home. Jax is sending her Dad to pick me up after supper for a sleep-over. I go straight to Mom in the kitchen. "Mom, did you know that Otto's mom left him when he was just one?"

She looks shocked. "Who told you that?"

"Otto did! He told me himself."

"Well, I kind of knew it and believe me, I wasn't trying to hide it from you, Sophie. It's just something people don't talk about. Your Aunt Dee used to talk to his mom in church. I have to wonder how his poor mother was even allowed out of the house to go to church."

"I don't understand the lives people lead, letting someone be mean to them like that. She got away, why didn't Otto? Why didn't she take him with her?"

"We don't know what the situation was, Sophie. Otto wouldn't either since he was only one. She may have had to just run, to save her own life."

"I can't imagine that. A mother leaves her child to save herself? I'd never do that!"

"Again, Sophie, we don't know the circumstances. Let's not judge someone until we know the facts."

"And when will we know that, Mom? He should have run away too!"

"And go where, Sophie? Where would a young boy go when his evil father would find him? It was easier for him to stay."

I suppose she is right. "Dad told me that when cobwebs are plenty, kisses are few."

"Yes, and it describes Otto's life perfectly."

I hate thinking about it. I'm not thinking about it anymore tonight.

I gulp down my supper so I am ready to go to Jax's for my sleep-over.

******

Saturday morning, Jax and I walk towards the tipple and beyond the boney dump. As we walk there, we talk about Otto. "He's a puzzle, Jax. Just a big puzzle I can't put together."

"And there is always going to be a piece missing, Sophie. Quit worrying. You can't fix him, you know. Let's go to the ice cave!"

Up a small hill near the woods is a small hole in the ground, in the side of a small hill. I look inside. "This is no cave. It's just a hole with icicles!" I declare.

"Well, it is like Shin said. It opens up when the ghost sees you, Sophie!"

"Do you think Shin was right about the ghost in there?"

She laughs. "Probably!" She gives me a push enough that I stumble towards it.

"STOP IT!" I yell at her.

"Awe, come on, Sophie. I was just kidding. There's no ghosts in there!"

"How would you know? Maybe Shin is right!"

She starts to walk away. "Then go ahead and wait until one shows up. I'm going to ride the hoodlebug!"

The hoodlebug is a handcar that sits on the tracks by the train at the Numine tipple. Some call it a *jigger*. I love going to the train tracks. Grant Davison is leaning on the rails near the tressle. He was a friend of Ruby's. He looks at us like he knows what we are up to, but he just smiles.

The guys that work on the tracks are called *Gandy Dancers*, but they are not around today. I catch up to her. We get to the train tracks, jump on to the hoodlebug, and start to pump hard. I don't think we are allowed to do this. But, my little voice in my head says DO IT!

The hoodlebug takes us towards Rural Valley. Pumping takes effort. The hoodlebug smells like the oiled floors at school. Pump, pump, pump we go, faster and faster. As we approach Meredith, we see the policeman, Hoot. He parks his car and starts walking towards us. We throw the switch into reverse and pump like nobody's business. He starts to run but he can't catch us. I don't think he can see that it is me. I hope not! He would tell my dad, for sure.

We get back to Numine before he can catch us. As we get off the hoodlebug, my arms are tingling and numb. There are some boys getting bicycle parts out of the trash pile that is near the boney dump. Maybe Hoot will blame them for being on the hoodelbug!

We run fast into Numine. At Alec Nagy's candy store, we buy pop and chips. I got twenty-five cents back in change. "Perfect." I tell Jax. "Just what I need for church collection on Sunday!"

Walking back to her house we see Snooky walking up the tiny lane from behind the elementary to Dr. Griffith's office on Main Street. When Mom was young, she used to be a friend of Doc Griffith's son, Wilbur. She told me how nice Wilbur was, and that she never knew what happened to him after graduation. He's probably off being a doctor somewhere too.

Doc Griffith comes to a house on the corner of Main Street once a week, though he is getting elderly now and probably will soon retire. Snooky sees us and invites us to go in with her. "Come in with me. I'm only getting a prescription for my dad."

We enter and sit in the small waiting room. It smells like medicine and mold. There is one old window with heavy velvet drapes. On the big windowsill, three plants sit there, all dead. I lean over to Snooky. "These plants here looks as sad as a weeping willow. I don't think your dad should go to a doctor whose plants have died."

She looks troubled. "What do you mean?"

I laugh. "I'm just kidding, Snook! Everyone knows Doc Griffith is the best!

Bud Davidson standing at Numine tressle

Monday, at school, it started to rain hard while we were on the playground.

We all started to race to the school when suddenly I felt something being held above my head. I turned quickly to see Otto holding his flannel shirt over my head. "Thank you, Otto." I smile at him.

He said only two words. "Rainin' bullfrogs." Something warm poured inside my heart. I was still smiling about it as I walked onto my bus at the end of the day.

When I got home, I told Mom about it. "Mom, he is coming around. I just know it. He is being nicer!"

Mom smiles. "I'm sure it's been hard growing up with no mother."

"But he could be happy if he wanted to, Mom! If he'd let me help him!"

"I'm glad you have faith, honey. But waiting for him to be happy might be like watching a tadpole getting his legs."

A school bus from the 50's

CHAPTER SEVENTEEN
SEVENTH GRADE
September 1962

I quit wearing my glasses. They were thick as molasses, as my problem was that I had a *wandering eye*. The thick glasses drew my eye forward. It isn't crossed anymore. I am so glad to get rid of those glasses! Ray, in my class, made fun of me. "Where'd four eyes go?" He asks laughing.

I look over at him with distain. "At least four eyes left! You, meanwhile, are stuck with that face!"

The teacher scolds us both and I must shut-up. I'm not done, though. I don't like him. Who does he think he is? He is just a short messy haired little twirp!

I stopped to see Nonna after school, and she likes me without glasses. She is very frail these days. I worry about her. I made cookies with her, had some with milk, kissed my mother's picture before I left, and headed home.

Ruby was home from college for the summer. I hated it when she went back. The only good thing about her leaving, is that I sleep in her room. She said I could, if I don't touch any of her stuff. Especially the red ribbon she has hanging on her mirror. She told me that it is sacred, and to never touch it.

Mom and Dad miss her, terribly. She is doing so well in college though. She gets all good grades. Ruby was a perfect daughter in every way. Much unlike me!

The New York Yankees won the World Series last October, and in February John Glenn orbited the earth.

The Beatles sing *Love Me Do* on the radio as I dance around the living room. That Paul McCartney is like a pure white light, breathtaking to behold!

Marilyn Monroe was found dead in August. That puzzles me. She had it all. What could have been so horrible for her to do that?

The first Walmart Store was opened in Rogers, Arkansas in July. I don't know what a Walmart is, but the news says it has everything from toilet paper to tents, whatever that means.

Recently, the Soviets aimed their missiles at us. JFK was on the television. He said that we will use military force if necessary. Julia is all worked up about that and I tease her. "Baby!"

She hollers back, "DO YOU WANT TO BE NUKED, SOPHIE?"

By Oct. 27 both sides came to an agreement, but we had been on the brink of a nuclear war for days. Julia says she is relieved. The thought of war has always put her into a tailspin.

Life goes way too fast for me. I am in seventh grade already! I was nervous, going into the big high school with all those older kids! Dutch assured me it would be easy. Maybe easy for her, because she is smart. I could be smart if I wanted to be, but I just don't want to get serious about it.

Julia and I watch *Ben Casey* on television every Monday night. He is a handsome doctor, and we are in love with him. Aunt Ina bought us both a Ben Casey shirt. Everyone has one. Now we do too!

In school on Tuesday, Mr. Peron in history class asks us who our President is and when was he elected. I know this! I put my hand up and he calls on me. "Our President is John F. Kennedy. He was elected in November 1960. He was only 43 and the youngest President ever! He is handsome. His wife is pretty too." The class laughs. Ray is howling. Ray thinks everything is funny.

Mr. Peron replies, "That's enough class. Yes, you are right, Sophie. Everybody likes him. He recently announced that his goal is to put a man on the moon."

That sounds crazy to me. I think President Kennedy must be dreaming!

In health class next, Mr. Abelman stands in front of the class in his plaid jacket. He is a little overweight with thinning hair. I find health boring, and he knows I do. Most times, Mr. Abelman is teasing students. He thinks he is funny. He told Charlie that his mother must have put a bowl on his head to cut his hair. He told Martha, who just got a new perm, that she must have stuck her finger in a light socket. He asked Larry, who is somewhat feminine, if he wanted to wear his wife's jewelry. He is not funny.

Ray, the rabble-rouser, asks Mr. Abelman, "How's your wife, King?"

Mr. Abelman shouts back at him sternly, "KING'S my HORSE! MAE'S my WIFE!" Just then the bell to end class rings way too early. It must be a malfunction. We all stand up ready to leave the room. Mr. Abelman hollers "WRONG BELL, WRONG BELL!"

Ray pipes up, "Ron Bell, heck, he graduated long ago!"

Mr. Abelman grabs Ray by his shirt to haul him to the principal's office. Ray won't stop laughing, as Mr. Abelman pulls him past my desk. Ray looks at me grinning. "Guess everything is funny as long as it's happening to someone else." I look away. I don't want dragged into this! Ray can sure be a bozo.

In Mr. Creag's class, Ray got into the classroom first and hid in Mr. Creag's closet. In the middle of class, as Mr. Creag is twisting his button on his jacket in front of the class, Ray comes out of the closet wearing Mr. Creag's top hat, his top coat, and he is eating Mr. Creag's lunch. Poor Mr. Creag. He is always being tortured by the rabble-rousers in class.

I've made a new friend, Betty Jones. She has a petite face and dark hair, always combed perfectly with a barrett on the right side. She invited me to go home on the school bus with her after school today. She is a little bit timid and quiet, but I like her.

When we arrive off the bus, we say a quick hello to her mom in the kitchen. We grab a warm cookie off the pan that just came out of the oven, then we go across the street to the barn. It is a run-down barn, and I can see her father in the field beyond. He looks burly and grouchy.

Betty sees that I notice. "Don't worry about him, Sophie. He's crabby all the time. He especially doesn't like when I bring friends home."

Why did she tell me that? I'm nervous now. But I forget about it as I pet her white horse in the stall. Then we start to play with the kittens in the barn. There are baby sheep here too. So sweet. Wait, one is laying still. Very still, but breathing. "Betty, something is wrong with this little lamb!"

She looks close at it and strokes its head. "It is breathing. Let me get Daddy." She runs to the barn opening, "Daddy! One of the lambs is sick!"

He walks to the barn like he is not happy she has bothered him. "Who's this?" he asks her, peering at me.

"My new friend, Sophie. She lives in Yatesboro."

He stares at me in a frightening way. "Sophie is an Italian name!"

"My mother was Italian, Mr. Jones."

"Umph!" he mutters. He glares at Betty next. He looks down at the lamb briefly, picks it up by the hind legs, walks just outside the barn door to a big tree clearly in our sight, and swings the lamb's head against the tree to kill it.

We scream. Betty cries hard, "Daddy! Did you have to?"

He doesn't answer. He throws the lamb in the weeds and gets onto Betty's white horse named Snow. She loves that horse. She talks about it all the time. Her Dad grabs a whip and starts whipping it and galloping fast up over the hill. I can see even in the distance the blood running down the side of the horse.

We run to the house to tell her mom. She just stares out the window, I think she is crying.

"Can I use your phone, Betty?" I ask. My hand is shaking, as I dial SUNSET33445. I wait. When I hear it pick up, I cry, "Dad, come get me!"

I absolutely am sure it is because I was there that these things happened. He didn't want me there. He doesn't like me. And, he obviously doesn't like Italians. I'm sorry for Betty, but I will never go there again. NEVER! Cobwebs are plenty there.

I tell Dad about it when he picks me up. "You have to forget about it, Sophie. Some people are just born crying, live complaining, and die disappointed!" That is supposed to make me feel better I suppose. But the feeling of unwantedness is consuming my soul.

******

The next day, Betty never mentioned it and in fact, didn't even talk to me. She knows. She knows we can't be friends.

Again, I notice how Otto is outgrowing everything. He grew probably four inches over the summer. I know the coat we gave him no longer fits. He is wearing a plaid flannel shirt again. Probably his dad's. It is worn, and dirty. His locker is right by mine. He struggles opening it. "Here, let me help, Otto."

He stands back as I turn the combination. "Do you like being in high school?"

"It's okay I guess."

As I look at him, I see more than one round burnt circle on his hand. I see several. "What is that, Otto?"

He slams his locker door shut. "Don't worry about it!"

"Why wouldn't I worry, Otto?" He walks away. "TELL ME, WHY SHOULD I NOT WORRY?"

He stops and turns. He glares at me. "Nothing you can do, that's why."

"Oh yes there is! I can help! I can do something, surely! "

"GO AWAY!" His face is rigid and he walks away from me fast and hard.

Mr. Bosco, Mr. Himes and Mr. Priestas are in the hallway. They could hear us, I'm sure. They heard Otto tell me to go away. Mr. Bosco smiles at me as I walk past him. "We'll just keep trying, Sophie."

I can't answer. If I try to talk, I'm going to cry. Why do I care so much about him? WHY??

Right now, I must forget about it, as we are having seventh grade physicals today. But I will catch up with him later and try again!

In the nurse's office, we girls must strip down to just our underpants and bra and stand in line. The school nurse, Mrs. Robinson, weighs us before we see Dr. Pitts. Betty Lou, his nurse is here. I saw Betty Lou walking last night on our street with her friend, Donna Lee.

141

I am humiliated standing in line, nearly naked. Finally, I am next. I step on the scale. Mrs. Robinson moves the little metal thing once, then twice, then a third time and announces as loud as she can, "You are getting fat, Sophie! You need to cut out the French fries!" I hear the girls in line giggle. I am mortified!

I am fat? I weight 117 lbs. and I am 5'2". Is that fat? I am embarrassed. I want to scream, I HATE YOU! I don't. I must be fat, that's all!

To make things worse, she hands me a little book to read. It says "Understanding your Body, Preparing for Menstruation." There is a girl on the front in her underwear. I am going to have to hide this in one of my drawers at home. It is a dirty book!

I go home feeling like I am so fat I am waddling, plus I have a dirty book tucked in my pocket.

Mom tries to tell me I'm not fat. "But I am. Mrs. Robinson says so."

Mom is angry at Mrs. Robinson. "I want you to respect your elders, Sophie. But between you and me, Mrs. Robinson is a bully. You are NOT fat, honey. Now her, SHE'S FAT!" We both laugh. But still, I know I am fat.

I run to my room. I hide the book in my underwear drawer, then join Mom in the kitchen.

"Mom, Otto got really tall over the summer. He grew out of those things we gave him."

She pauses a minute to think. "There's a football parents meeting tonight at the school. I'll go to it and see if I can get some clothing donations. You can go along if you like."

Mom and I drive up to the gym for the 7 pm meeting. The parents have their football meeting first then ask if there are any other concerns.

Mom stands up. "I am here on behalf of a boy in seventh grade that needs clothing. Your boys on the football team would all be much bigger than him. I am just asking, that if you have things your boys outgrew, or are done with, would you please bring them to my house? I will get them to this boy." I am so glad she didn't announce his name.

******

The next day, clothes, coats, boots, shoes, hats, gloves started to show up at our house. I am so excited to take them to Otto. Dad doesn't want me to go. "I think it is better that I go myself." He knows what happened last time.

"Otto's dad works at the car garage, and I know he works Saturdays," I tell him.

"Okay, then. You can go."

We drive out the lane early in the day. The lane is the same, narrow with lots of ruts and holes. As we approach the house, nothing much has changed. The porch is still falling off, the barn with the chicken feet and deer horns looks the same. The blue bus with paint falling off has more weeds covering it. Dad drives right up to the house. We walk across the broken porch. Knock, knock, knock.

Otto comes to the door. "We have some things for you, Otto." I smile at him. He doesn't smile back.

Dad has two large garbage bags full of clothing. "May I set these inside?"

"No, leave them here on the porch." Otto looks scared. "Leave them right there." He points to just in front of the door, and Dad sets them down onto the rotting porch.

I can see through the screen door, past Otto, the old grandpap sitting in a chair. There is a whiskey bottle beside him. His head is down. He is sleeping.

"Have you eaten yet today, Otto?" Dad seems worried.

"Some," he timidly replies.

Dad looks at his slim frame and hollow eyes. "Come home with us, son. We'll do a good cooked meal for you today for supper."

"No! Thank you, but you need to go!" He reaches out, grabs the garbage bags. "Thanks." He slams the door and we see him go through a tiny hallway to the back of his house. I look at dad, he looks at me. The silent cloud of a dragonfly passes by as a snake withers across the grass. I hear frogs in the distance and the caw of a raven. But the sound I want to hear is Otto coming back out the door. I never hear that sound.

We walk back to the car. "You can't keep obsessing about Otto, Sophie. We are doing all we can to help him. You must remember we cannot overstep our boundaries as it would not go well with that dad of his. We don't want to cause Otto more grief than he already has. You can see he is scared to death."

We drive home in silence. I try to not worry about Otto, but it is hard not to. I decide to take a walk to Rural Valley to get my mind off Otto. At Mrs. Waryu's house, her daughter, Mary Ann, plays records in her upstairs bedroom. She is playing Patsy Cline on her record player. I want my own record player. I know if I ask, Dad will get me one. Her son, Charlie, is mowing. I give him a quick little wave and he nods.

I walk up around the Community Building to see if anyone is there. There isn't. I head down the hill towards Yatesboro.

I am thinking about Christmas again. I wonder if Otto gets any presents.

Since aluminum cans came out just last year, I am allowed a can of soda in the evenings. I'm going to save it and bring it to Otto. I know he would never get any soda. I can't quit thinking about him. I need to know more about him. I NEED TO HELP HIM! I just do. Maybe I WILL buy that hammer to knock that wall down!

Shannock Valley High School built 1954

CHAPTER EIGHTEEN
THE DAY THE COUNTRY CHANGED
November 1963

Ray talks to Otto often now and as odd as he is, I'm glad Otto has a friend. Well, sort of glad.

Last May, on prom night, Ray showed up with us to watch the couples going into the gym and he wasn't being stupid for once. He, in fact, was acting like he likes me, but I could never like him that way. His older brother had gone on the senior class trip to Washington DC so he was chatting a mile a minute about that.

We knew most of the girls at the prom, even though they were older than us. Nancy, a junior, wore a gown that was a beautiful soft blue and the skirt was full and luscious with little butterflies on it. I dream of wearing a pretty gown like that and dancing at the prom someday! I'm thirteen already. It won't be long now that I'll get to go to the prom. It gives me something to dream about.

I've become friends with Brenda, Renie, Linda and Judy. Brenda is just slightly older than me. She is my exact height and I like how she talks in a soft voice. She lives on the road to Dayton. Renie is most likely the tiniest person in our class. She has very blonde hair and I always tell her that I think a strong wind would blow her away. Judy is bubbly and happy all the time, and her make-up and nails are always perfect. Linda lives in Numine, on Main Street. She is quiet but friendly. She has a boyfriend, Andy. Linda thinks the sun rises and sets on him, but I am not so sure. Just something about him isn't right for her. I suppose it is none of my business, though.

There is an exchange student in the senior class this year. His name is Swiet. Such a strange name for a guy. It is Saturday night and Mom and Dad have him down for a meal. His English isn't great but we manage. He is tiny, and he is homesick. It is as obvious as daylight. A girl from the senior class came along, Linda Swanson. I am glad, as she helps him with his English and makes the conversation easier. He needs the help. He will be here until May when he goes back to Indonesia. Mom and Dad want us to learn about other countries, but all I learned is that I never want to go as far from home as he did, seeing how homesick he is. It is sad.

Swiet

I like high school, except for the homework. I am all about football games and friends.

Doug Buffone graduated from here, and we hear he is doing swell playing football for college. They say the Chicago Bears are looking at him to go pro. He was good in high school football. We might be a little town, but we've had some big athletes come out of this town. Bob Pelligrini was another. He played for the Philadelphia Eagles. Hard to think that two great football players got their start on our football field at the top of the hill. Who says big stuff can't come out of a small town?

In baseball too, Steve Souchock played for the NY Yankees, Chicago Whitesox, and the Detroit Tigers. Mike Goliat played baseball for the Philadelphia Eagles Whiz Kids and Billy Hunter played for the Baltimore Orioles. Ron Shoop played for the Detroit Tigers. I just think that is all really something!

******

Mom is having another baby soon. I was watching American Bandstand one evening with Julia when I found out. Julia was fighting me for the television. She wanted to watch about the brutal police attacks on young demonstrators that happened in Birmington. Mom settled that by turning off the television to tell us another baby was coming in late November. I didn't even know what to say about that. I hadn't noticed her belly, although I must say I thought she was eating too many sweets and gaining weight. Theo is just four now. Mom just loves babies and a big family. Dad loves it too. But not me. It's too many kids! Dad was kissing her and smiling and I was growling inside. I don't want to help with another baby, I want to be with my friends!

I made up my mind when November came, I was going to figure out how to get a Thanksgiving meal to Otto. I run into him as we all walk to Bull Fischer's science class first period. "Hey, Otto!" He says nothing. "You look nice today!"

"Thanks." He is in his silence mode today. He is now wearing the clothes we took to him. He is still a little dirty looking, but does wear different clothes now and then. I know they never get washed.

He always grabs a seat way in the back of the room. I grab one right in front of him. I turn around and smile, "Gum?" as I hand him a stick of juicy fruit.

He takes it. "Thanks." That's all.

"Otto, my dad says that your cobwebs are plenty and kisses are few. Is that true?"

He looks at me puzzled. "I don't even know what that means."

"It means that your life is bad and your happiness is very little."

He puts his head down. "I guess you could say that."

"Well your life can get better. You just need to work at it, and let me help you. I'm going to come to your house on Thanksgiving with a meal for you. That okay?"

"NO, DON'T!" he answers sternly. Why did I ask? I should have just done it. Darn it!

"Why, Otto? It's Thanksgiving. I'll have enough for your dad and grandpap too!"

150

"I DON'T CARE ABOUT THANKSGIVING!"

"Honestly, Otto. I don't know WHY I care about you!" I turn away.

From behind me I hear the word. "Sorry." I don't turn around. I don't respond.

I feel Ray staring at me across the aisle. I look over. He circles his ear with his index finger, meaning *crazy* of course. If anybody is crazy, it's Ray!

It is Wednesday, November 20, 1963. When we get home from school, Aunt Ina is at our house. "Your Mom has gone to the hospital to have the baby!" She is excited. I should be too, but not quite. "Do you want a boy or a girl, Sophie?"

"I want a puppy!" I tell her. I'm kidding, but I really DO want a puppy.

Aunt Ina just laughs at me.

My new little sister, Isabelle Betsy, arrived at 3:15 pm. I think I will call her *Izzy* for short. I won't be getting my puppy. Dad gets home by early evening happy as a clam. Most men would be saying "Oh my god, seven kids!" My Dad says, "Thank you God, for my seven kids!"

I laugh at him. "You are awfully happy, Dad. Happy for a guy with seven kids!"

He laughs back. "I am, Sophie. I know you think that is a lot of kids. Why does that overwhelm you so bad?"

"Because I read something that says you should never have more children than you have car windows!"

He broke out in a full belly laugh. "Then we'll need to get another car, so we have enough windows!"

******

Two days later, November 22, 1963, Mom is still in the hospital. I am in gym class just after lunch. Our teacher is playing *Sugar Shack* and *Louie Loui,* as we bounce on the trampoline.

Suddenly the big double doors to the gym open with a bang. Roseann from the sophomore class is in the doorway. "PRESIDENT KENNEDY HAS BEEN KILLED!" She hollers. The music stops. We all get down and gather on the floor. "You sure?" our teacher asks her.

"I'm sure! The office is playing the broadcast in classrooms! President Kennedy was in Dallas Texas with Mrs. Kennedy. He was in a convertible in a parade. Someone shot him!"

Everyone starts to cry, students and teachers alike. What a strange feeling it is to have loved somebody we never met. But we loved him.

Finishing the school day was hard. In Mr. Creag's class, he twirled his button so hard one fell off and rolled down the aisle beside Margie. She picked it up and gave it back to him. Kids didn't even laugh. Not even Ray. Mrs. Brown, the Librarian, usually is very strict about us talking in the library. She always wears thin white sneakers so she can sneak up on us, but she didn't even try to sneak today. She didn't have to. No one feels like chatting.

Changing classes, I pass Mr. Stroupe and Mr. Boarts, our custodians. They always tease me, but not today. They are leaning on their brooms with their heads down, talking in almost a whisper.

School lets out and we are all glued to the television. They show the moment he was shot over and over again. Suddenly I realize, "Oh my, it's Sammy's birthday today!" He is ten years old. Old enough to know we missed it and quiet enough to not remind us. Dutch jumps up to start making a cake. A couple hours later we sing to Sammy, and eat cake, still glued to the television. I doubt Sammy will forget this birthday.

President John Fitzgerald Kennedy   May 29, 1917 – November 22, 1963

Another day passes and we again flip the television on immediately. They've got Lee Harvey Oswald in custody. He is the assassin. He is only twenty-four years old, and a former U.S. Marine. How can you be a Marine for our country and kill our President? It is all so troubling!

Today they are marching Lee Harvey Oswald through

a crowd at the courthouse. BANG! BANG! He falls. He has been shot. Secret service pile onto a guy in a trench coat holding the gun. Lee Harvey Oswald is dead. A man by the name of Jack Ruby shot him. He is a night club owner. Why would he do that? Is he mad that Lee shot our President? Or is he part of something bigger, part of the assassination, and afraid Lee will start talking?

I will never forget where I was the day that I heard President Kennedy was shot. Never. The funeral a few days later is so hard to watch. Poor little John-John is saluting his dad. We cry our eyes out. Vic Firment's mom came to visit. She is a friend of ours. Vic is in Korea. She told us that as soon as President Kennedy was shot, Vic told her they were all put on high alert. This assassination is bigger than we could ever know.

I watch a few days later as they are moving Mrs. Kennedy out of the White House. They load President Kennedy's rocking chair onto a moving van. Poor Mrs. Kennedy. Her life changed in an instant.

In school, in science class, I turn around to Otto. "What did you think about President Kennedy getting killed? Wasn't that awful, Otto?"

He looks at me and says firmly, "We are all going to die, Sophie."

What a strange thing to say. What a very strange thing. "Well, of course we are all going to die! But, I'm afraid to die, aren't you?"

"There isn't much I'm afraid of anymore."

Of course not, he has lived every day in fear. I suppose he'd have to, at some point, must just stop being afraid, in order to survive.

He reaches into his pocket and brings out a small key. He hands it to me. "Keep this and don't ask me any questions. I will tell you when it is time to use it."

What could it be for? Strange. "I'll keep it, Otto. Is everything okay at your house?"

"You're funny, Sophie. Nothing is ever okay there. You know though, Fred Wilson moved into Kiser's place. I go over there a lot. He is very kind to me, just like Kiser was."

"I'm glad, Otto. You deserve to be treated nice."

"Fred used to drink, but he doesn't now. He told me he took to the bottle when he lost his twin brother in the Korean War. They were close. He took it pretty hard I guess."

"It would be horrible to lose a sibling. It would be the worst thing ever! At least Fred is okay now. I'm glad he's a friend to you."

I love that he is talking to me more now. He smiles and I see a slight dimple on his right cheek. I never saw that before. It's cute.

SVHS Class Trip in Washington DC 1962

SVHS Prom 1962

CHAPTER NINETEEN
THE GOOD WITH THE BAD
February 1964

Nonna died. She was ninety-five. Mom told us as we were getting ready for church this morning. Zio Dom had come earlier, to tell her. "She didn't suffer honey. Your Zio Dom found her dead in bed."

Our Nonno had died a year ago, now Nonna. I am sad. So sad. I feel the guilt creep up my body like a dense fog. I hadn't visited her much lately. I wanted to be with friends more. Mom sees my guilt.

"You were good to her, Sophie. She really enjoyed you. It was just her time. You'll see her again someday."

Words are easy to say, but are they true? I think words hold too much water. How do we know what is true? Will I see her again someday? Will I?

We skip church, and Mom and Dad go with us to Nonna's house. Zio Dom is here. I look around. So empty. So very empty.

Zio Dom smiles at us. "She loved you, girls."

Does he think we don't know that? We know that! I am swallowing hard to keep the lump in my throat from coming up. "I know." I say, still holding onto my stiff upper lip.

He puts his arms around me. "We'll sure miss her, won't we?" My tears start to flow. Dutch and Julia are crying too. Mom and Dad have their arms around them.

Zio Dom takes the picture of my mother and him down from the wall and hands it to me. "You've given your mama lots of kisses on this picture. I think you should have it."

I hold it to my chest and cry. It means a lot. It is the only picture I have of my mother.

Zio Dom looks at Mom and Dad. "My mother was always sad that she couldn't raise the girls. I was sad too. I would have, if it weren't for my wife. I've always regretted that, but I had to keep peace, you know."

Dad replies to him. "It was for the best, they've been happy with us. And they are my daughters in every way. We love them."

"Just the same, what I have to give you hopefully makes up for what my family couldn't do for them." He hands Dad a large envelope. "In this envelope is money for the girls. My parents saved it for them. Dad put it in my care just before he died, in case we needed it to provide care for my mother and if not, it was to go to the girls." He smiles. "I guess that wine that my old man sold in the kitchen was for a purpose. It should be enough for each of them to go to college."

Dad takes it sheepishly. "I don't know what to say. That would be a lot of money from just selling wine!"

Zio Dom laughs, "Well, I am seventy-five years old, and he's been selling that wine since the day I was born. So, it added up! You don't need to say anything, Sam. It is the least my family can do for yours."

"What about Ulla?" Dad asks.

"What about her?" Zio Dom answers firmly. "This is none of her business! She kept me from having the girls, so this money is definitely not for Ulla!"

Dad understands. He tucks the envelope into the inside of his coat and shakes Zio Dom's hand. "Thank you doesn't seem enough, but thank you."

I can't stop crying. I am miserable. "I want to go home, Mom." We do.

I go to my room and take a picture of The Beatles down to hang the picture of my mother. I sit on the bed and stare at it. She was a pretty baby. "I only know you as a baby," I say out loud.

The evening is long and we all stay up late. The Beatles are on the Ed Sullivan show. Watching them makes me forget my sorrow somewhat. When it is over, we don't go to bed. We chat until midnight with Mom and Dad about Nonna and Nonno. We talk about the money they left us.

Dad wants us to make our plans for the future. "You girls need to start thinking about what you want to do with your lives. Dutch, you especially. Start looking at colleges and think about what you want to be. My hope is that you'll all go to college, but I know college isn't for everybody. Whatever it is you choose in life, this money is here for that purpose."

"Okay, Dad." Dutch replies. "I've been thinking of something in education."

Jules chimes in. "Whatever it is I do, it will be something to help people. Maybe a nurse."

I say nothing. I've got no idea what I want to be. No idea at all.

Shortly after midnight, we hear fire sirens. There is a fire somewhere close. Dad could hear the fire truck speeding down the street with their sirens blaring, and he could see smoke. "Come on girls. You want to go watch a fire?" We race to the car.

As we get close, we can see it is the Goldstrohm barn. We jump out of the car. Sam Goldstrohm is in the yard. It's his family's barn. Sam is in my class. He is a quiet boy, and he works hard on this farm. He even works before he can leave for school in the mornings. "What happened, Sam?" I ask.

"Seems as though a drunk went in there by the hay to sleep off his drunk. He had walked to Greendale earlier to drink and was walking back. The drunks do that all the time, you know. They'll sleep wherever they land. He was probably smoking. The barn went up in flames. Unfortunately, so did he."

It was totally engulfed in flames. I had a flashback of the Doms fire and I shivered. It is troubling to think about the man inside.

"I never saw my dad move so fast." Sam said. "When he saw the fire out his bedroom window, he started running down the stairs, putting his pants on at the same time. I didn't know that was even possible!"

I'm glad he can chuckle. This is a big loss. Alcohol can bring so much heartache. So much.

Greendale has been here for as long as I can remember. Dad said that Angelo Milicia opened the bar in 1938, and Mary Geary kept it going when he served in the army for three years. He added a kitchen and an apartment when he came home, and eventually married Cecelia Londino. They lived in the apartment above the bar with their children, Beatrice, Cynthia and Michael. The dance hall was built two years later. Dad says there were dances and wedding receptions there. He said Johnny Murphy and his orchestra played in the grand opening. After a few years, they turned it into a bowling alley. Dad knows a lot about a lot of stuff.

Dutch has a couple girlfriends over the next evening, Suzanne and Mary. I hear them giggling in Dutch's bedroom so I peak in. Mary is teasing Suzanne's hair! "Does that hurt?" I ask. Dutch laughs and slams the door.

Mary Lias and Suzanne Coleman

I don't care that I'm not included in the *big girl* moment. Dad is taking Julia and I bowling!

We walk through a hallway outside of the bar as I hear the ding-ding-ding of balls coming in and the sound of the pins being knocked down. After we rent our bowling shoes, Dad leaves us to bowl and he goes over to the bar for a beer. When he comes back, he sits down at the scoring desk beside me. "Guys in the bar are saying that the police have suspicions about who killed the guy at *The Bucket of Blood* years ago."

"Really?" I'm rather shocked. "That was like six years ago!"

"Never too late to catch a criminal, Sophie."

"I hope they catch him. It has always creeped me out that he could be living among us."

"For now, it just seems they have only suspicions. It still may take them a long time to make an arrest."

I throw my ball down the gutter, as usual. As I wait for my ball to come rolling back to me, I look across two lanes. There is a boy from school here bowling. I recognize him. He is one year older than me. He is very tall, and handsome. His light blonde hair is always neatly combed and the square shape of his face gives him a striking look. I hear the kids call him Buck. He lives somewhere near here, on Route 85, I'm pretty sure. I think he has noticed me staring at him.

Original Greendale Tavern

Cecelia Milicia

That little bit of eye flirting I did must have done some good. In school the next day, walking to the band room for first period, Buck stops me. "Hey there."

I'm not sure what to say. "Hey there, yourself!" That was all.

After fourth period, I'm heading towards the cafeteria. He comes beside me. "Do you want to stand at the windows and talk?"

"Sure." He buys two ice cream sandwiches out of the machine.

That was the day it started to grow. Our lunchtime became standing at the window, eating an ice-cream sandwich. Just standing and talking. I like him. I like how this is feeling. Everything about it is right. The best thing about it is that I get to save twenty cents of my lunch money every day. Mom gives me thirty cents for my lunch and the icecream sandwich is only ten cents. She doesn't need to know I'm eating icecream sandwiches instead of broccoli.

It is all couples standing at the windows. One couple is kissing, another is arguing.

"There's a fan bus going to the basketball game Friday night. Can you go?" he asks.

"I'm sure I'll be allowed." I answered. My little voice is telling me NOT to tell Dad I am going with a boy. But really, I am fourteen. I am old enough.

******

Friday comes, and the bus leaves the school at 5:30 pm and we are on it. Buck runs to the back seat of the bus to grab it for us. "Why back here?" I ask.

"I don't like kids," he laughs and I think he is kidding, but I'm not sure.

The games start at 6:30 and we make it in time. The last game is over by 9 and we head home on the bus, still in the back seat. It is dark outside. Some of the kids are sleeping. Buck starts to kiss me. Holy crap, I don't know how to kiss! So, I just lean into it. It is exciting. His lips are soft and warm, but he is slightly aggressive. Honestly, I don't think he knows how to kiss either. He is sucking in my upper lip. That is strange, but is that how you do it? Must be! I let it happen. What do I know? It is an hour ride home, and we kiss the solid hour.

When the bus stops and we part, he looks at me and says, "Oh my, sorry about that!"

"Sorry about what?" I ask him. He is staring at my lip, so at that point I touch my lip. My top lip is HUGE! It's swollen so big it almost touches my nose! My dad is going to kill me! "WHAT DID YOU DO?"

"Well, I didn't mean to!" He is laughing. He thinks this is funny!

I leave the bus and run home. Mom is in the kitchen. I try to get in the door and get to the stairway so she doesn't see me, but she does. "WHAT happened to your lip, Sophie?"

I had to think fast. "Those darn kids got off the bus and started throwing snowballs at me!"

"That so?" she says and goes back to what she was doing. She bought it! I think.

******

The next morning my dad got us three girls out of bed. "Let's go! We are going for a drive!"

After breakfast he makes Dutch and Julia come along and sit in the front seat of his big old Mercury station wagon with the wood panel down the sides. I am the only one in the back seat. He starts to preach, and he is merciless. "I don't ever want to hear that you girls let a boy kiss you! If you let a boy kiss you, you've given him an inch. Then, he won't be happy with that inch and he'll want a foot. You give him a foot and he'll say he wants two feet, and before you know he will want a yard!"

Julia and Dutch keep turning around on the front seat giving me horrible dirty looks. Dad never turns around. He couldn't say this stuff face to face, hence the car ride.

By the next day, my swollen lip went back to normal. When I saw Buck on Monday, I scolded him. "If you're going to kiss me, you can't suck my lip in!" He just laughs and walks away. He doesn't care. He doesn't care at all.

I sat in front of Otto again in Mr. Briskell's class later in the day. Otto taps me on the shoulder. "Heard you got in trouble for kissing on the bus."

"Who told you that?" I can't believe he knows that!

"Julia is yapping about it all over school."

"I'm going to kill her!"

Otto laughs. I rarely see him laugh. "Don't tell Julia I told you!"

As much as I hate that the whole school knows, I love the fact that Otto is saying more than just a few words. But that can change on a dime and he'll be silent. Right now, I love that he laughed. Even if it is only once.

Rabble-rouser Ray is at it again. Mr. Briskell's eyes are closed. He is in one of his naps. Ray sneaks up to his desk and takes the class roster that is a list of our names. When Mr. Briskell grades us, he writes our grade beside our names on that list and passes it around class. Ray quickly wrote the name *Ruby Begonia* at bottom. He shows me as he passes my desk to put it back. I laugh. It's funny. When Mr. Briskell woke up, he knew none the better.

I turn to Otto. "Ray's going to get in trouble for that, don't you think?"

Otto looks down, then up. "Probably."

I'm about to lose my mind with him. One minute he talks, the next minute he doesn't.

"Sometimes you don't say much, Otto."

"Oh well," he laughs. "Does your boyfriend say much?"

"This has nothing to do with him!" I whip myself back around.

"Whatever!" he mumbles.

Whatever? What does that mean? There is that moment again, where pulling conversation out of him is like trying to pull an oiled pig out of wet mud!

******

The next day Otto seems in just a little better of a mood. I even saw him exchange a couple words with Larry who sits beside him in Mr. Briskell's class. I'm not trying to talk to him today. I'm still mad about his change in mood yesterday.

Mr. Briskell passes around that class roster that contains our grade beside our names, so we can all see our grade, and everyone else's actually. He has made a copy for everyone. As they come back the aisle, I take mine and hand Otto his. "Thanks." He smiles ever so slightly.

"It talks!" I say and whip back around.

On the roster, Ray and I got a B, the brains of the classes got an A, several got a C, and I was sad and embarrassed for Otto to see the D beside his name.

At the bottom of all those names was: Ruby Begonia A. I heard Otto chuckle when he saw it. Good. He can at least laugh occasionally, even if it is just a little chuckle. I smile at the thought of it. I turn around, "Good to hear you laugh, Otto."

"I'm, not ALL bad, Sophie."

"Didn't say you were. But what *little* bad you are, we need to work on!"

Students in science class at SVHS

SVHS Football Team 1966

CHAPTER TWENTY
FRUSTRATION
Spring 1964

Lately, my conversations with Otto have grown into more words. He still seems apprehensive to have a friend, yet I think he likes it. I asked him yesterday what he does for fun. "I work in the barn." It was a short answer but at least he answered.

"What do you do in there?"

"Just stuff. When I'm in the barn, he leaves me alone."

"That makes me sick! You have to stay in the barn to stay out of harm's way?"

"I love being in the barn, Sophie."

I give him a warm smile. "Then that is exactly what you should do!"

He smiles and opens his math book. "Get busy, teacher's watching."

With the excitement of summer break approaching, my excitement of summer fun grows.

Things between Buck and I got way beyond that first kiss. I told Dad I won't ever kiss until I'm older and he believed me. It is so sad that he is so naive.

I really don't like going further than the kissing but I don't know what to say. I think this is the way things are supposed to happen, so I keep my mouth shut. Buck gets mad when I try to stop him anyways. He comes to my house every Saturday night. He also gets mad if I plan something and he can't come. I don't like that.

I told him I want to work at Boyer's Potato Chip factory. He got mad about that, too. Mom told me that the Boyer brothers, Jesse and Harry, used to peel potatoes by hand in their kitchen twenty-five years ago. That was where it all started. The factory was built three years ago and the newspaper said they produce 1200 to 1500 lb. of chips per hour.

I asked Mom if I could work there. "Absolutely not! You are only fourteen!"

I'm mad. "Well, Jaci Boyer works there and so does Georgine Jordan, and they are younger than me! Heck, there's even a Thomaswick girl that works there that drives out from Ford City. Why can't I?"

"Because you are not! You can babysit for people. Mrs. Hayes just called last night asking for a babysitter. You can do that!"

"Me? Me who isn't crazy about kids? I won't make much either!"

"You like kids, Sophie. You just don't know it. Look how Izzy hangs on to you. She won't leave your side." She goes back to the pot she is stirring. "You know, Sophie, my friend, Virginia, used to work for Linus Olsen for twenty-five cents a day!"

"Well, that was in cave man days!" I run upstairs, but I can hear Mom laughing.

I must agree about Izzy. She sure grew on me. She turned into a cute little girl. There is no more sense in arguing this point. Buck will be glad I lost this argument anyways.

******

It is the last day of school and Otto isn't here. He has had more bruises on him lately. Two were as purple as iris in sunlight. I'm worried. It is Friday and tomorrow is the weekend. Brenda, has a car now. A green Volkswagon Bug. "Will you take me out to Otto's tomorrow morning?" I ask her.

"I don't know, Sophie. Do you think you should be doing that? He is weird!"

"I know he is, but there is just something about him. Something that makes my heart ache."

Brenda looks concerned. "I'll take you if you know his dad isn't there. I want to get right back though, some of the girls are going to the Roundtop after lunch."

"Jax checked with Doc Crawford and he's working tomorrow. You'll be home in time to go to the Roundtop."

Ray is eavesdropping. He has heard our conversation. Suddenly idiot Ray is serious. "You girls might want to think about that. I feel sorry for the poor guy too, but it might be dangerous out there."

"Shut-up, Ray." I scold. "You don't know what you are talking about."

"Whatever, Sophie! Shame on me for caring about you!" He stomps away.

Kids hanging out on the Roundtop
Behind them are the rows of company houses on the hill in Yatesboro

After an uneasy night's sleep, I awaken ready to go. I walk to Palilla's Market so Dad won't see I'm getting into Brenda's car. She picks me up there at 9 a.m.

Brenda seems uneasy. "It's okay. His dad isn't there. Don't worry." I tell her.

We go up through Numine and past Shannock Bar. "Turn right here." I tell her.

"I don't know about this, Sophie. It scares me."

"It will be fine. Stop worrying. His dad isn't there, and Otto is harmless."

"You sure about that?" she asks.

After navigating the narrow lane, we approach Otto's shack. She still stays back a hundred yards or so, and I walk across the high grass, past the well, and onto the broken-down porch. Knock, knock, knock. "Otto, you there?" No one answers. I peak through the living room window. His grandpap is asleep again in his chair, the empty whiskey bottle beside him. He doesn't hear me.

I walk to the wooden barn with the chicken legs over the door. There is a padlock on the outside of the door. He can't be in there! I go to the back of his house, to the blue school bus, with weeds growing all around it. I hear something rambling around inside. "Otto? That you?"

His head pokes up. His eyes look wild as he peers at me through the broken glass.

"It's just me!" I holler. "What are you doing in there?"

"Doing nothing. You need to go home!"

"Come out here!" I demand.

He has a bloody cut by his ear. "Come on Otto. I came here because I care about you. Who did that to you?" With his head down, he answers. "Who'd ya think?"

"Your dad? Is that why you weren't in school yesterday? You don't have to put up with that. I can get you out of here and help you."

"Don't want no help! Go be with your boyfriend!"

"You are driving me crazy, Otto! I am trying to HELP you! Tell me what to do. JUST TELL ME WHAT!"

"Leave!" He turns and walks away. "Just please leave!"

"Listen, Otto. We can talk to the Principal and Guidance Counselor and they'll get us help to get you out of here. You could have a good life somewhere else!"

He stops and turns to look at me. His face is troubled and his eyes wild. "You EVER tell anyone about me, Sophie, I'll disappear and never return. I MEAN IT!"

He scares me. "Disappear? Are you threatening me, Otto?"

He says nothing. I turn to walk away while hollering at him. "You know, Otto, I am trying to be your friend!"

I start back towards Brenda's car. I hear him holler, "Sophie!" I turn around, waiting for him to continue. I stare at him. He puts his head down then up again. He says two words. "Never mind."

I have no more words. He is exhausting. How can I help someone who doesn't want help? One thing for sure, he is being beaten here and often. I don't think that his old drunken grandpap cares either. And what is Otto doing in that broken-down old school bus? I will leave for now, but I WILL be BACK!

Getting into Brenda's car, it is clear she doesn't like what I'm doing. "What do you hope to accomplish, Sophie? It is obvious he is beyond repair!"

"Nobody is beyond repair! I can't sit back and let his dad kill him, because he will! I could get a family in town to take Otto, or even maybe my parents would. I could do something! But now I'm afraid to tell anyone, he threatened me he would disappear if I told anyone."

"He threatened you? Isn't that enough, Sophie?"

"He is just troubled. So very troubled. I have to figure it out, that's all."

When Brenda drops me at the basketball court, I go to the football field to just sit and think. I go to the top of the hill, where the bleachers are high. I sit on the top bleacher. The band is practicing and I hope it will distract my thoughts but it doesn't. Otto has never been a baby chick tucked under his mother's wing. I take the key out of my pocket. What is it? What is it for? I look up as a flock of birds float by. Why is life so difficult and unfair? I have it all, yet Otto has nothing. How is that? My parents love having seven kids, yet his father can't stand having one. How can that be? Yet, I try. How can I help someone who refuses to help himself? And at this point, how damaged is he? Why can't I just forget about him? Especially when I know he is probably hopeless.

It is still late morning as I walk to King's Drug Store. Maybe a vanilla coke will lift my spirits and that will help me think this through. Lenny and Gene are sitting at the counter, having their vanilla cokes which they tell me is their breakfast. I tell them about Otto, and how worried I am.

Gene speaks up first, "Don't worry too much. Lots of kids grow up in horrible circumstances, and they turn out alright! My dad was always cleaning my clock! Back in my hay day, I was always in trouble. The town cop then, old Charlie Dinger, was after me all the time. He had a 48 Plymouth and he'd always forget to shift from 2nd to 3rd. So, I'd lay rubber on one end of town, and he couldn't get there fast enough, because he never shifted to 3rd. Then I'd go to the other end of town and lay more rubber. He'd try to get there and couldn't. He just kept going back and forth. He never caught me, but he did tell my dad. Charlie told him that when he catches me, he will put me in jail and throw away the key!"

"That's not quite Otto's situation though." I tell him.

"I'm just sayin' that kids can take a lot. When Charlie told my dad that, I'd say that was the worst beating I ever got. You can just survive things, that's all. I'm okay. I'm normal."

"You think so?" Lenny says, chuckling.

I can't laugh at anything right now. "Well, Otto can't possibly be normal, living the way he does. And looks like as he gets older, the abuse gets worse. There is no way that won't affect his mind." I am sad saying it, but that is what I think.

Just then Norm King and Jack Arbuckle come up from the basement. Zelma Kirkpatrick is with them. She works here. She was in church last Sunday with her twin sister, Thelma and their younger sister, Erma.

Lenny is curious, "What's going on?"

Jack laughs, "We're down there to see what we got to fix the hole."

"What hole?" Lenny asks.

Jack points above the pharmacy. We hadn't noticed. We look up. We can see the sky through a hole about two feet in diameter.

"What happened?" I ask.

Norm answers. "We got robbed. Funny thing about it is that old Jessop saw the whole thing. At night he sleeps in his sister's shed behind here when he is sleeping off a drunk. He woke me up at 2 am and insisted there were robbers going down through the roof of the drug store. He told me they had on black hoods and black masks. I told him to not bother me and go sleep it off. Imagine my surprise when I came to work this morning and found that big hole in the roof. Jessop wasn't so drunk as I thought he was, I guess. I'm so frustrated with myself that I didn't believe Jessop. We could have caught them red-handed!"

"Yes, and you might have gotten yourself killed too!" Lenny tells him.

"Suppose so. The frustration may kill me though. Just a matter of fixing it now." Norm walks away.

Frustration comes in all different forms. I'm stressed, I'm frustrated, I'm scared for Otto. So scared. Mom tells me stress is when you wake up screaming and you realize you haven't fallen asleep yet. I am at that point.

THE SVHS Band practicing in the late 40's
To right is Company Store, behind them is Dr. Griffith's Office

SVHS Band on football field in the 60's

CHAPTER TWENTY-ONE
BIG TROUBLES
November 1964

The war in Vietnam has escalated, since the Gulf of Tonkin incident on August 2nd. There are so many different conversations about the war. I don't understand it all, but it does not affect me. At least not yet.

Although the trees have lost their leaves. It is an unusually warm day for November. Julia and I decide to walk to the gym, to sit on the steps.

I meet two sisters, Lynda and Susie. Lynda is shorter than Susie and her brown hair slightly darker than Susie's. She is bubbly, they both are. Their friend, Karen, is here with them. Karen is tall and chatty, and she laughs a lot. Since I idolize the older girls, I am excited I am in their company. They are in the junior class, all except Susie, she is a sophomore. I saw them last Friday at Homecoming on the football field.

Visiting on the gym steps

Homecoming on the football field

Lynda is telling us about how she and Susie came to live in Rural Valley. "There were five of us kids. We used to live in Sagamore with our real mom and dad, but my dad was killed in a car wreck when he was only thirty-two."

"I'm so sorry." Julia replies. "That would have been hard on your mother."

Lynda frowns. "We wouldn't know. It didn't take her very long to give us away!"

I am surprised. "Give you away? Just like that? Give five kids away?"

"Yep. Just gave us away. She had better things to do, I guess."

These things really interest me. "So, what happened to you?"

"Our Aunt Floss lived in Sagamore then too. She didn't have any kids of her own. She took Susie first. Other relatives took my other sisters, my brother and me. I cried buckets because I missed Susie, so Aunt Floss agreed to take me too. Before we knew it, Jeannie and my brother came there also. Just my oldest sister stayed where she was. Then after a few years, we moved to Rural Valley. We still go up to Sagamore now and then and hang out with some of our friends at the restaurant there."

"I'm glad it all worked out for you, Lynda. Your Aunt was brave taking on all those kids."

"Yes, she was. And she is not my aunt anymore. She is my mom. She became a true mother in every way."

Julia speaks up. "I get that. Our Mom and Dad are true in every way too, and they aren't my real parents either. You have a steady boyfriend, Lynda, don't you?"

"Yes, I do, and so does Karen. I don't like what happened in gym class yesterday over that."

"What happened?" I ask.

Our gym teacher, Mrs. Negal, singled us out by name. I mean those of us who have boyfriends. She handed us a form we were to fill out. It had questions on there as to how 'heavy' we pet!"

"How 'heavy' you pet? What does that mean?"

"She wanted to know how far we had gone with our boyfriends! We were furious!"

"Did you fill it out?"

Lynda laughs. "I sure did, I put on there that I pet my dog, Sparky, pretty heavily!"

We all laugh. Lynda sure has guts!

Three young boys just came. They start up the cement steps and hang onto the steel banister as they strike up a conversation with us. I know two of them, Richie and Andy. The third I don't. He is missing part of his one arm. They are all maybe in just fifth or sixth grade.

"I rode my bike past your house last night, Sophie. Did you see me?" Richie says. He lives on my street. He is sweet but very silly. His hair is always wild. He must like me. Who knew.

I remember that puppy love when I was his age. "No, Richie. I didn't. Who's your friend?"

"This here is Gary Devivo. Bet you wanna know what happened to his arm!"

Gary doesn't look embarrassed. He seems not as silly as the other two. He is just balancing himself on the pipe banister leaning out, then in. He just laughs. He knows Richie is silly.

"I didn't Richie, but why don't you let Gary tell me."

Gary smiles. "Got it caught in a meat grinder!"

I am a little shocked. "Oh my! When did that happen?"

He talks as he walks up and down the cement steps holding onto the steel banister, like boys do. "I was only fifteen months old. I don't remember it. My sister said I was lively. It happened so fast. It was no one's fault but my own. It's no big deal. It doesn't stop me from doing anything at all!"

"That's great to hear. You can be anything you want to be, Gary!"

They all laugh and jump down off the steps and start to run to the football field. Richie hollers, "See ya' later, Sophie!"

Lynda is amused. "He likes you, Sophie. Ain't that cute!"

"Well, gosh, don't tell Buck. He'll beat the poor kid up!" I laugh, but is it funny? I don't think so.

I walk back home thinking again about how the gym teacher asking Lynda how heavy she pets. I'm not sure what heavy is. It is possible I am already there with Buck, though I don't like it. I wish he would back off. But I don't ask him to. I don't want to make him mad.

******

The next morning Dad takes me to Numine, to Jax's. "You feel like a long walk?" she asks.

"How long of a walk?" I want to know.

"From here to Yatesboro, but on the Shamokin Trail, so it won't seem that long." I agree to go. We start out and pass the tipple. The tipple was full to the top with coal the last time I was here. The coal is all gone now! The boney dump smokes as we get to the path. Leona lives at the end of the street past the boney dump. She waves as we pass by. We start to walk from Numine to Yatesboro on the Shamokin Trail. On our walk we could see every coal bin to every house full to the top. I guess that is where all the coal went. Everyone has stockpiled their coal getting ready for winter.

Once home for the evening, Buck and I talk on the phone, but the party line is miserable. And besides that, every three minutes we get clicked off. I call him back a couple of times after being clicked off, then I throw my hands in the air and say FORGET IT! Mom and dad only allow me three click-offs anyways. The third click-off, when I hang up, Dad is staring at me. "You are getting too serious with this boyfriend, Sophie. You are only fourteen."

I think he is right, but I don't know what to do.

Otto talks a little more than he used to in school, though many times he seems troubled. Can't say that I blame him. Buck tells me I'm wasting my time. In fact, most times, he is mad at me for even talking to Otto. I am NOT giving up!

Today I am entering school just as Otto is getting off his bus. He is just a little cleaner than usual. He looks nice. "Can I walk with you?" I ask.

He just does a very slight nod, yes.

Mr. Hopkins teaches history, and is the first classroom. He is chatting with Mr. Taylor who has the art room across the hall. I like art, and I like history. I think Otto does too. They both look up as Otto passes and Mr. Taylor speaks to him. "Morning, Otto!" Otto keeps his head down. Mr. Taylor walks up to Otto. "Everything okay, son?"

As usual, Otto answers with one word. "Yep."

Mr. Hopkins smiles at us. "I'll see you two third period!"

"Sure thing!" I reply. Nothing from Otto.

Mr. Uhron is next. He is an older man with dark hair with the bald circle showing in the middle. He always wears a dark colored suit. "You look nice today, Otto."

Otto says nothing.

I poke Otto in his arm, "You're supposed to say thank you when someone compliments you, Otto!"

He glares at me.

Mrs. Midock sees what just happened. She is so pretty and always dresses fit to kill. I hear the *click, click, click* of her high heels as she approaches us. "Hi Sophie and Otto! How are you both doing?"

I am praying Otto answers, but he doesn't. I answer for us both. "We are both fine, Mrs. Midock."

When we walk past her, I shove him. I'm so mad. "I'm sick of you, Otto! I keep trying to help you, but you just won't let me! You don't even answer people who talk to you!"

"Can't talk," he says, barely legible.

"What do you mean you can't talk?"

With his finger he pulls down his bottom lip. I see nothing but blood.

"Oh my God! What happened?"

He just waves me off. "No worries." That's all he says. He walks away quickly.

Buck came around the corner. He is mad. "Why do you care so much about that idiot? I don't like you talking to him!"

Just then, *SNAP!* Joe Malec just took our picture! He takes pictures for the yearbook. I sure hope he doesn't use the one he just took. It's hard to smile when your mood is bad.

A basketball player comes around the corner. He is wearing his Varsity S jacket. He is always friendly, so he waves and says, "Hi!"

I reply, "Hi!"

Buck is angry. "Why are you talking to that guy?"

"It was just 'Hi' for heaven's sake!" He gives me a little shove to keep moving.

"Stop it!" I holler. Yet, I keep walking as he has directed me to.

A couple more days pass and I watch Otto. Maybe he needs a doctor. "Otto, let me see your lip again."

"No, it's better now." He is prying a paperclip apart and shaping it into something.

"Otto, what are you making there?" I ask him.

"An apple pie," he answers, looking at me with a grin.

"You know, Otto, that one day you told me about your mom and everything. You talked to me! Then you turn around and you don't talk at all. Do you hate me?"

"I don't hate you. Just go be with your boyfriend."

I am puzzled. "Why can't you and I be friends? Sometimes I think we are, then I don't!"

He keeps his head down. "There's no use. I can't have friends!"

"Why can't you have friends? That is ridiculous!"

"To you, maybe. Would you invite a friend home to where I live?"

With his head down I see several marks on his neck. "What's that on your neck, Otto?"

He keeps his head down. "Don't worry about it, Sophie. I'm not worth it."

"What do you mean you're not worth it? That is a ridiculous thing to say! You are worth it to me!"

He blushes ever so slightly. "Otto, come home with me tonight for supper. We can talk."

He puts his head down. "Don't want to talk. There's no use."

189

I can't keep asking him about his injuries. There are too many. I think I should tell someone, but who? He's got troubles. Big troubles. His cobwebs are so plentiful. I don't know what to do next. But I can't seem to stop caring about him. I just can't.

A greeting in the halls of SVHS

CHAPTER TWENTY-TWO
BEWILDERMENT
Summer 1965

Otto missed most of the last week of school but was there on the last day. I heard Ray asking him how he was. Recently, Ray is trying harder to be his friend. I heard Otto reply a simple "okay." That was good enough for me. I don't know, though, if Ray can be good for Otto. Ray is a little out there. Lately he acts like he is Elvis Presley. I heard a couple of the guys say that Ray is about half a bubble off plumb. He is just odd. Just odd, even though he looks normal. But they say that it is the odd ones that make it big sometimes. Maybe we'll all be shocked someday.

Izzy is two now, and after school I take her for a walk to the basketball court. Otto is here. "Why didn't you go home on the bus, Otto?"

"Didn't want to. Who's that?"

"This is my little sister, Izzy. Isn't she cute?"

He smiles ever so slightly. "S'pose so. Where's the boyfriend?"

"I'm not with him non-stop Otto. Why are you so worried about him?"

"He isn't right for you, that's all."

"Isn't right? In what way?"

He won't answer. With his finger, he takes a few strands of Izzy's hair, lifts it up then drops it. "Yeah, she's cute."

"She is attached to my hip!" I laugh. "I sure hope this is the last baby mom has! There are seven of us now!"

His face is in a frown. "If my dad had seven kids, he'd throw them all down the well."

"That's a horrible thing to say, Otto!"

"It's the truth!" He walks away. The heel of his shoe is unattached and it flops as he walks. He is limping.

"Why are you limping, Otto?"

He just keeps walking. He doesn't reply. Such a strange, poor, creature he is.

******

I am looking forward to summer. Since I play trumpet in the band, we'll get to go to the Dayton Fair and perform. And then there will be football games I'll be in when fall comes. It is exciting, but Buck doesn't like that. He says the boys in the band flirt with me. Sometimes I think he just has a few screws loose!

Mom is always busy, with so many kids and all. I don't have a lot of time to help her, with band practice, school and all. But, thankfully, she doesn't let the messy house bother her too much. She told me that cleaning your house while your kids are still growing is like shoveling the walk before it stops snowing. She has a point there.

Dutch, Julia and I went on the skating bus to Cicero's Friday evening. I was shocked that Dad let us go. It was fun. Buck was mad that I went, though. He is always mad when I go somewhere without him. He gave me his class ring last week. I hesitated, but he insisted. "This means you are my girlfriend and mine only!"

I suppose that is okay. A lot of the girls have steady boyfriends. I put mohair yarn around it to hold it onto my finger.

******

Four days later, there is scuttlebutt about town that they caught the murderer of the man found dead in *The Bucket of Blood.*

I am anxious to hear who it is, but tonight I've got plans. We are going out to the Blose Farm to look for UFO's. Mitchel Blose is a teacher. It is his farm and he is the one that says that aliens come there. He must be right, since he is a teacher and all.

Brenda picks me up. "Let's go to Dimaio's Store in Numine for snacks first."

"Suits me! They've got those good corn curls there."

"Does Buck allow you out tonight, Sophie?"

"He wouldn't like it but he doesn't know, does he?"

"You let him run your life too much, Sophie."

She may be right. I don't respond. She stops at the carwash to pick up Renie, Judy and Linda. Once we arrive at the farm we get out of the car and lie in the grass. "You think we'll see any UFO's tonight?" I ask.

"Probably," Brenda replies.

I chat with Linda about her boyfriend. They are talking about marriage. "You sure that's what you want, Linda? You are awfully young to be talking about marriage."

"Well, I'm not getting married right away, Sophie. I mean as soon as I graduate."

"If you say so, Linda. But I'm beginning to think that having a serious boyfriend keeps you from living your life the way you would want."

"I'm living the way I want! Aren't you? Stop worrying!"

After an hour I'm bored, but a bunch of boys from the junior class pull alongside us in an old green and white 1955 Chevy Bel Air. I've seen that car. I recognize the one boy, Jeff Snyder. Jax and I saw him a couple times picking up his dad from Zamperini's Bar in Numine in that car.

The boys take ropes out of the back seat. They put the couch on the top of the car, tying it with the ropes. Then two boys climb up to the couch. They are smoking, and it doesn't look like cigarettes. They start to ride around the field smoking and hollering. I don't know how that couch stayed up there! Finally, they come back to where we are and jump down.

I know most of them. The one they call Roach thinks he is hot stuff. His real name is Roland, but everyone calls him Roach. He comes over to me. Immediately, his hands are all over me. "WHAT ARE YOU DOING?" I scream at him.

"I want to touch your boobs!" I can smell the alcohol on him and the potent aroma of weed. I push him hard. He falls. He is mad. "Don't try to be a little goodie-two-shoe! Buck brags all over school that he touches your boobs! It doesn't matter anyways, 'cause your girlfriends will let me touch theirs!"

They hear him. We all at once push them all away and jump in Brenda's car and get out of there. As we look back, they are making a lame effort to run after us, but they are so high they can't stand up.

I am troubled. Buck is bragging about touching my boobs? Really? That was so traumatic for me in the first place, and to know it is not even private. Really?

I will certainly be talking to Buck! And, so much for finding any aliens. I do think aliens come there though. A boy in the senior class, Francis, said he saw burned circles in the field there. He said one week it would be in one place. The next week there would be one in another place. I'm coming back here for sure. Only thing I'll do different is have a weapon!

When Brenda leaves me off, Mom and Dad are sitting in the kitchen waiting for me. I right away get defensive. "I didn't do anything wrong. We were just looking for aliens out at the Blose farm!"

Dad looks serious. "Sit down, Sophie."

I sit. "What's going on?"

"They've arrested the guy who killed Kiser Wilson years ago at the Bucket of Blood in Numine."

"They did?" I ask. "Who was it?"

"Dastard Black," Dad says.

My heart jumps into my throat. "Otto's dad?" I think for a minute. "I KNEW he was evil!"

"Apparently was," Dad answered.

"Why did he do it? And, why did it take them so long to catch him?"

"For years they had suspicions, because someone saw Dastard and Kiser arguing at Doc Crawford's garage earlier that day of the murder. Until now, there was no hard evidence."

"What evidence do they have now?"

"A knife. He was dumb enough to keep the knife. Didn't even clean all the blood off I hear. They found the size ten boot too in his house. It had the one tread missing."

"At least he'll go away now and won't be there to beat Otto."

"Sophie, there is something else. Otto hid the knife for his dad in the blue school bus."

My mind spins. That is what he was doing in there! "Why would he? How? I don't understand."

"Well, Otto was foolish enough to tell a bunch of young boys that was out there hunting what he was doing. He told them his dad asked him to hide it years ago, he was just moving it to a new spot."

"Oh my God! What does this mean? Is Otto going to jail?"

"He's a juvenile, honey. That will help him a lot."

I run up the stairs so I can cry uncontrollably with no one stopping me. Poor Otto! And, why did he do it? I don't understand! His dad was so mean to him. Why would he do that for him. How could he?

Dimaio's Store (Frank and Catherine Dimaio pictured)

Zamperini's Bar, Numine

CHAPTER TWENTY-THREE
EVIL AND INNOCENCE
Fall of 1965

Otto's dad's trial was in September. His dad got life in prison with no parole. Otto was taken to Sherman Juvenile Detention Center for Troubled Boys. He was charged as a juvenile for a misdemeanor. The detention center is only forty-five minutes away and he will be allowed visitors.

I start to write letters to Otto. I never expect an answer. I send him pictures of Izzy and me. I tell him everything that is going on. After three months, I beg Dad to take me to visit him. He agrees.

Buck got mad at me when I told him I'm going to see Otto. We've been fighting ever since I found out he bragged about touching my boobs. Still, I've stayed with him. Why, I don't know. We walk together down the hall. He is going to woodshop and I am going into home ec. We stop at the woodshop doorway. He is glaring at me. "Your top is too tight! What are you trying to show off?"

I look down at my body. I have a lovely ribbed sweater on that mom bought me. It is perfectly fine. It is made to fit tight. "This is how it's made, Buck!"

"Don't wear it again! AND, you have no business going to see Otto!"

"I'll do what I want!" I spurt at him.

He pushes me hard. I hit the lockers.

Mr. Biuth comes running out of the wood shop. Ray is behind him. "Whoa, whoa, whoa! What's going on here?"

Buck is silent. I am angry. "He pushed me. He doesn't like me visiting Otto!"

Mr. Biuth grabs Buck by his collar. "Ray, take him into the woodshop for me! Buck, I will deal with you in a minute!" He looks at Ray. "Make sure he gets there, Ray."

They did what they were told. I hear Ray say to him, "Really, buddy?" Buck glances back at me with a dirty look.

Mr. Biuth looks at me with great concern. "Sophie, it is none of my business, but is that the way you want to be treated?" I start to cry. He puts his hands on my shoulders. "It's okay, Sophie. Just think about it. You deserve to be treated better than that!"

I nod yes and go into my home economics class a mess. Mrs. Snyder catches me as I enter. "What's wrong, Sophie?"

"I have a bad headache," I lie.

"Linda, come here and walk Sophie to the nurse!" she orders.

I don't want to go to the nurse. I don't like her. She'll tell me I'm fat again!

Linda takes my arm. "Come on, Sophie. It will be okay." Linda knows. She knows Buck.

As we walk to the nurse, Linda tries to console me. "Why are you with that idiot, Sophie. You can do so much better." I don't answer.

The nurse believes my headache story and calls my dad to come get me.

When Dad picks me up, I am still near tears. "What's going on, Sophie?"

"Nothing, just a headache. A bad one." We are headed down Main Street. "Dad, did you ever push Mom?"

"Push your mother? NEVER! She is my life! Why would I ever push her? I LOVE HER!"

He pulls the car into the parking lot of Bishop's Funeral home and turns the car off. He stares at me. "Did Buck push you, Sophie?"

I am ashamed to admit it. "Sort of."

His face is beet red and he is biting his lip. I can see he is trying to calm down. "Are you okay?"

"Yes. I hit the lockers but I wasn't hurt. Mr. Biuth came out and stopped it. He sent Buck into the woodshop and I suppose he hollered at him for it."

He is trying to stay calm. "And, what are you going to do about that, Sophie?"

My tears flow steady now. "I'm breaking up, Dad!"

He hugs me and lets me cry. "There, there. That is what I wanted to hear. You deserve so much better. You don't even need a boyfriend just yet. Have fun with your friends, Sophie. Enjoy your young life."

I can see why Mom fell in love with him. He is so warm and loving. I hope someday I have the same luck Mom had, and I get a boyfriend who loves me like that! "Can we go see Otto tomorrow, Dad?"

"We'll go tomorrow right after school. Now you put a smile on that pretty face of yours, okay?"

After supper the phone rings. It is Buck. His voice is shaking. "I'm sorry! I won't do it again!"

"We're done, Buck. I don't want a boyfriend. Go live your life. Find someone else." I hang up.

He rings again. I pick up. "You'll get your ring back tomorrow!" I hang up. He calls again. I pick it up and hang it up, saying nothing. The phone rings a fourth time. I pick up. "Go away, Buck. IT'S OVER!"

******

The next day, the drive to the juvenile center to see Otto seemed long. As we enter the gate, I see a magnificent two-story red brick building with a porch the whole way around. It looks rather nice. It is not what I expected.

Dad went in with me to sign in. "I'll be sitting on the porch, Sophie."

I was led down a long hallway to a visitor's room. There are couches, chairs, and round tables. In the corner is a ping pong table. I sat down at a round table. I was so excited when a man wearing a suit coat instead of a police uniform, brought him to me. "He can be here an hour if you wish." He said, and walked away.

Otto sits down across from me. He looks clean and healthy. "How are you, Otto?" I ask.

"Fine. How are you?"

I can't wait another minute to ask him. "Why did you do it, Otto? Your dad was so mean to you. Why would you protect him?"

"I didn't know I was protecting him. I did anything my dad told me to do, and I never asked questions."

"Did you know he had killed someone with that knife?"

"No, I didn't. He told me to hide the knife and I did. It became a game for me. I kept moving it."

"Did you know there was blood on it?"

"I never really looked at it. He gave it to me in the leather sleeve and I never took it out."

"Why didn't he hide it himself, and leave you out of it?"

"The day he asked me to hide it, he had come home limping. He said he killed a deer and fell in the woods. He told me to hide the knife, in case the game warden came after him." He puts his head down then looks up again. "The bastard probably tripped on Kiser's body, and that was how he hurt his foot. Anyways, he couldn't walk. That was the day he told me to hide it. He was always killing deer illegally. I had no reason to question what he said. Forgive me for using a curse word, Sophie."

"If anybody deserves to use curse words, it is you, Otto! But he would have had to kill the deer with a gun, so where did you think the gun was?"

"I didn't think about it, Sophie. I know it sounds stupid. I never asked questions about anything. If I did, I got beaten. So, it wasn't so unusual that I took the knife without asking questions and did what he said."

"I understand, Otto. Really, I do. I am just so sad that you are in here."

"It is better than home, Sophie. People are nice here."

"I'm so glad to hear that. How long will you be in here?"

"Five years and maybe less for good behavior. Lucky for me I'm charged as a juvenile."

"Five years? When you are innocent? That's a long time."

"To the court I wasn't innocent. They didn't believe that I didn't know what he used the knife for. But, it's okay, Sophie. I'm happy here. The food is good, I am warm, and I have clean clothes. I even have a woodshop to work in here. The only bad thing is that I'll miss seeing you."

That warm thing just poured over my heart again.

"You'll miss seeing me? Me? You acted like I bothered you most times."

"Well, you did!" He laughs a hard belly laugh.

"Well, I suppose you are right. It will be okay. You are better off here anyways. And you're happy here then?"

"Happy is hard to define for me. I never had it. But, I think this is happy I am feeling."

That makes me so sad. "I can try to come more often, Otto. I'll ask Dad."

"Will your boyfriend allow you to come?"

"I don't have a boyfriend anymore, Otto."

"What did he do?" Otto demands. "Did he hit you?"

"No, he didn't. He pushed me but it wasn't just that. He was demanding things of me. I didn't like it."

"I'll kill him!" Otto spurts out.

"Kill him? What kind of talk is that!? Are you a killer now? I took care of my problem with Buck. You need to forget about it!"

"I knew he was a piece of shit. You deserve better!" He leans back on his chair. "Have you heard anything about my dad?"

"Why would you care, Otto? He beat you, he starved you, now he has you in this mess!"

He is silent for only a moment. He looks down. "I don't really care about him, but he's what I got, and that's it. I got no one. Just him."

"How about your grandpap? You've got him?"

"A worthless piece of crap," he answers. "Pays the taxes, that's all."

I feel so bad. Even his grandpap is worthless. "You have me! I could have helped you. I could have gotten you into a good family. You could have had a good life, but you refused! Now, that path you took is keeping you here!"

"I couldn't let you help me. If I did, it would be you dealing with my dad."

Such a sad thing to say, but it is true. His cobwebs have been so plentiful.

He is glaring at me. "Did you know Kiser Wilson helped my mother escape?"

"He did? Is that why your dad killed him?"

"Yes. The cops told me. It took my dad a long time to figure out how she escaped, I guess. Kiser made the mistake of telling Slick Bowser at the bar that my mom had run to his farm that day after Dad beat her. Slick kept the secret a long time, but he was telling a guy at Moore's Hardware about it one day and my dad was around the corner listening. Right after Dad found out, Kiser went to Doc Crawford's garage to get his car fixed. My dad argued with him, then he followed Kiser to the bar and waited for him to come out. Seems as though he pushed him into that building and slit his throat with the knife, the knife he had me hide. I know the whole story now. I hate him for what he did. Kiser was a nice man."

"You know your mom had to run, right? Would you want your mother to take the beatings you have taken all your life?"

"No, I don't suppose so." His head is down.

"Your mother loved you, Otto. I'm sure she did. When you get out of here, we'll look for her. Okay?"

He looks at me and his eyes have softened. He smiles softly. "Okay, but even if we find her, I don't know how she could explain why she didn't come back."

I don't know what to say. Especially since I agree. It is best to just change the subject. "What's that key for, Otto? The key you gave me."

"Oh, that key. Just hold onto it. I'll tell you someday."

"Will you answer my letters, Otto?"

He put his head down, his eyes fill with tears. "I can't write very well."

I am confused. "How can that be? How did you go to school, if you could not write?"

"It is called dysgraphia. It is a condition. They made allowances for me in school." He answered.

"Is there treatment for that?"

"I never knew there was, but they gave me a therapist in here who is helping."

"That's wonderful, Otto! And you can do it! I know you can!"

"Thanks for your faith in me, Sophie."

"Otto, this is the most you've talked to me since fourth grade. I wish we could have talked like this all along. Why didn't we?"

"I didn't want you getting too close. I lived in fear. I don't have to do that now."

"I can tell you one thing, Otto. You are going to get through this. You are a good person!"

He stares at me, then leans towards me. His hazel eyes turn to dark gray. He talks in a low tone. "How could I ever be a good person, coming from what I come from? Thanks for coming, Sophie."

He stands up, and walks over to the door. He is gone. What do I do now? I wasn't done talking!

Dad tells me I must forget about Otto for now. At least he is being fed daily and he is warm, he says. I hope when he comes home, he will be a better man. I will just keep praying for him.

Two days later I'm walking up street with Julia while she is on another one of her soap boxes. "There is so much hatred in the world, Sophie! The war in Vietnam is escalating, and there are protests over the war and protests over civil rights. Martin Luther King led a civil rights march in Alabama last March and police attacked peaceful protestors. Did you see it on the news? The hatred is so ugly! On top of that, Black Muslim leader, Malcom X was assassinated in New York."

"Why don't you try watching happy stuff, Julia!"

She won't stop. "I feel like the whole world is going to shit! Nothing makes me happy."

"That's because you are always doom and gloom, looking at all the bad stuff!"

"And YOU don't pay attention, Sophie! There is so much poverty and inequality in the world! I'm going to sign up to be an exchange student and go to South America! The guidance counselor told us that, as exchange students, we would be ambassadors and other countries will judge the U.S. by how we present ourselves and act."

"Well, I hope if you want to help people that much it will work for you. It sure didn't work for me!" I think of how hard I tried with Otto. For sure, it did not work for me. Well maybe, just a little.

We go to the gym steps. Karen is here again with Lynda and Susie. Karen is talking about when she went to elementary school in Margaret.

"Margaret has a school?" I ask.

"It did! It closed two years ago and Guy Spera bought it. But when I was in second grade, in Mrs. Bofinger's class, a boy named Clarence was exposing himself to us!"

"What did you do?" I asked.

"I went to the teacher, and here is what I said. She is trying not to laugh as she recites what she said. "Mrs. Bofinger, Clarence is showing us his gall bladder!"

We all start to laugh, almost falling off the steps. I really needed this hearty laugh!

"Well, I was only seven, and I never knew what a wiener was!" she laughs.

"Oh Karen!" My belly hurts I am laughing so hard. When I look up, I see Buck is at the corner of the gym staring at me. I look away. Is he stalking me?

Moore's Hardware (L to R) Milo Gibson, Philip Frederick, Marshall Melson, Chauncey and Janice Moore, Tom Covola

CHAPTER TWENTY-FOUR
GOOD FRIENDS
October of 1965

Sammy is twelve already. He has a new friend, Frankie Brochetti. He lives on Swede Alley. He is just slightly older than Sammy. He doesn't look it. Frankie is a sweet boy, petite in stature with small facial features. His sandy brown hair is usually messy and he has dark brown eyes. I tell him he's going to be a woman killer because he is so handsome. He just laughs at that.

We just finished supper. Sammy and Frankie are bouncing a ball off the back of the house. I go to my room to write to Otto.

> *Dear Otto,*
>
> *I hope you are doing good.*
>
> *Are you learning to write? I bet you are doing swell.*
>
> *How is the food there?*
>
> *Izzy is getting big. She is two already!*
>
> *Sammy has a new friend, Frankie. He is a nice kid.*
>
> *Theo is six and started school in September.*
>
> *School is school, long days and boring.*
>
> *All for now. Will write again soon.*
>
> > *Love,*
> >
> > *Sophie*

I hope he can answer my letters soon. It's like writing to Santa Claus. He never answered my letters either.

Mom hollers up the stairs. "Sophie, don't forget you have a dentist appointment after school tomorrow!"

"I know, Mom. I won't forget." I wish I could forget though. I hate going to our dentist, Dr. Griffith. I think he might be a brother or cousin of the Dr. Griffith that was our town doctor. It always hurts when he drills my teeth, then I must spit into a little sink sitting beside me. It is disgusting and painful. I'd be happy to have false teeth, then I wouldn't have to go back there ever again!

Sammy and Frankie are in the living room as I go down the stairs for a snack. It is evening. Mom and Dad have gone to visit Aunt Ina. He and Frankie are laughing. "Okay, what's going on?" I'm asking.

"Don't tell Mom and Dad. We're going out Halloweening a little bit!" I can see the lump of soap in Sammy's pocket.

"Is that soap in your pocket?" I look at Frankie. "You in on this, Frankie?"

He just laughs. "Yep!"

Sammy is begging. "Don't tell Mom and Dad. They'll be gone for a good while anyways. We're just going out for an hour." I can't help but smile at them. I look at Frankie. "I trust you, Frankie. Can you keep Sammy in control?"

He just laughs. "Sure can!"

Out the door they go as I am hollering at them. "One hour! That's all you got! Come in the back when you get home. AND, you have to stay in Yatesboro!"

An hour later, they aren't home yet. I look out the front door and see Mom and Dad walking hand in hand crossing the road, coming home from Aunt Ina's. I run out the door towards them, hoping Sammy gets home and runs in the back door. "How was Aunt Ina tonight?" I ask.

Dad laughs. "Same as always. Trying to educate us on stuff we already know!"

"It's a nice evening. Let's walk awhile!" I propose, trying to kill enough time for Sammy and Frankie to sneak in our back door.

The three of us walk across the road passing the Roebuck house, then Mary Hockenberry, Margaret Jean Smouse, the Whitacre house then Mrs. Hilliard's. As we round the corner to proceed past the Catholic Church, we see Sammy and Frankie running with the priest in hot pursuit.

Dad stops. "What the heck? SAMMY! FRANKIE! GET HERE!"

The priest is in front of us now. "These boys were soaping the windows of the church, Sam! I think they should clean them now, don't you?"

Oh boy, I sure flubbed this one! Sammy looks worried, but Frankie is just grinning.

"I absolutely do!" Dad turns to the boys. "You two be here at the church tomorrow morning with your buckets and rags at 8 a.m.!"

211

"I wanted to sleep in, Dad!" Sammy argues.

"Well, isn't that just too bad. I did too. But guess what? I can't, because I will be the one supervising you two while you clean those windows. What were you two thinking? What were you doing out here?" he demands.

Sammy's head is down. "Halloweening! Sophie said we could!"

Oh crap!

CHAPTER TWENTY-FIVE
SIBLINGS, FRIENDS AND BUBBLES
Spring and Summer 1966

As I enter school on Monday, I see Linda coming out of the guidance office. She is crying. I run up to her. "What's wrong?"

"Oh, Sophie! I have to quit school!"

"Quit school? What are you talking about? Why would you quit school?"

She wipes her eyes and takes a deep breath. "I'm pregnant."

I don't know what to say. It takes me a moment to collect myself. "Pregnant? Oh, Linda." I want to cry but I try not to, for her sake. "Why can't you keep going to school though? You can have the baby and come back."

"They won't let me. You can't be pregnant and be in school. As soon as I start showing I can't be here. I will be showing soon. At least Andy says he'll marry me, Sophie."

I tell her I am glad, but I am so sad. For her and for me. I hug her and she starts sobbing again. "It will be okay, Linda. Once the baby comes you can come back and finish school." I know the chances of that are slim. She is going to miss so much. Our last two years of high school when we should be creating memories, we can't.

I don't know. I just don't know how this is going to turn out. She is so young. I am going to miss her. Why does life have to keep getting more complicated?

******

Linda didn't come to school after that day, and she no longer joins us girls on outings. We all miss her.

They are putting a new road in which will bypass Rural Valley. It will be the new Route 85 and the town of Rural Valley will be the old Route 85. It's been under construction for a while, and each day when the workers are done, I ride my bike on the new road. There are no cars, no workers, no one to stop me. Julia rides with me sometimes, but Dutch is playing girls basketball now. She has basketball practice every day after school.

In gym class today our teacher seems to be on a high horse. There is another Linda in my class I started chatting to. Seems as though we are becoming friends. Seems funny that I am drawn to girls with the name Linda. I started calling her Linda Lou, just to be funny, and found out that was her middle name anyways.

We sit to tie our white tennis shoes as we complain to each other how stupid it is to have to polish white canvas tennis shoes. The shoes as well as the laces are stiff as a board. Not to mention starching our white one-piece uniform. For what? To run around a gym?

Our teacher heard us and after scolding us, she ordered the entire class to run out the door and up the hill to the football field, then around the field twice. Judy has asthma and is having a bad day. She forgot her inhaler at home. She immediately asks if she can be excused from it. The teacher scolds her as well. "No one is excused! You all want to complain, so you all run!"

214

Judy started up the hill at a slow pace. We can see her gasping for air. "She can't do it!" I say curtly to our teacher.

"She is going to do it! GET GOING!"

I sat down with a thump onto the grass. She is staring at me. Then one after another, the girls all sat down with me in protest. Before we knew it, the principal was in front of us. By now, Judy only made it to the top of the hill and she is sitting in the grass trying to breathe. She is crying. We told him what happened. Shockingly, he was on our side! "You girls all go get your showers and get dressed and when the bell rings, just continue to your next class." He walked up the hill and helped Judy down. I waited for her and took her with me.

The principal had our gym teacher go with him to the office. I hope he cleaned her clock! She needs it cleaned, bad!

Linda Lou hates showers as bad as I do. It smells like wet dog there. She is laughing. "No teacher, no shower!"

I heartily agree. For once I don't have to get naked, be embarrassed, and smell wet dog.

Linda Lou came to my house after school to hang out. She brought her sister, Sue Ann. Sue Ann is four years younger than Linda. They are both pretty, but different. Linda has very dark hair and eyes, and Sue Ann has blue eyes and her hair is brown. Since Linda Lou and I are sixteen now, Sue Ann follows us around like a baby duckling. Linda Lou has a younger brother also, Michael. She has a boyfriend too, Tad. I hope he treats her good. Tad is handsome, but I've learned not to judge a book by its cover. Buck was handsome too, but ugly inside.

When I had the class ring Buck gave me, I bought different colors of mohair yarn to wrap around his ring, so it would fit on my finger. Linda does that too. "Here, Linda Lou. Take all my mohair. I don't ever intend to have a boyfriend again!"

"Oh, Sophie, that's crazy. You just picked the wrong one, that's all."

Sue Ann laughs. "I told my mom I'm never getting a boyfriend!"

Linda Lou nudges her. "You don't know what you'll do until the time comes. No one does!"

It is a rainy spring day, so we are stuck inside. "Let's set our hair!" I get out the jumbo rollers, hair spools, bobby pins and a glass of water. After getting all the rollers in, I comb my bangs straight down and tape them with pink hair tape. We have two hair dryers, so when we're done rolling our hair, we put the hoods of the dryer onto our heads and lay on my bed looking at Teen Magazine.

Sue Ann was doing cheers the entire time we were setting our hair. Now she is doing her nails.

Twenty minutes later, Mom is hollering. "Sophie, your cousin, Bob, is here. Can you come down?"

Bob Burns is my second cousin, but we don't see him much. He has always kept to himself. They say that when his older brother, Jimmy Burns, was killed in WWII, Bob was never the same after that. Mom told me about that horrible day that she found out Jimmy was killed. She had been close to Jimmy. She said he was a comedian and made her laugh. She was at the Company Store that day and heard men talking about a soldier being killed. She said when she realized it was Jimmy, she got hysterical. She said it was awful, but my dad helped her through it. She said Bob was just a little kid when he lost his brother. He really wasn't old enough to realize, but she said that the grief of it all was so heavy a burden on Jimmy's mother, Aunt Maude, that it trickled down onto Bob and grew like fungus grows on trees. I didn't know grief could do that. Bob always seems sad.

I pull the plastic hood filled with hot air off my head and scurry downstairs. "How you doing, Bob?" I ask.

He always keeps his visit very short, as conversation is hard for him. "Doing okay, I guess."

Mom insists he have a piece of her pie and I sit and try to chat, but it is hard. He lacks the ability to converse easily. He looks at me funny. "You go to bed with those things in your hair?"

I forgot I even still had rollers in my hair. "When I have to!"

He didn't stay long. "Gotta go. Thanks for the pie, Patsy." He is kind of like Otto. A troubled soul, and his cobwebs are plenty.

Getting back to my room I see Linda Lou has her rollers out. She teased her shoulder length hair high and fashioned a huge flip at her neckline. "Wow, that's a good flip, Linda Lou. I think I could lay my pencil in that and it wouldn't fall out!"

"Thanks to Aqua Net!" She laughs. "I forgot to ask you; did you hear about the cops catching the kids at the carwash last night that were on their way to party out Kime Road?"

"No, I didn't. What happened?"

"That girl in eleventh grade that lives on the hill, Debbie, was there in her bell bottom pants. She told me that when they saw the cops coming, they all hid their bottles of booze under her bell bottoms. She said she had Mad Dog under there, Boones Strawberry Hill and Ripple. She just stood still while the cops looked in all their cars and stuff. So, as long as she didn't move, they couldn't see the bottles. That would be wide bell bottoms, no?"

"That is hilarious. I wouldn't be smart enough to think of that!"

"Yes, you would, Sophie. Hey, I heard you quit the band. Why did you do that?"

"Every time I had band practice and blew that darn trumpet, my lips swelled. It was embarrassing. I'm DONE with band! Who wants to walk around school with swelled lips?"

She laughs as she heads out the door with Sue Ann trailing behind her. "Gotta get home. See you in school tomorrow!"

Sue Ann hands me my pink nail polish she was using and holds up her hands. "You like, Sophie?"

"Of course. Pretty pink for a pretty girl!"

She giggles and runs off.

******

Back at school the next day, everyone is chatting about our basketball team. Everyone except Ray, of course. Ray doesn't like sports. He only likes music.

Our team won the section this year. The players are Schrecengost, Craft, Shoop, Emery, Brewer, Sabo, Brown, Sakash, and Krizmanich. That Krizmanich moves like the wind!

Bud Schrecengost from the team is from a big family. He lost a brother a few years ago. Jimmy Schrecengost crashed his car back in 1954. Two other boys were killed too, a Brown and a Troutman. He was older than Bud, but they say Bud remembers it and talks about it a lot. That would be awful.

I am painfully aware how many kids lose siblings. It grinds on me. From the day that Darla lost all her siblings, I fear it. When I find out someone lost a sibling, I cry like it was my own. That little bubble lying in my heart that came there when the Doms kids died, stays there. Seems as though it simply took up residence. It surfaces now and then. It floats up and comes to the surface, then I cry. I wish I could burst that bubble so it would go away, but I know I can't burst it, and it never will go away.

School is almost over. Everybody gets silly towards the end of school. Even the teachers. Mr. Hopkins has a rubber chicken and he throws it at us to scare us. Mr. Abelman is teaching drivers ed now, in addition to health. He puts an empty glass milk bottle on the floor in the middle of the front seat, and if it falls, you fail. Ray told me that when he took him out driving, that at every little turn, the bottle tipped over. Mr. Abelman just kept hollering, "FAILED….FAILED!" Ray got mad and jumped out of the car. He says he'll drive without a license and just not get caught.

******

Once school lets out, the summer is in full swing. Linda Lou and Sue Ann come by often and tan with me in the back yard. Jax and Debra never want to tan, they say when we get old, we'll wrinkle faster. That's ridiculous!

As we lay in the back yard today piling the baby oil on so we will fry better, a car goes by. It is Buck. Why is he driving around my house? I wish he would leave me alone!

Linda Lou and Sue Ann head home and Mom asks me to go out and look for Sammy. He is always somewhere. He and Frankie go to Cowanshannock Creek to dissect crabs, or they ride their bikes, play football on the field, or whatever. Wherever Frankie is, that is where Sammy is. I suspect today that Sammy and Frankie are at Cowanshannock Creek.

I throw my clothes on and begin to walk. As I cross the black road heading to the creek, I hear tires screech to a halt beside me. It's Buck. "Where you going?" He asks.

"I'm looking for my brother. Why are you following me?"

"I'm not following you. Just was around town, that's all. How about we get back together, Sophie?"'

I look at him in shock. "Back together? Absolutely not! You are mean!"

He opens his car door and grabs my arm. His grip is hard. I am scared. His eyes are piercing. "You better think about it girl!" As he jerks me harder. Just then Sammy and Frank come up from the creek.

Sammy runs hard and jams his body into Buck, knocking him off balance. "Leave her alone!" Frankie is right behind him.

Buck gives them a look of disgust. "Big guy now, are you?" He laughs an evil laugh, then gets in his car and leaves.

"Thanks, Sammy. Are you okay?"

"I'm fine. He's a jerk!" Sammy is upset. "I'm telling dad what he did."

"No, Sammy. Please don't. Dad will just worry. I can handle this."

Frankie looks at me pitifully. "You sure, Sophie? He seems awful mean to me."

"I can handle it I said, but thanks for your concern." Frankie is so sweet.

We walk home for dinner and I try to forget about what just happened. Sammy doesn't tell.

Dad is talking a mile a minute about Doug Buffone playing for the Chicago Bears. That helped get my mind off Buck, to think about something else. Yet, should I be scared?

CHAPTER TWENTY-SIX
SENIOR LIFE AND DISASTER
Fall 1967 through Spring 1968

Ray has become a little more behaved, but not totally. I suppose he got tired of being in trouble. He has also become somewhat of a singer. He has a decent voice, so he started a band with some of the younger boys. He asked Sammy, Richie, Jim and Ed to join him. They call themselves *Andelic Religion.* Sammy plays the tambourine and he sings pretty good too. Ray writes the lyrics and the other guys put music to it. I must admit they are not half bad. The freshman class asked them to sing at their fall fling. They got hired to sing at New Bethlehem and East Brady too. I heard they did pretty good.

It is my senior year. Buck graduated last May and I can breathe now. I grew to hate him. He went to live with an uncle in Detroit after graduation. His uncle got him a job at a car factory. I hope he stays there.

We got to preview our yearbook yesterday and the cover. It's nice, but it still says SH-WAN-EE on the cover instead of Shannock Valley. I was telling Mom how the school continues to honor the Shwanee Tribe. "You know, Sophie, that when the Shwanees left here, their journey was called The Trail of Tears?"

"Sounds sad. Do you think that HAD to leave?"

"Yes dear, they did, from what I have read. So, I think it is nice the school continues to use their name."

"I feel ashamed about things our ancestors did way back then. We studied in history class the Holocust and we studied all about slavery. I hate that those things happened, don't you, Mom?"

"Yes, I do. But we can't change it. The only thing we can do is to be better and always be kind."

"Maybe I'll name my first baby Shwanee, in honor of the tribe, if it's a girl I mean."

Mom chuckles, "you don't have to go THAT far, Sophie!"

"I wonder how they got the name Shannock Valley?"

"This is Cowanshannock Township and there's the Cowanshannock Creek so it was taken from there."

"They should have called it Shwanee High School. It's on the yearbooks anyways! I'm really interested in this stuff. Do you think there is some way I can learn more about the Shwanee Indians?"

Mom smiles. "We'll start with the local libraries and see if we can find something. We will do what we can."

Sh-Wan-ee

Classroom mischief is at an all-time high. Mr. Uhron teaches business law. I sit beside Darlene. She is always happy. She is *down-to-earth*, which is what I like about her. The kids are chatting, as usual, and Mr. Uhron announces, "I see you kids want to play the *game*."

The *game* is when he writes names on the board for talking, and when it reaches three names, they all three get paddled. Everyone is in such a devilish mood. Mr. Uhron speaks louder, "Who wants to be first?"

I am surprised when I see out the corner of my eye Darlene raise her hand. I look at her, she is laughing. "Why did you do that?" I want to know.

"Poor guy needs a name, so I'll give him one." She laughs out loud.

Joe and Bud are sitting in front of me side by side. I see Bud poke Joe in his side. Quickly their hands went up. That makes three names. They want to see Darlene get paddled, even though it means they get paddled too! Darlene's chuckle has subsided. She glares at them with a look that could kill if daggers came out of her eyes. They all three got paddled. Not a good day for Darlene. She walks out the doors with me on the office side after school, since we are both walking home. "Why did you do that?" I ask her.

"I don't know. Just wanted to get a laugh, I guess. The laugh ended up being on me!"

The Varsity S is having their picture taken for the yearbook at the front of the school in the grass. Those guys sure are handsome! Especially in their Varsity S jackets! I smile at them as I pass, and most smiled back. There is one on the left in the front row that is especially handsome, but I'm not interested, really. I don't need a boyfriend.

Varsity "S" Club 1967

Linda Lou asked me to go along to Pina's tonight for pizza at 8:00. Sue Ann made it for junior-high cheerleader and they are celebrating. I'm so happy for Sue Ann. She deserves it. She is a very sweet girl. When I arrive, I give her a hug. "Hey you, you cheerleader girl!" She laughs.

"Were you ever a cheerleader, Sophie?" She asks.

"I wasn't pretty enough, like you!" I laugh.

"You're crazy. You're pretty!"

"Okay, if you say so, Sue Ann."

After pizza, we drive to the gym to sit awhile and see who is hanging out. It is getting dark. Sammy, at fourteen, is now hanging out with a bigger group of teen boys. Frankie is always there too, of course. I look over towards the school and I see Sammy and Frankie standing near the cafeteria talking.

I go over to them. "What are you guys up to?" I know for sure it is something not good.

They look nervous. Sammy looks towards the roof of the school. "I don't think you want to know. Go home."

"No, I'm not going home. What's going on? You better start talking!"

Just then three boys jump down off the roof. They have chocolate on their faces. They are shocked to see me. They look at Sammy.

"What were you guys doing? Start talking!" I scold them.

Sammy speaks for them. "Ah, Sophie, it's no big deal. They go up there on the roof and they can go down through a door that opens into the janitor's room. Then, they go into the home ec room and eat the cookies the class made today." They all laugh.

I am trying not to laugh, but it's funny. I just turn and walk away, but first scold Sammy. "It better not be YOU going up on that roof! You know dad wouldn't like that!" I look back. Frankie is bent over laughing. "You too, Frankie!" I holler.

I am amused by the things kids do. I never had the guts to have fun like that. I turn my back to head back to the steps and the boys all race around me to beat me to the steps of the community building. They start singing Christmas Carols at the top of their lungs starting with *Better Watch Out, Better not Cry, Better not pout I'm telling you why* and they are all pointing at me and laughing. I laugh too. Gosh it's funny.

******

October is here before we know it. Linda Lou is at every football game to watch Sue Ann cheer. I join her most times on the bleachers. I always oversee Theo and Izzy at football games. We all love when the Friday night lights go on.

Sue Ann is good at cheering and she is really becoming a pretty girl. She is popular too. It is nice to watch the sisterly bond she and Linda Lou have.

We take our seats on the high bleachers, on the hill. Theo and Izzy are playing on the embankment directly in front of the bleachers. All the young kids are. I try to watch the game but my eyes are on them also. Up and down, up and down the hill. They come to the top, run across in front of the bleachers and go down again. One if not both will certainly get hurt, but I can't stop them. And, Mom is used to them coming home from football games all dirty.

The game ends with no major injuries to the players or to Theo and Izzy. Walking out, I stop to greet Sue Ann. "You did a really nice job." I lean over to her ear. "You know you are the prettiest cheerleader here, right?"

"Stop it, Sophie!" She laughs.

******

On Saturday morning I watch the news. It says that 100,000 protestors marched on Washington DC yesterday, protesting the war. They burned draft cards, and they marched on the Pentagon. I don't understand this. I hear cowards are moving to Canada to avoid the draft. This war in Vietnam is getting ugly. But, why is everyone protesting it? I just don't get it.

Putting the war out of my mind, I try harder to get better grades, now that I'm a senior. I race to beat everybody in shorthand and typing. Mrs. Bauer teaches shorthand. She is easy to learn from, and she wears the most beautiful clothes! A girl in my class, Diane, is my competition. I like her a lot, but I also like to beat her. I hate losing. I think Diane likes *the thrill of the chase* too. I know for sure Mrs. Bauer likes that we both are fast. It is the competition between Diane and me that has made us fast, even though many times Diane beats me. Dad scolds me for that. He says, "Wisely and slow. They stumble that run fast."

"Speak English!" I tell him. He just laughs.

I am more faithful than ever listening to the evening news. Julia finally got through to me and got me interested. On April 4, 1968, Martin Luther King Jr. was assassinated. He was the leader of the civil rights movement. He was so well-spoken. Julia called me from nursing school. "I'm super sad. I loved his message of peace and equality." I agree with her, though I wish she would relax some and not take on the world's problems like she does.

******

My senior year is going fast. I write to Otto often, and visit him when I can. We have conversation now when I

228

go. Real conversations. And he is always well kept, clean, shaved, nice haircut. As I visit today, I give him a pack of Mars bars. He laughs. "You trying to make me fat, Sophie?"

"It won't hurt you. Eat just one a day. Anyways, a couple more pounds on you would look good."

"I don't look good now?"

"I didn't say that, silly. You actually look wonderful." I gaze into his eyes and he returns the favor. He has intense, pretty hazel eyes. "I wish you could come to graduation Friday night."

"I wish I could too. I'll be thinking about you."

Now, when I leave from visiting him, the warm stuff is just spilling all over my heart.

May 31, 1968 is graduation night. It is a warm night. Mom bought me a white dress for under my graduation gown. Ruby is here, and all my siblings, making a big deal about it. I just want it to be over. I never really liked school. At the end of the ceremony, we throw our hats in the air and greet our families at the entrance to the Community Building, in the grass.

Dad hands me a box wrapped in gold with a gold ribbon. I open it. It is from Pribicko Jewelers. I lift the lid to find a silver necklace with a crescent moon on it. The edge of the moon has tiny sparkly stones. I look at Dad. He is laughing. "I wanted you to have a crescent moon. It will help you forget about the full moons you hate so bad! Did you know that a crescent moon represents new opportunities and optimism?"

I laugh. "And I am OPTIMISTIC! I love it, Dad!"

He takes it out of the box and puts it around my neck. It is so delicate. The crescent moon lies at the base of my throat, as a sweet little choker necklace would. It is perfect.

As I hug him, and my cheek meets his, I look beyond him into the parking lot and I see Buck. What is he doing here? He is supposed to be in Detroit? I won't acknowledge I even see him. "I'm going to the Roundtop with some of the kids, Dad. They are making a fire for hot dogs and smores."

"You go have fun, honey. No drinking though, okay?"

I nod okay, but I might have just one......or two. That little voice in my head is telling me to. Once again, what he doesn't know won't hurt him.

1968 SVHS Graduation, Community Building

On the Roundtop everyone is gathering. There must be forty kids here. The beer is plentiful and cheerfulness abundant. We are graduated! Linda Lou is with Tad, sitting by the fire. I take a beer out of the cooler and sit with them. After a couple hours I need to find somewhere to relieve myself. I hate this part......going to the bathroom in the woods. I excuse myself and start to walk. It is dark, but I must get far enough away from everyone. I'd die if anyone saw me. It would be humiliating! I keep walking, through some trees and down the hill just a little. If I keep going just around this bend, those big bushes there will hide me well. I find my spot and first look back towards the campfire to be sure I can see no fire nor kids. I figure that if I cannot see them, they cannot see me.

Suddenly, I feel like a truck hit me from behind. I am on the ground, face down. Someone is on top of me. I fight. It is a man. I feel his strength. He is pulling my clothes off with one hand, and his other hand covers my mouth. My face is in the dirt. I am screaming but it goes only into his hand. No one hears me.

I feel pain. Terror consumes me. I fight and I fight. Something hard hits me on the head.

The next thing I remember is everyone standing over me. I am on my back. There are firemen here, taking my blood pressure and wiping a gash on my head. They have me covered with a blanket. "What happened?" I ask.

Linda Lou is by my head. "Just relax, Sophie. You are going to be okay. The ambulance is on its way."

There are faces over me. They all seem to be fussing with my head and tucking the blanket around me. Through the little bit of dark sky that I can see between their faces, I see the moon. It is full. I fall into darkness.

When I wake up, I am in a hospital. Mom and Dad are here. They are crying. "What happened?" I want to know.

Dad takes my hand. "You were attacked, honey."

"Attacked? Who attacked me?"

"Just rest, Sophie." Mom says, caressing my arm.

"NO! I don't want to rest. Who attacked me? What did he do?"

I close my eyes, trying to remember. I start to remember bits and pieces. "Dad, it was a man. A strong man. I remember fighting. And pain. I remember pain. Oh, Mom. What did he do to me?"

She is trying to hold back her tears. "They caught him before he could do more, honey. Your wounds will heal."

"Before he could do more? WHAT DOES THAT MEAN?"

Mom looks at Dad for reassurance. He nods yes. "It was Buck, honey. Your friends saved you. Some of the boys got him off you and held him to the ground until the police got there. He was trying to do more than just attack you, but he failed. You are okay now. You hear me? You are okay. He is in jail. He will do jail time over this. I promise you, honey." Dad grabs my hand. "He will pay, Sophie. I promise!" He reaches into his pocket and comes out with my crescent moon necklace in his hand. "He pulled this off your neck, honey, and broke it. I will have it fixed for you."

I start to sob. "The crescent moon saved me!"

My right eye hurts. I touch my cheek. OUCH! I feel pain on my head and try to touch it.

"Don't touch it, honey. You have several stitches on your head. He must have hit you with a rock. You have a black and blue eye and there is a gash below it. It didn't need stitches though. Let's let it heal now, okay?"

I look over at Dad and he looks beaten. The tears run down his face. "It's okay, Dad. I'll be okay."

I don't know if I'll be okay, but I can't stand to see Mom and Dad so distraught. How could he have done this to me? I look at Dad. "Dad, I saw Buck in the parking lot after graduation. He was watching me."

Dad bites his lip. "If he weren't in police custody, I would kill him!"

Ruby comes minutes later. I cry when I see her. She immediately crawls onto my bed with me and holds me. I've missed her. "It's going to be okay, Sophie. You'll see." She feels warm and loving.

I am starting to feel my body relax and my crying stops. "Ruby, how could I have been so stupid? I thought I was in love with him when I had his ring. How could that be? When he was so evil."

"We see only what we want to see, honey. We all make mistakes. The law will take care of him."

I hope so. But what if it doesn't? I'm petrified.

CHAPTER TWENTY-SEVEN
EVIL NEVER WINS
Summer and Fall 1968

I was in the hospital two days. When Mom and Dad bring me home, I just go to my bedroom. I don't want to see anyone. I can't look at my brothers and sisters. I am ashamed.

After a couple hours, Ruby comes into my room with a tray of food. As I eat, slowly, she sits on my bed to talk. "It wasn't your fault, Sophie. You have to let it go."

"I feel so stupid. And I ruined everyone's graduation celebration. Who was it that saved me?"

"Joe and Bud were walking towards where you were with their dates when they heard your muffled scream. They are big guys. They held Buck down while the girls ran for help."

"Oh God, did Joe and Bud see me naked?"

"No, honey. You weren't naked. Buck had ripped at your clothes, but you weren't naked."

I give a sigh of relief. "I want to kill him, Ruby!"

"Don't worry, Sophie. He'll be going away for a very long time. And, you did NOT ruin anyone's graduation!"

Mom is hollering. "Sophie! Linda Lou is here! I'm sending her up."

When she enters my room, I can see she is trying not to cry. "We're not shedding any more tears over this, Linda Lou."

She starts to cry anyways. "I should have gone with you when you left, I'm sorry."

"Stop it, Linda Lou. I didn't want you with me. I never let ANYONE see me pee!" We both laugh.

******

Within the week, Buck was taken to a prison in another town to await trial. I felt better once I knew he was not near our town.

I keep trying to get back to my old self, but it is hard. Then, on June 5, Bobby Kennedy was assassinated. President Kennedy was murdered five years ago, and now his brother. What is happening in this world? I am troubled. My cobwebs are plenty.

I haven't written to Otto for a couple weeks. I haven't seen him for a very long time. First, I was so busy with graduation, and now I need my head and my soul to heal from this. At the hospital, they shaved my hair around the cut on my head. I can't hide it, so I don't want Otto to see it. I did keep up writing to him, though. Now, I do not know what to say. To tell him or not to tell him. I decided not to tell him. But my letters are short. The words just won't come to me.

> *Dear Otto: How are you? I*
> *graduated. I am going to get a*
> *job and buy my own car.*
> *I hope you are well.*
> *………Love, Sophie*

My letter looked skimpy and pitiful, but it was all I could say.

A week or so later I walked down the hill to the post office to find an envelope in our mailbox addressed to me. It just said SOPHIE. Under my name it said, YATESBORO. I am the only Sophie I know of in Yatesboro, so the post master must have figured it out. I go outside of the post office and across to Dr. Griffith's office to sit on his cement steps. I open it. The writing is elementary but readable.

DEAR SOPHIE: SOMETHING IS WRONG. I COULD TELL IN YOUR LETTER. PLEASE TELL ME WHAT IT IS. Love, OTTO

That warm thing poured over my heart again. Otto wrote to me! He has learned to write! I smile at the thought of it. I knew he could do it! I KNEW it! I must go see him. He knows something is wrong. I must tell him. I can't put it in a letter.

I ask Dad to take me on Saturday and he agrees. I pull my hair back into a ponytail and in doing so, I hide the bald spot on my head. I wear my ribbed knit sweater that Buck hated and my bell bottoms. I try to cover my black and blue eye that has now turned to yellow with makeup but it still shows slightly. We leave at noon so we are there just after lunch. Dad pulls into the parking lot and looks at me. "You want me to stay here or go in with you?

"I've got to do this alone, Dad. I'll be fine."

The man who brings him to me is just inside the door as I enter. "Go to the back garden, Sophie. It's a nice day and there's a bench there. I'll bring him out in a minute."

I go through the building out the back door and find my place on the bench. When I hear the door open again, I turn around. It is Otto. I am surprised. He looks very different. He looks better yet. He put on a few pounds, so the lines in his face have filled in. He looks healthy.

He smiles at me. I smile back. "You look wonderful, Otto." He smiles and sits beside me.

He is staring at me. "I learned to write in here. I am taking my GED test next week."

"I am so very proud of you, Otto!" I stare back at him. Our eyes lock. I never noticed the long eyelashes on top of his deep green-gray eyes. He is clean shaven, yet his face has the shadow of his beard. It makes him so handsome! I didn't know he was handsome!

His eyes do not leave mine. "Tell me what's wrong, Sophie. What's that mark on your eye?"

I take a deep breath. I look down. As I look back up, his eyes never left me. "I was attacked, Otto."

He closes his eyes tight and drops his head. He is silent. He looks up. "Who?"

I tell him the whole story. Start to finish. I see his hand tightening into a fist. His knuckles are white.

"Are you alright, Sophie? How do you know he didn't......?" He chokes on the mere word.

"He didn't. Chet and Bud stopped him. I am fine. My wound on my head healed. I can't say mentally I am wonderful yet, but it will come. I am determined to put it behind me, Otto."

"I WILL KILL HIM, SOPHIE!"

"You won't need to, Otto. He is in jail and he is hopefully going away for a very long time. Besides, don't talk like that. I can't wait for you to get out of here and get home!"

Conversation is strained after I tell him that news, but we try to chat about me getting a job and a car. "Taking the business course in high school paid off. I really like my job as a secretary at the phone company."

"I'm glad you do." He tells me what he has been doing and what he has been learning. His growth has been amazing. It is obvious. I am so proud of him. He has been in here nearly three years already. I hope the next two years goes fast. And, I hope he doesn't go back to that shack.

"Will you do me a favor, Sophie? Will you go out to my house so I'm sure it will still be there for me? Grandpap would have kept up the taxes, but see what the situation is, so I know. Fred Wilson wrote me a letter that he is keeping the grass cut and he was getting Grandpap groceries and dog food for Thor. You don't need to be afraid of my grandpap. He wasn't physically abusive. His abuse was all verbal. Just tell him I'm coming back and see what his reaction is."

"Of course, I will. I'd be glad to, Otto. But you don't need to go back there when you get out. You can live with us!"

"No, but thank you. I have my own house. I've tried to call him but he doesn't answer the phone. He never did. Just need to be sure it is still there for me. Such as it is."

As I stand up to leave, he is staring at me. "I was just thinking the other day about this, Sophie. You never went to a prom. Why didn't you?"

"Because I never was asked by the right guy, I guess." I smile thinking how funny it is the silly things he thinks about, but I guess he has a lot of time to think in here. I finally have to say goodbye. Things have changed so much. He not only has come around like I said he would, but he is different in every way.

******

The next day, Dad and I drive out the narrow lane to Otto's shack. I walk across the tilted porch. Knock, knock, knock. The Grandpap doesn't come to the door. I peer through the screen of the door. I can see him in there, sleeping in his chair. The door isn't locked. I open it quietly. "Hello! Mr. Black! I'm a friend of Otto's. I'm coming to check on you!"

No response. We walk slowly towards him. I nudge him on his shoulder. Nothing.

Dad comes around me. "Wait over there, Sophie."

My heart is pounding as I back off towards the television. Dad nudges him harder. "Mr. Black!" He falls over. He is breathing, but something is badly wrong. I see the phone in the corner. "Call the ambulance!" Dad orders.

Otto's grandpap survives in the hospital only hours. He had a stroke. It took his life. After the doctor tells us that he is gone, we drive straight to tell Otto. They bring Otto to us. "We went to check on your Grandpap, Otto. We have bad news."

"He's dead, isn't he?"

"How do you know, Otto?"

"Just felt it. It was time. He's been dead to me for years. It's nothing new."

"There had to be some good things about him, Otto."

"Can't think of any, Sophie. I find it ironic that God took him before I must deal with him again. Maybe someone is on my side after all."

"I've always been on your side, Otto."

"I know."

We told him then how we found him in the condition he was in and called the ambulance, and went to the hospital with him.

"Thanks." Otto said. "He didn't deserve you. If you don't mind going back there, just be sure the door is locked and save the key for me. It is hanging on a nail to the right of the porch. I don't want anybody getting in there before I get home."

"What about a funeral or something, Otto?"

He looks at my dad. "Do you think the state would bury him? I owe him nothing, and I have nothing. Better yet, could his body be donated to science? I'd love for them to figure out what made him tick. It could explain a lot!"

So very sad. Poor Otto. What must his childhood have been like in that shack?

Dad assured him we would plan for the body. As I go to leave, I give him a little hug. "I'm sorry, Otto."

"Don't be sorry for me. My life is just beginning. Thanks for what you and your dad did."

We go by the shack before returning home and I get the key.

I go to bed thinking about the little key he gave me long ago. I was dreaming it opened a chest and in the chest were mice. It was an awful dream. I am glad when morning arrives. I have had so many nightmares since I was attacked. One is worse than the last. My head is not in a good space just yet, but I pray it will come.

******

The trial for Buck finally came in late August. Buck tried to lie out of it, but he lost. He said he had been drinking and must have blacked out. Sure, he did! Luckily, no one believed him. His trial was short. The jury was out only twenty minutes. They found him guilty of aggravated assault, and sentenced him to ten years in prison. And, after his release, he cannot be within ten miles of the Yatesboro, Rural Valley area.

My whole family is here with me. I cried when we heard the verdict.

Dad hugs me. "Don't cry, Sophie. It's over. You can't change what happened, but you can move forward and rise above it."

I know he is right. When we get home, we have a nice meal together, and sit on the front porch until dusk falls around us. As I'm getting ready for bed, I hear church bells ringing. First the Catholic Church and a few seconds later, the Rural Valley Presbyterian Church bells are ringing. I run downstairs, "Dad, something is wrong in town. Do you hear the bells ringing?"

"I sure do! Let's take a drive and see what's going on!"

We drive up through Rural Valley and people are standing out in their pajamas. Everyone is concerned. Suddenly, we see Hoot Gibson with his bubble light blaring running through town. He is heading towards the Catholic Church. We park on Macaroni Street at the Waryu house and stand on the sidewalk talking to Mrs. Gosetti, when Hoot's car comes back through, heading the opposite way. The Catholic church bells seem to have stopped. His bubble lights are squealing and flashing and two boys are in the back of his car. I think I recognize them. I've seen them in school. Next thing you know, the Presbyterian Church bells stop. Hoot is coming back down the street, bubble light off, and now four boys in his car. He pulls into the borough building below us and we walk down.

"What is going on, Hoot?" Dad inquires.

"These four hoodlums are what's going on! Damn kids set their watches to ring two bells on two different churches at the same time! They think it's funny!"

The boys are laughing. Dad is trying not to laugh as he talks to them. "You had a lot of people scared, boys. Do you know that?"

They nod yes. Hoot grabs two by their collars. "Gonna get their parents in here and have a talk!"

I look at Dad. "Oh boy, they are going to have their clocks cleaned!"

We head home laughing and get to bed at long last.

******

The next morning, Dad takes me to Curly Moore Chevrolet for a car! I am so excited! "So many to choose from, Dad!"

"Yes, and take your time. I would have taken you to look other places too but I like to stay with people I know. When you are dealing with strangers, you have to be sure to not take any wooden nickels."

"Wooden nickels? What does that mean?"

"It means, beware of the ruthless." He hands me an envelope. "This is some of the money your Nonno had left you. There is $1,000 in here. Use it for your car. It isn't all in here. I saved some in case you want to go to college someday. Now, you want to buy a used car. It's the smart thing to do."

"Thanks, Dad."

I chose a tan Wrangler. It was $850. Perfect! It's used, but it's new to me!

My first plan is to go visit Otto. Mom and Dad always laugh at me, "There she goes, off to Never Never Land again, The Land of The Lost Boys!"

I know Otto was lost, but he isn't now.

CHAPTER TWENTY-EIGHT
A PRECIOIUS LOSS
August 1969 to September 1, 1970

The phone was ringing as I come down the stairs. It's Otto. "I'm being released!" He announces happily.

"Oh, Otto. I'm over the moon. When are they releasing you? I'll come get you."

"Tomorrow, Saturday. Can you? Come get me, I mean."

"Absolutely. Do you know the time?"

"Noon, they say. I'll be ready." He is quiet for a second. "Thanks, Sophie."

"You don't have to thank me, Otto. I will see you at noon tomorrow!"

Mom sees my excitement as I hang up. "I'll bet he's coming home, right?"

"How can you tell?"

"That smile on your face that almost touches your ears is the tattle tell." She laughs.

Julia comes down the stairs and we tell her the news. She is happy for Otto, but she is in one of her moods because of the news on the television she watched last night. Charles Manson and his followers killed actress Sharon Tate and five others in a gruesome rampage. She wears tragedies like a cloak. She obsesses too about the figures going across the bottom of the screen of the deaths in Vietnam too.

Mom tries to get her mind off all that. "Did you know that your dad joined the Ding-A-Lings this week?" They are a sports booster club. Dad loves being involved, especially when it comes to kids. They do a lot for our sports teams around here.

"He'll love that." I answer. "Now maybe our basketball team will get new uniforms."

Frankie graduated last June and had been a star basketball player for Shannock Valley. He told us how bad their uniforms were. He is at college now. I suspect Sammy will pick the same college when his time comes, just to be with Frankie.

Mom is popping in more toast. "Did you hear your cousin, Bob, is going to marry a girl named Glenda? I hope she brings him some happiness. THEO AND IZZY, COME ON, YOU ARE GOING TO BE LATE FOR SCHOOL!"

Theo is eleven and Izzy is seven now. Mom and Dad had a hard time when she started school. They didn't want her to go. I suspect she is their last child. After all, Dad is forty-nine-years old now. Mom is thirty-nine. I think the date on the baby making machine has expired.

******

I was so happy when the next morning came and Otto would be coming home.

Izzy is having a meltdown as I get ready to go pick him up. "I wanna go too!"

"Quit your fussing, I'll take you!" I holler to Mom that I've got Izzy, and out the door we go.

As we arrive, he is on the front porch. "Was waiting for ya'!"

Izzy runs to the flower garden at the front and sticks her hand in the fountain. Otto laughs. "Every kid has to put their hands in water when it's moving!"

He picks up his one lonely bag and we head down the porch stairs, as I feel water splash my face.

"Stop that, Izzy!" I grab her by her hand.

"Don't holler at her. You won't melt, Sophie!" We all three break out in laughter. It is funny how he defends her. She is naughty. Even naughtier than I was when I was young.

Forty-five minutes later we are pulling up to his shack. He sits for a moment. "Just as I remembered it, a piece of crap."

"Don't worry, Otto. It can be made nice. Looks like Fred just cut the grass."

"Thank God for Fred. He is as nice as Kiser was."

Izzy and I go in with him and I help do a few dishes and straighten up the kitchen.

"You get going now, Sophie. You've done enough. It's going to take more than one afternoon to get this place in shape."

"We'll help you, Otto. A little bit each day, okay?"

He nods yes and walks us to the car. He picks Izzy up and swings her around, planting a soft kiss on her cheek. "Thanks for bringing me home, Izzy."

"That's silly, Sophie brought you home. I can't drive!"

I'm chuckling as he puts his arms around me. "Thank you isn't enough, Sophie. Will you come back?"

"Does a woodchuck chuck?" I laugh, and climb into my car to head home.

As we return home, Linda Lou pulls in behind me.

"Did I catch you at a bad time, Sophie?"

"No, absolutely not. Just got home from delivering Otto to his house."

"He's home? That's great! Are you and Otto an item?"

"Oh no. Just friends. We'll always be just friends. I'm lucky I even got to the *friend* stage with him, but he sure has changed a lot. He's friendly and he talks now. Sometimes too much!" I laugh.

"Then he surely is different than he was."

"Very different. Very different for sure. What's up with you?"

"Just bored. Just came to hang out with you."

"You're just missing Sue Ann, aren't you?"

Sue Ann took off in late May to be an exchange student in Peru, in the city of Cuzco.

"Yeah, it's different for sure."

Linda Lou had a campfire for Sue Ann with her girlfriends for a send-off before she left, and I was there. I hated to see Sue Ann go. Paula Prugh was there too, since she was an exchange student also, leaving the same day as Sue Ann. I am so used to Sue Ann being with Linda and me. Sue Ann started calling her Linda Lou too. She always laughs when she says it. We will miss her, but she'll only be gone three months. "She'll be home before you know it!" I tell Linda Lou.

We sit in my back yard in the grass chatting for an hour. She is just getting up to leave when I hear a car horn. It's Ruby! She is home for the weekend with her new boyfriend in tow, Charles. He teaches in the same school as Ruby. I run to the car and hug her. "Home at last!"

Mom and Dad come out to the car too. After the initial niceties, I tease him. "Better marry her, Charles. She's twenty-nine already!"

Mom doesn't think that is funny and gives me a nudge which means I should shut up. "You'll have to forgive my daughter, Charles. She often speaks before she thinks."

But, by the end of the weekend, Charles proposed to Ruby when they were on the Roundtop. He said he knew the Roundtop held special meaning for Ruby. It sure doesn't for me.

The wedding will be next June. Everyone is happy. Charles went fishing with Dad and spent one afternoon helping Mom cut up vegetables. He definitely passed the *meet your parents test* with flying colors. He is not only tall and handsome, but he is so very friendly. He is interested in all of us and conversation is so easy with him.

******

The week they are home goes so fast. We walk them to their car and I give her a hug. "I'll miss you, Ruby!"

"Not as much as I'll miss you! See you soon. Start looking at bridesmaids' dresses!"

It is so exciting, thinking about the wedding.

As soon as she leaves, I go to visit Otto. I want to tell him about Ruby and Charles. He'll be happy to hear it.

I can't believe how far he has come. He takes such good care of himself now, and he always smells good. It is the Jovan Musk I gave him for Christmas.

I take the little key he gave me years ago, out of my pocket. "What about this key, Otto? What is this for?"

He smiles. "You will see when the time comes. When I gave it to you, I didn't know I'd be away for so long. But I'm glad you kept it. It's still going to work."

That puzzles me. "Okay." I tuck it back in my pocket.

I help him take the old curtains off the windows, as he asks me to go shopping with him to buy new ones.

"Sure, I will."

I stand up to leave. He stands up too, and put his hands on my shoulders. "It's good to be home, Sophie." There is that warm thing pouring over my heart again.

I get home and go to bed with a warm heart and a smile on my face. I knew in fourth grade I could help him. I have. At least I think it was me.

******

Sunday morning comes and we go to church as a family, as always. We have our Sunday meal together and I spend the afternoon at Otto's, helping clean out his kitchen cupboards. "I have a long list of stuff I need, Sophie. Can you go with me next Saturday to shop?"

"Of course, I can."

As I'm walking in our door at 8 pm, Dad suggests we all go for ice cream at Kings Drug Store. They are open until nine on Sundays. We jump in the car and Dad drives us to the drug store where we fill up five stools. Mom, Dad, Me, Theo and Izzy.

We sit on the high stools, but no one waits on us right away. Jack and Norm are at the end of the counter talking with Zelma. They look serious. Jack walks over to us. "Sam and Patsy, may I have word with you?"

"Sure!" Dad answers and they head to the end of the counter and into a small back room. What is this about? Why a secret? Oh boy, did Sammy or Theo do something?

When they come out of the room, their faces look gray. I get off my stool and stand-up, expecting to hear about some boyhood devilishness. Dad puts his head down. I can see him swallow hard before he looks up again. He puts his hands on my shoulders. "Honey, Sue Ann was killed in a plane crash in South America today."

I stare. I am speechless. I don't know whether to try to talk or just throw up. My stomach is working its way up my throat. Jack comes up to me. "Take a minute, Sophie. Breathe, just breathe."

"How do they know?" I manage to ask. "Maybe it's a mistake."

"It is not a mistake, honey. She was in a plane going to see Machu Picchu with other students. The plane crashed. There was some confusion because she wasn't on the manifest, but Harry Fox had connections and he worked hard to find out for sure. It is true. She was on the plane. It was Sue Ann's sister from Cuzco that was to go, but she had given her seat to Sue Ann. It is true, honey. She is gone."

My head feels like it is full of clay. I start to cry. Mom rubs my back and cries with me. "Where's Linda Lou?" I ask.

"She is with her family. You can see her tomorrow or maybe the next day. They will need time. This won't be easy."

"Take me home," I cry. My heart is heavy. My legs feel like rubber. I think of Linda Lou, and her family. How can they get through this? I think of Sue Ann, so pretty, in the prime of her life. IT ISN'T FAIR!

We didn't get our ice cream, nor did we care. As we walk outside of the drug store, I feel like the night sky is not pitch black, as it should be. That means there could possibly be a full moon in the sky, but I refuse to look up. I refuse to look at another full moon. Damn the moon!

I put my hand around my crescent moon of my necklace. I make it to the curb. I throw up. I feel numb. The sadness consumes me. How will life ever be normal again? August 9, 1970 is a date I will never forget, the day we lost Sue Ann.

Sue Ann Nagy, just months before the deadly crash

Two days later I go to see Linda Lou. My heart is pounding as I knock on her front door. When it opens, she is standing there. She looks like a statue. Her eyes are dark and her face is drawn. She just stands there, in silence. "Oh, Linda Lou!" I cry, as I throw my arms around her. She is stiff. It doesn't feel like Linda Lou. I feel and hear her cry, yet she is different. I fear that maybe Linda Lou is gone too.

* * * * * *

Just two days later, as the Nagy family is still waiting for Sue Ann's body to come home, Julia has the nerve to coax me to go to Woodstock. It is taking place August 15 through 18. It is a three-day festival of *Peace and Music* on Max Yasgur's Farm in Bethel, New York. "You should go, Sophie. My friend Colleen is driving. We can take Dad's tent and food and spend all three days. It will be good for you!"

"I don't feel like having fun at all! How could I, Julia? Do I look like I'm in the mood to sit in cow poop and listen to music?"

"You are such a Debbie Downer, Sophie!"

I want to hit her, but I don't. I just walk away.

******

Julia and Colleen left for Woodstock on August 14th. They arrived home on the 18th. I was sitting on the front porch when Julia crawled out of the car covered in mud. Her hair looks like birds have built nests in it.

"What happened?" I ask.

"It was awful, Sophie! There were so many people it was like being one ant in the middle of a million. There wasn't enough food. People were smoking weed and having sex everywhere. Then it rained and turned into a mud bath. I'll never do that again!"

On August 19th the news reported of the nightmare that Woodstock was. Thank God I didn't go.

******

Days and weeks passed. It took a month for Sue Ann's body to arrive home for the funeral. The pain of losing Sue Ann stayed with me, like little fruit flies swarming a rotten piece of fruit. I was numb through the funeral and knew not what to say to Linda Lou. What would one say? Now Linda's cobwebs will be plenty. Forever.

253

When the funeral service is over, I give her a hug, "Oh Linda Lou, are you okay?"

She just stared into space. "I don't know if I will ever be okay again."

She starts to cry and I cry with her. "Oh Linda Lou, I'm so sorry."

She gets a hold of herself and parts the embrace, keeping her hands on my shoulders. "I have to ask a favor of you, Sophie."

"Anything. What is it?"

"Don't call me Linda Lou anymore, okay?"

"Sure, it's okay. But why?"

She weeps softly. "I liked it, Sophie. No one ever called me that and I thought it was funny. But, thing is, so did Sue Ann. She started calling me that and laughed every time. I'm afraid now that when I hear that name, I will hear Sue Ann's voice, and hear her chuckle. I don't think I can take it. So, just call me Linda, okay?"

"Of course. But, Linda, it won't be a bad thing to think of her and hear her voice. Memories are a good thing. Don't push the memories out of your way. You still have a life to live, and Sue Ann would want you to live it, wouldn't she?"

She nods a faint yes. I hand her a card I made for her. She takes it and walks out the door with her parents and her brother Michael. I feel like I am watching a slow-motion movie. They are moving through life in slow motion with all the wind knocked out of them.

My handwritten card said this:

Grief never ends, but it
changes. It is a passage, not a
place to stay. Grief is not a sign of
weakness, not a lack of faith…..it
is the price of love. I love you
Linda Lou.
Love, Sophie

I return home thinking of Sue Ann and look at the pink nail polish on my dresser she used. I can see her face and her smile. I remember her giggle. I hope it never leaves me. I cuddle my pillow into my chest and curled up like a baby I fall asleep, hoping I see Sue Ann in my dreams.

CHAPTER TWENTY-NINE
A NEW BEGINNING
September 1970

Saturday morning, I arrive at Otto's shack before noon. He opens the door before I even hit the porch. He is smiling. "Guess what I found!"

What did you find?"

From behind his back, he shows me a coffee can that must be fifty years old. The lid is all rusty. "Is it an antique?" I ask.

He laughs. "The can is, but not what is inside. It was on top of the cabinets."

He opens it and leans it over to show me. There is money inside. Lots of it.

"Oh my God, Otto. Did you find that here?"

"Yep. Looks like my Dad was stashing away money for years. Maybe for his get-a-way?"

"How much is there?"

"Six-thousand-nine-hundred and twenty-two dollars."

"Holy crap! How do you know it was him saving that and not your Grandpap?"

"Grandpap couldn't reach that high. Anyways, I've seen my Dad getting into this can. Can you imagine, Sophie? Him stashing away this money when he wouldn't even get the things I needed, including food?"

"It's hard to understand for sure. Very hard."

"Well, too bad for him. He won't get to use it. I'll be fixing up this place with this! And guess what! I got a job!"

"You did? Where?"

"In contracting. Fred Wilson knew a guy that needed a new man. He builds new homes. He hired me!"

"Oh, Otto! I'm so happy for you!"

"Not as happy as me! Let's go shopping!"

We shopped for groceries, for cleaners, for paint, and the last stop was the State Store for wine. "We're celebrating!" He laughed, as he bought six bottles of wine.

We arrive back to his place and I help put everything away. We have the cupboards nice and clean so the task was easy. Once done, we sit down with a glass of wine. "I have a problem, Sophie."

"What?" I still find myself staring at him finding it hard to believe he was once that frail, dirty cold boy in fourth grade.

"You'll need to help me get a driver's license!"

I laugh. "You call that a problem? I was expecting something big! Okay, we start tomorrow. You will learn on my car!"

"Thanks, Sophie. How about going with me to Johnny Lavosky's later today? I want a new refrigerator and stove. I can't stand these. They are filthy."

"Sure, I'll go. Johnny and his wife Ann really like my mom and dad. I know they'll like you too. I would think they'd give us a good deal, since we Kaminskys are so well liked and all." I laugh.

"Who wouldn't like the Kaminskys?" He chuckles. "Hey, been meaning to ask you, I heard Ray moved to Florida. Do you know anything about that?"

"No one has said much about it but I knew it. He finished college in May. I guess he went down there to join another band. Maybe he'll make it big. You know, they say that a lot of big artists were very odd in high school. We could say that about Ray."

"I agree. He was odd. I must give him credit though, for being nice to me. Most boys wouldn't give me the time of day in high school. Of course, I wasn't Mr. Bubbly Mush either." He laughs.

"You had good reason. Besides, Bubbly Mushes aren't attractive."

He smiles and puts his head down. "I'm not attractive, Sophie."

"Says who? I am telling you that you are, silly!"

We finish our wine and go to Lavosky's. Johnny is happy to help and seems to like Otto immediately. He gives him a good deal and he will even bring it out and set the stove and refrigerator up for him on Monday. We go back to his house and I must head home. Before I leave, I try to give him back the key he had given me long ago.

"Not yet," he says, smiling. "You are going to need that key. I will tell you when."

As I drive home, I think of how Otto was back in fourth grade. Skinny, poor, cold, and dirty. It is hard to believe he looked like that at one time. As I pass Kiser Wilson's farm on my way out, I think of Otto's mother.

What was she like? Did she love her baby as she should have? What could have happened to her? We don't have Kiser to ask now. Surely there is some way we can find out!

Lavosky's Appliance Store.   John and Ann Lavosky pictured

CHAPTER THIRTY
HE'S A CATCH!
October to December 1970

I go to Otto's when I can, especially on weekends. Today we are painting the walls of the kitchen. I started while he was at the store. As he walks in the door, I tell him. "Don't touch that wall on the left, I just painted it."

He reaches over and touches it. With paint on his hand he replies, "Yep, it's wet."

"Boy oh boy, Otto. Tell a man there are 300 billion stars in the universe and he'll believe you. But, tell him the paint is wet and he'll have to touch it to be sure!" I take my paintbrush and dot his nose with paint. We laugh heartily.

Every time I go, I take him driving the dirt lanes that go different directions in Owl Hollow. Two weeks later, he passes his driver's test and buys himself a used pick-up truck. He is so proud.

He also bought himself new clothes and wonderfully smelling soaps. He takes such good care of himself now. With his talents and a little money, he fixed up his old shack to be quite nice. He replaced the boards of the front porch and steps. He hired a couple guys to repair the chimney and put on a new roof. He restored the broken-down fireplace in the living room back to being in working order. He tore down the old wooden fence out front. He plans to paint the outside of his house white. I will help him.

******

A week later, I went with him to purchase some new furniture and a decent bed. His entire life he had slept on a mattress on the floor.

"The furniture will come tomorrow. Can you help me carry this old furniture out, Sophie? I think I'll just burn it all."

"Sure, Otto."

After the end tables are out, we go to lift is his Grandpap's chair, an overstuffed ugly flowered monstrosity. It is too big to get out the door. "Turn it on its side, Sophie."

Together we flip it. The cushion falls off. A ball of something wrapped in a rubber band falls out. It's money!

We put the chair down and he picks it up. "Well look at this, will ya'." He says as he unrolls it and counts. "Four thousand six hundred dollars. Can you imagine, both hiding their money while a little boy was hungry!"

That makes me so sad. He sees my face and grins, "I'm not hungry now! Heave–Ho!"

We get all the furniture out and sit down to a cold lemonade, chuckling about the money wrapped in the rubber band. "This I'm going to save for something special." He tucks it into his shirt pocket.

It is fun seeing his shack come to life and seeing Otto as a normal person, no longer beaten and poor.

******

The next day, he went to the Rural Valley Bank on Main Street. Stella helped him open an account and Charlie Dill called him into his office. Otto insisted I go in with him.

261

We take the two seats across from Mr. Dill. "There's an account here son, with $10,000 in it. Your dad opened it. He has not only his name on it, but yours also."

Otto looks shocked and blank. Mr. Dill knows of his history with his dad. "Here's the thing, Otto. Your dad is not going to come home. You can take this money out whenever you want. It is yours."

Otto clears his throat. "Forgive me if I seem rather shocked."

Mr. Dill taps his desk with his pen. "He owes you something, I figure."

"I will leave it there for now, if you don't mind. I'll get it when I need it. Thank you."

We walk out of the bank and get into his truck. "See there, Otto. Your dad did care about you."

"No matter what, I can't even think of him as a dad. He wasn't. This money doesn't make up for a lifetime of misery."

"I know, Otto. But perhaps he had a serious problem you don't know about. I mean a mental problem."

"He was mental alright, Sophie! That's for sure! It scares the life out of me that I might inherit any of him. I've thought about it a lot. Especially if it was a mental problem. That stuff is genetic!"

"You are not like him, Otto. You could NEVER be like him!"

He looks so serious. "Only time will tell."

******

The next day, he called a tow truck to haul the blue school bus out from under the pine trees and the old cars that were sitting around with no tires and the old refrigerator. He cleaned up the yard. He works hard. As I help him rake the grass, I ask him about the well. "Was that a working well at one time? I see there's no water in it."

"I suppose years ago maybe it had water, but it's been dried up as long as I can remember. It's not all that deep. In fact, my dad always had me rake the grass and throw all the grass clippings in there. I hated him for that. The leaves in the fall too. I had to rake and gather them and put them in the well. He didn't give a rat's ass that we lived in poverty and our house was falling down around us. Yet, I had to pick up all the grass and all the leaves and throw them in the well. Can you imagine the way his mind worked? I've been throwing grass clippings and leaves in that well for probably fifteen years. I started raking when I was five."

"Holy Moses, Otto. The life you lived should be made into a book. Then people who complain about little things can read it and know they don't have it so bad!"

"Everything is relative, Sophie. Did you know that Kiser's brother, Fred, has been coming over here from the farm and mowing while I was away? That was awful nice of him. I think I should do something for him."

"We can make a gift basket. I'll help you. Maybe like different jellies and homemade bread. We won't give him alcohol, that's for sure."

263

We finish the grass and sit on his porch swing with tall glasses of iced tea.

He swings back and forth quietly, thinking. He looks at me. "There's something I want to tell you. I have to tell you that I'm sorry that I hid that knife for my dad."

"I'm sure you are, Otto. It caused you a great deal of pain."

"I've spent my life being mad at my mom for leaving me. I think as mean as my dad was, I did not want to displease him or he would leave me too. That would have maybe been a good thing, though." He laughs.

"I know what you mean. But you were young, Otto. You needed him. Even as he was."

"It wasn't Kiser's fault my mom left. It was my dad's fault. I don't know why he blamed Kiser. Poor old Kiser. He never hurt anyone."

"What's done is done. Your Dad is paying for it. That's all that matters."

"Kiser was nice to me. I'd go over there and he'd talk to me like a father would and should. I missed him when he was gone. Had I known my dad murdered him, I dare to think what I might have done."

"So don't think, Otto. You didn't know AND you could not have stopped what happened. Quit blaming yourself."

"I'll try. I'm thankful for Fred. He is as nice to me as Kiser was."

"It wouldn't be hard to be nice to you, Otto. You are a special person."

264

"I won't be special if any of my dad's personality comes out in me."

"Stop that, Otto! That WILL NOT HAPPEN!"

* * * * * *

Before we knew it, it was Thanksgiving. Otto comes to our house to eat Thanksgiving with our family. He seems to be happy. Mom and Dad welcome him easily and conversation is never lacking.

Christmas came. I bought Mom and Dad their first colored television and it was delivered two days before Christmas. It sits on the floor in a big wooden case. They were so appreciative and said they want to pay me for it. I laugh at them. "It's a gift, silly people! A gift to you, for being such good parents!"

On Christmas Day we opened gifts at home, then I went to Otto's. I bought him a new type of saw. They just came out this year. I also got him his first wrist watch. He loved both.

He hands me a large wrapped package. I open it slowly. It is a soft plush baby blue robe. "I love it, Otto!" I stand up to put it on and push my hands into the soft pockets. There is a small box. I pull it out. I hesitate. Surely, it's not……?

"Get that look of fear off your face, Sophie. It is just a friendship ring!" He laughs.

I open the small black box and it is a pearl and jade ring. A pearl on one side, a jade beside it. "It's beautiful, Otto."

265

"I hope it fits!"

I put it on my finger and it is perfect.

He is laughing. "That look on your face was priceless!"

"I wasn't scared exactly."

"Yes, you were! Don't worry. I don't expect more than friendship. After all, I'm no catch!"

"Why would you say that, Otto? You certainly are a catch!" I've embarrassed him. His face is fifty shades of red. He is adorable when he is embarrassed.

"I can never be more than a friend, Sophie. I don't dare to dream otherwise. I must always remember what I came from. At any point I could see those things in me that scares the shit out of me."

"That's ridiculous, Otto! Put that out of your mind! You are not him!"

"Whatever you say, Sophie."

But I can see him thinking. I know he cannot put that fear out of his mind.

CHAPTER THIRTY-ONE
GONE AGAIN
January 1971 into February 1972

My cousin, Annie, has an exchange student living at her house. Her name is Maria. She is from South America. I walk over there today to visit. It is just three houses over. As I go around the front porch, I laugh at the snowman they've built. I can hear them laughing out back. Annie and Red are standing in the alley, helping Maria onto a sled. Maria loves sled riding, since she never saw snow before.

Maria waves. "Sophie! Watch this!"

She jumps on her sled and speeds down the hill. She loses control and she lands in Leona Fear's Garden. She topples over onto her side and the sled keeps going without her. For a second, I hold my breath, then I hear her laughing. Mrs. Lucas is on her back porch laughing, too. Maria laughs and she laughs and she laughs. Then I start to laugh along with Annie and Red. It's fun to see someone loving snow that much!

Later in the day, I go to Otto's. "Where you been?" he asks.

"Just stuff! Got a visit in with Annie and Red. The exchange student, Maria, was sled riding. She was having a ball. She crashed and scared me, but she laughed. She loves the snow!"

"It's funny how we take snow for granted. Imagine being in it for the first time ever. It would be neat, for sure. Weren't your sisters exchange students, Sophie?"

"Yes, they were."

"Why weren't you one?"

"Because Buck was my boyfriend. He didn't allow me to go."

"Oh my God. He truly controlled you!"

"Yes, he did. Let's not talk about him."

"Sorry. I agree."

"You don't have to be sorry. I'm sorry for the time I lost while I was with him, and the decisions I made because of him. It's funny how you don't see that at the time."

"At least you came out alright!" I see his cheeks getting flush again. "Let's watch television!"

As we watch Gilligan's Island together, he gets quiet. I see his is thinking. "I was beginning to wonder if I'd ever be home for holidays again, or if I wanted to be, Sophie."

"I know, but look at you now! You have a home, and a nice one. You have everything you deserve right now."

"The only thing I don't have is resolution."

"What do you mean, Otto?"

"I need to know what happened to my mother. I doubt I will ever know. I asked Fred yesterday if he knew that Kiser helped her get away, and he didn't."

"Keep the faith. You never know. We may be able to find out." But I know it is doubtful too.

After Gilligan's Island, the news comes on about Vietnam. The figures going across the screen at the bottom are frightening. "So many, Otto. So many are dying."

"I know, Sophie. Maybe we shouldn't watch it."

"I agree I shouldn't, but I know I can't NOT watch it. I better get home, it's getting late."

As I drive out the lane, I think about the news and the figures at the bottom of the screen. They keep growing.

******

The next day is a normal work day, until I get home. The phone rings. It is Otto. "Sophie? Did you just get home?"

"Just walked in the door. What's up?"

"No easy way to say it. I got a letter in the mail today. I am drafted!"

My heart sank. I never thought about this happening. How unfair is life? He just now GOT a life, and it is being taken away again. He hasn't even turned twenty-one yet. "I'll be right over, Otto."

When I arrive, he is still holding the letter. I don't know what to say. I sit down beside him. "It will be alright, Otto. Maybe you'll fail the physical."

"I doubt that! I'm healthy and strong! I wouldn't want to anyways. If I am to fight for my country, I must. Sophie, will you look after my house for me while I am gone?"

"Of course, I will. The time will go fast, you will see." But I know it won't. I'm feeling a little weepy. I don't know why. After all, we are just friends! But I love my friends. All of them.

******

I take him to the Kittanning YMCA on January 30th for his physical and plan to pick him up at noon and take a half day off. I didn't get a call to pick him up. At 4:00, I drive to the YMCA. Just one Army Sergeant is sitting at a desk. "I'm here to pick up Otto Black. Is he done?"

He looks up at me with no emotion. "He's more than done. He is on a bus on his way to South Carolina to basic training at Ft. Jackson.

"What do you mean? You took him? Just like that?" I pause, "he doesn't even have a toothbrush!"

I know it sounded silly, and he laughed at me. "They'll give him a toothbrush there, miss. He'll call you probably by tonight. We had your phone number and I was just starting to make my calls. I would have called you."

I am angry. "So, you can just take someone away, just like that? And make a phone call like it was nothing?"

"You need to relax, miss. I don't make the rules. This is the United States Army and this is how it works."

I left there in tears, feeling so very bad for Otto. It seems insane what happened here today. He has only me. I drive home angry and fast. I get to his shack to turn off the water and turn the thermostat down. His truck would be in the barn, and it's locked, so it's okay. I start to rid out the refrigerator since he won't be coming home to use up this stuff. I find our half empty bottle of wine in the refrigerator that we had the last time I was here. I crumble into a kitchen chair, and I cry.

Otto called me a day later, in the evening. "I'm sorry they did this. I had no say, you know."

"Of course, I know. Are you okay?"

"I'll be fine. Don't worry. Were you able to go to the house and take care of things? There's stuff in the refrigerator that will spoil."

"I got it, Otto. I turned down the heat and shut the water off."

"Thanks, Sophie. I'll be sending you money to pay the bills. Go ask Kiser's brother, Fred, to keep an eye on it, and in grass cutting season I'll send him money to keep it mowed. Let's hope the next two years go fast."

"It will, Otto. I know it will. In no time at all you'll be home."

******

The weeks and months begin to drag. Two months later, Frankie got drafted too. He had left college in November. Said it wasn't for him. That left him wide open to be drafted. Sammy is upset about Frankie. I assure him it will be okay. "He'll do his two years, just like Otto, and they'll both be home in no time." I tell him. Though, I don't really know, do I?

On March 14, Otto calls me from South Carolina. "Sophie, are you sitting down?"

"Why do I need to sit down?"

"I have something to tell you."

I chuckle. "Okay, I'm sitting down." Even though I wasn't.

271

"I am going to Vietnam, twenty-four hours from now. I'll be gone a year."

The wall phone I am on won't hold me up. I slide down the wall onto my bum with the phone at my ear.

"You there, Sophie?"

I shake my head to get the cobwebs out. "I'm here. "Twenty-four hours? That quick? I don't, I can't....I.....I....."

My body shivers and I am cold.

"I know. You don't have to say anything. It is happening. We must accept it. I will be sending you how to get letters to me. You will write, won't you?"

"Of course! I will write every day. I promise!"

"I'm sorry you're stuck with taking care of the house. I'd be glad to pay Fred to do it if it's too much."

"No, Otto. It is not too much. I'll be glad to do it. Don't worry."

There isn't much more to say. We end our conversation feeling robbed of more. It just doesn't seem fair. And he'll be gone a whole year? That is a long time. I go to my room and stare at the ceiling. Now MY cobwebs are plenty!

The world seems out of control. I watch the news religiously. This past January, Charles Manson was sentenced to death for his murders, but it was overturned. He just got life. That is a shame. He deserved to die. There are evil people in the world, and it scares me bad.

The news of Vietnam is more troubling now than ever too. The figures that flash across the bottom of the television screen during the news of how many were killed that day, are hard to grasp. So many. So many mothers who have lost sons, wives who have lost husbands. Families lost brothers, uncles, fathers. I can't stand it. There are women in danger too. So many nurses trying to help the wounded. I hope Julia doesn't get a crazy idea to go there once she gets her nursing degree. The figures go around in my head for hours. I must fight to make them leave.

******

On August 1st, Sammy met me at the front door as I got home from work. "What's wrong, Sammy?"

"It's Frankie."

"What about Frankie?"

"He is going to Vietnam!"

I know the color just left my face. I am upset, but I try to stay upbeat. "It will be okay. He'll do his tour of duty and be home, Sammy. Just like Otto." But the truth is, the figures on the bottom of the television screen just grew legs. At any given moment, Frankie or Otto, or Frankie AND Otto, could be in those figures.

CHAPTER THIRTY-TWO
COBWEBS ARE PLENTY
March 1972

The girls in high school now are wearing their skirts so short, you can almost see their bums. They wear high boots called go-go boots. Only two years have passed since I graduated and fashion has changed that much. I had to wear my skirts down to my knees when I was in school!

Time is going so slowly. I go to work, come home, eat, then sit in front of the news every day. I do nothing but that. I write to Otto every day, and he writes me. He is in heavy fighting. I must pray, a lot. I keep busy going out to his house. I keep it clean and many times I'd like to just stay there overnight but it wouldn't seem right to do so.

In his last letter he told me about his new friend, Bobby Jo. He is from the state of Indiana. He said he was a good old hometown boy from a farm, and he loves listening to him. They seem to have become good friends. I'm glad that Otto has someone.

As I watch the news, Dad tries to make conversation to help me forget about the war. "Did you hear that Mike Krizmanich is playing for the Yankees? He graduated in '66 I think. He was really good in basketball in high school too."

"Yes, Dad. I knew that. He was good in every sport that he played in high school." I go back to watching the news.

"That news channel will drive you crazy if you let it, Sophie."

"I'm okay, Dad. I just need to know." He leaves me alone after that.

******

As spring is beginning to poke it's sweet head up, I get a letter from Otto that he is coming home. I am so excited. I knew it would be soon. This means Frankie will be coming home soon too.

On March 15th I am standing at the airport with Dad as Otto comes down the ramp from his plane. He is thin. So very thin. He looks like a kid. I give him a hug and I feel like I am hugging just bones.

"It's so good to see you, Sophie."

"It's good to see you too, Otto."

Dad shakes his hand. "Good to have you back, Otto!"

"Good to be back too. You have no idea!"

Otto sets down his duffle bag. "Do you mind if I take a minute to go to the restroom and get this uniform off?"

"Why would you want to do that, Otto?" I ask.

"Because when we changed planes in Seattle Washington, someone spit on me. I just want out of this uniform."

"Spit on you? Why?"

"Where have you been, Sophie? Most people think we shouldn't have been over there."

"That's crazy!"

"I know it is, but still, I'm getting out of this uniform."

How sad. How very sad. He nearly lost his life for this country, and someone spits on him? I can see in his eyes how it troubles him. His mood feels dark, like the night sky.

I study his face. I see a scar at his hairline. "What's that?" I ask as it put my finger on it.

He pulls my hand away. "Just a mortar scar." He rubs his right torso, "I had some shrapnel removed from here too. It still hurts a little."

He walks away from us towards the restroom with his duffle bag. When he comes out, he looks like any ordinary person. He isn't ordinary though. He should be proud of his service.

We head home and Dad asks him if he'd like to stop for a beer.

"If you want to," Otto replies.

Dad stops at a bar and we all walk in and sit up to the bar. Dad orders a beer for him and Otto, and I get a Coca Cola. The bartender looks at Otto. "Are you twenty-one?"

Dad is perturbed. "This young man just almost lost his life fighting for our freedom. Are you serious?"

"Gotta be twenty-one, sir. Sorry."

"It's okay." Otto said as he shows him his license. "I'm twenty-one going on ninety-one."

I think what a sad thing that is to say. Yet, could it be true?

The bartender seems embarrassed. "Forgive me, and thank you for your service." Otto just nodded.

From there, we go straight to my house. Mom has made us a meal. Otto is quiet. I can't stop looking at him. That same gaunt look is in his face that was there in fourth grade. He is so very thin. His eyes seem heavy and his hand trembles as he puts his fork to his mouth.

Dad and Mom ask him questions about the war but he answers short and vague. He doesn't seem to want to talk about it. Mom picks up the dishes to take to the sink and one slides off the pile onto the floor. It banged loudly as it shatters. Otto jumps a mile.

"You okay, Otto?" I ask.

"Just a little jumpy, I guess. Do you mind if we go home now?"

I take him home in my car and go inside with him. I cleaned yesterday so the smell of Pine sol is in the air.

"Smells nice." He walks to the kitchen and takes two bottles of beer out of the refrigerator. "Thanks for shopping for me, Sophie. Let's sit down now."

We sit down on the couch.

"You want to talk about it, Otto?"

"Can't. Maybe someday."

What did these boys go through? How very horrible was it? Poor Otto. His cobwebs were always plentiful but I thought we had them all cleared out. His cobwebs are plentiful again. I feel like we are starting from scratch.

"How about we go for pizza tomorrow to Charley's? We'll celebrate your homecoming!"

"Charley's? Where's that?" He asks.

"The old Pina's Restaurant. It is no longer Pina's; it is Charley's Place now."

"Is it the same pizza recipe?"

"Yes, it is. Maybe even better!"

"Then I will go."

"Pick me up at 6:00 then?"

"Sure thing." He yawns. "I'm pretty tired."

I laugh. "You should be! I'll get going." I look into his eyes. They aren't the same as before. "I'm so glad you are home, Otto."

Charley's Place Main Street Rural Valley
(Owner, Joanne Kreutzer pictured)

The next day I am ready when Otto picks me up.

"I'm starved!" I tell him as I jump into the front seat of his truck.

Rocket Man by Elton John is at the top of the charts, and it is playing on his radio. He seems okay, but still subdued. "Nothing like a Pina's pizza! Oops…. I mean a Charley's pizza!" He doesn't respond or even smile.

278

"I meant to ask you, Otto. Did you hear about Watergate?"

"No, I didn't."

"Well, they say former FBI and CIA agents broke into the offices of the democratic party months before the elections. They were members of President Nixon's re-election campaign. Nixon is in big trouble."

"That doesn't look good for Nixon. Hope they impeach him. He did nothing to bring troops home."

"He's probably done as President because of Watergate, anyways, Otto."

In Charley's, we order our pizza and two beers. Otto asks for a whiskey chaser. He is drinking more than he did before. He sees me raise my eyebrows when he orders it. "Don't worry, Sophie. Just something extra to celebrate being home."

"Oh, okay. I get that."

Half-glass Harry is here at the bar. He is just a guy in town that only drinks half a beer when he goes to a bar. So, they call him half-glass Harry. Sly Mancini is sitting beside him. Sly is the gigolo around town. He likes ALL the women. In the men's restroom here, there is machine that dispenses rubbers. Sly goes into the restroom and comes out mad. The machine was empty. He throws up his hands to half-glass Harry and announces loudly, "NO SEX TONIGHT!"

I am embarrassed. Otto doesn't like it. He starts to get out of his chair and I grab his arm. "Sit down, Otto. That doesn't bother me. He's just a drunk!" He sits back down.

A few people stop to say hello to us, knowing Otto just got back from the war. He does not encourage conversation. He just says hello and thank you.

We eat our pizza with few words said between us. He just doesn't seem to want to talk.

A guy we call Bumblebee just came in carrying flowers for the owner, Joanne. He is as wide as he is tall, and his round moon face is always red. He often walks Main Street, stopping into the bars he passes. On any given day, he is outside of Charley's Place washing Joanne's car. He pulls her garden hose across the road and washes her car in the parking lot across the street. Dad stopped one day and told him that the garden hose is going to get ruined with cars running over it. Bumblebee always answers with the same words said twice. "No worries, no worries!"

He picks Dick Leonard's flowers out of his yard. Everyone knows it, and Dick can never catch him. Today, Bumblebee gives the flowers to Joanne.

"Thank you, Bumblebee! Where did you get these?" She knows very well where he got them.

"No worries, no worries!" Out the door he goes. Everyone chuckles, including Joanne. But Otto doesn't laugh.

"Don't you think that's funny, Otto?" I ask, smiling.

"Wasn't paying attention, I guess." He is looking across the room.

There is a guy here with his wife sitting at a corner table. He was arguing with her when we came in and he still is. Otto is watching. I see Otto clench his fist as he watches. The guy suddenly grabs her arm, hard. Otto stands up quickly. I grab his arm. "No, Otto. Sit down."

The man sees Otto's reaction and withdraws from her arm. They get up and leave.

It scared me. It all happened so fast. Otto didn't have a temper like that before. It is like he just wants to hit something. "Let's go home, Otto."

He pulls into my house and I tell him good night. He doesn't answer. He is just staring out the windshield. "Otto, I said good night."

He shakes his head like he is shaking out the cobwebs. "Oh, sorry. Good night then."

I see my neighbor's car backing out of his garage. He is leaving for his night shift at the coal mine. His car backfires. Otto's body drops to the seat. He is trying to fit under the steering wheel.

"Otto! It's okay. It was just a car backfiring!"

He sits up very slowly, looking all around with fear in his eyes.

"It's okay, Otto. You're okay." But I don't know if he is okay.

I know for sure that the man that left for Vietnam a year ago, didn't come home. This man that came home, is different. His cobwebs are plenty, once again. He is the fly, trying to get out of the web.

CHAPTER THIRTY-THREE
A HERO GOES HOME
April 1972

I'm not worried all the time now, since Otto is home. Soon, I can quit worrying about Frankie too. He should soon be coming home.

Some girls from work asked me to go to a movie Saturday night. I haven't done very many fun things in the last year. I'm going to go!

On Saturday, April 8 at 2 am, I jerk awake when a chill runs through my body. It is strange. I sit straight up. I look over to my window. It is closed. My room isn't cold. It is a calm night. What was that? I go back to sleep.

When I awake again at 8 am, it is a nice sunny April day. Mom and Dad got Izzy two rabbits for Easter, and Dad and I have been busy building a pen for them. We plan to finish it this morning.

Dad and I do a lot of laughing throughout our hammering of boards. "This is going pretty fast, Dad. Don't you think?

"Many hands make light work, Sophie!"

"Do you ever run out of sayings, Dad?"

"Pretty much no!" He laughs.

"You know, Dad, this is a big pen for two rabbits. Especially when we'll probably end up eating them!"

"Who would eat a child's pet, Sophie?"

"Just saying, Dad. Izzy is eight already. By the time she is thirteen she won't give a hoot about these rabbits. That is just five years from now."

"You're right. I better keep the rabbit stew recipe handy!" He laughs and pounds another nail. It is a fun time, spent with Dad. "Are you going to the funeral with us this afternoon, Sophie?"

We have a funeral to go to. It is Billy Pompelia. He was killed in a car crash three days ago. His wife was with him. He married Jackie Nelson just six months ago. They were driving Jackie's little Volkswagen bug, on their way to work at Robertshaw in Indiana. Jackie was injured badly, but she survived. They lived in a sweet little house across from the Catholic church in Yatesboro. They were young. So young.

I know I should go, though I don't want to. "I guess I'm going. Yes."

We finish the pen in plenty of time to get ready for the funeral.

My heart is heavy as we enter the church. There are so many families from town in the church. The Enterline family is in the back row on the right, and in front of them are the Vicini and Formaini families. To the left is the Samosky and Skummy families talking in whispers to Mr. and Mrs. Bernardi sitting with Helen Kashur. Liz Brochetti motions for us to sit in their pew with them. The entire family came, minus Frankie, of course. Everyone is silent. So silent. Billy's Mom and Dad look beaten. I am sure they feel beaten too. Billy's brothers are here, Bobby and Larry.

Bobby is in a wheelchair. Bobby got through Vietnam and came home to work in the coal mines. He was so proud the day he bought his 1971 Chevy Nova. He and Ed Lucas went together and both bought the same car. Only eleven days later, he swerved to miss a deer and wrecked. He was paralyzed. How much tragedy should be bestowed upon one family? When will it ever end? The bubble in my heart floats straight up and I feel the dampness on my cheeks from my tears.

After the funeral there is a luncheon at the church hall. We all attend. It is a quiet luncheon. Not much talking. A few ladies in the kitchen are chatting as I go in to return my plate. "She's injured pretty bad." I hear Mrs. Moore tell Mrs. Andryka.

"Are you talking about Jackie?" I want to know.

"Didn't see you there, Sophie." Mrs. Moore says. "We just heard that Jackie's life will never be the same, because of her injuries. She is in a coma."

Poor Jackie. A young girl just in her prime. I tell Mom and Dad that I will walk home. I need to walk and hope the sand in my heart passes through. I've changed my mind about that movie tonight. I don't want to go.

******

Saturday morphs into Sunday, and after church, Dad and I finish the rabbit pen. After our Sunday family meal, I visit Otto for a couple hours. He is planting a garden, so I dig in and help.

"You sure you want to get your hands dirty?" he asks.

"That's what they make soap and water for, silly!" I grin at him.

He smiles back at me that soft smile where the little dimple appears on his right cheek.

We finish just as the softness of evening sets in and the fireflies light the yard. "I must get home, Otto. Work tomorrow you know."

"For us both!" He laughs. "I hate when weekends end!"

* * * * * *

Monday is a normal work day. Too much work to do with too many interruptions. When I drive home from work at the end of my day, and pass Swede Alley, I see many cars lined along Swede Alley near Frankie's house. Are they having a party or something?

I walk through my front door and it is quiet. Dad and Mom are sitting at the kitchen table holding hands. "What's going on?" I ask.

Dad looks at me. "Sit down, Sophie."

I'm scared. What could be so serious? I quickly sit. "What is it? WHAT'S WRONG?"

Mom grabs my hand. "Honey, Frankie was killed in Vietnam."

I jump up from my chair and both my hands go to my heart. I feel like it is going to fall out and I need to catch it. "Frankie? OH MY GOD!" I sit back down still clutching my

285

chest. My tears flow, as mom embraces me. "Where's Sammy, Mom?"

"On his way home. We just let him know."

"Sammy will be devastated!" I am devastated. My mind is spinning. I think of the Brochetti family. How did they find out? Two of his sisters would be in high school. Did they tell them there? How do you tell kids they just lost their brother? HOW? And his brother, John, in college. How do you have enough strength to drive home when you just found out your life changed forever? Where was Frankie's mom, Lizzy? She works at the hospital. Where was his dad, Spy? Where was his sister Linda? Where were they all when their world came crashing down? How does one deal with that kind of news? HOW?

My head feels like it is going to burst. I run to my room and shove my face into my bed pillow to cry uncontrollably. A half hour later I hear the front door open. It is Sammy. I hear him wail. I can't go to him. I just can't. I think of the figures going across the bottom of the television. Frankie is in those figures! OH MY GOD!

By early evening I manage to collect myself. I must for Sammy's sake. We must go to the Brochetti house. Dad says we will walk down Tarzan Hill instead of drive. He says it will give us time to get ourselves in the right head space, to be of support to the Brochetti family.

The walk feels long. The woods that surround us are thicker than before and the decline steeper than before. As we enter, there are many people around. Food is pouring in. Mom brought fresh baked cinnamon rolls. Conversation is all in low tones, some just whispers. We sit around Lizzy and Spy at the kitchen table, and just let them talk. Lizzy speaks first. "The army told us our Frankie was killed at 2 am Saturday morning." She cries.

We are silent. Mom holds her hand. Sammy runs out the back door. I think to myself, that was when I woke up with that chill! Could it be? Am I a psychic, or maybe just a freak? Why would I wake up with a chill the exact moment Frankie died? And, we were all at the Pompelia funeral on Saturday. Oh my God! The Brochetti family was beside us. There they were, at a funeral, and they didn't know that Frankie was gone too!

We say nothing. What would one say? What words would possibly be appropriate?

Spy takes a letter off the counter and shows it to us. "We received this just today. From Frankie. He wrote it on April 7th at 3:05 am. Just twenty-three hours before those bastards took my boy from me."

The date and time on the letter were at the top, just as Spy had said. Frankie wrote:

> *"The situation is really getting bad over here now. The Viet Cong have been attacking a place twenty miles north of us. On my radio I can hear U. S. troops who are under attack, talking to planes that are dropping bombs on the Viet Cong. It doesn't matter how many*

they kill, more seem to be coming
back. I've started to get a little
jumpy lately."

Frankie told of the horror of his situation, yet tried to be uplifting at the same time. He included a poem at the end: Spy reads it out loud to us:

> *I shall pass this way but once; Any*
> *good thing therefore that I can do*
> > *Or any kindness that I can show,*
> *Let me do it now.*
> > *Let me not defer it or neglect it, For*
> *I shall not pass this way again.*
> > *Remember me is all I ask now, If*
> *remembrance be a task,*
> > *Forget me!"*

Spy drops the letter to the table and drops his head as he sobs. Dad puts his arms around him as Spy cries into his shoulder.

I know this letter they will cherish. Yet, it is painful. Painful to know what he was going through, to feel his fear. And to think he took the time to write such a traumatic fearful moment.

Dad rubs Spy's back. "Your boy is a hero, Spy." Spy just keeps his head down and slightly nods yes.

Mom and I are trying not to cry, but it is impossible.

Lizzy gets up from the table. She wipes her eyes with her handkerchief and walks over to the cabinet. She brings out a document they had received from the army. "I want you to see this." She says, handing it gently to Mom.

Dad stands up and we gather behind Mom so we can all read it. After the lines at the top that say, *Awarded, then Date of Action, Theater,* and the words *By Direction of the President*, my eyes then go to *reason*.

AWARD OF THE SILVER STAR
(POSTHUMOUSLY)

PFC Brochetti distinguished himself by gallantry in action on 8 April 1972 while serving as Radio Telephone Operator of the Third Regional Assistance Command's Kui Ba Dem (Black Virgin Mountain) Radio Relay Site, Tay Ninth Province, Republic of Vietnam. On this date, the radio relay site suddenly began receiving extremely intense mortar, rocket propelled grenades, and small arms fire from three directions. Taking immediate action, PFC Brochetti ran to the radio relay building fearlessly exposing himself to this intense fire. Upon

reaching the building, he engaged the attacking force with small arms fire while his Non-commissioned Officer-in-Charge prepared to destroy classified equipment and publications even though the building was receiving intense fire and was burning. The mortar fire was lifted and enemy sappers assaulted the radio building using small arms, grenades, and satchel charges. Enroute to man one of the prearranged fighting positions, PFC Brochetti was wounded by an exploding grenade. Although wounded, he still directed fire on the attacking enemy forces until he succeeded in reaching the fighting position. Numerous enemy assaults were directed at his fighting position until it was totally demolished by satchel charges and rocket propelled grenade fire. He continued directing fire at the enemy until he was mortally wounded and his position was overrun. PFC Brochetti's conspicuous gallantry in action was in keeping with the highest traditions of the United States Army and reflected great credit upon himself and the military service.

It was hard to read. The words written there, GALLANTRY IN ACTION, describes what Frankie did. He was gallant. He was brave.

Mom stood up and took Lizzy's hand. "He was a hero, Liz." Liz just nodded her head up and down as her tears fell. She buried her face in Mom's shoulder to cry. Mom rubs her back and cries with her.

******

The telegram came the next day informing them when Frankie's body would be returned to them.

Frankie's funeral is April 18, 1972 at 11 am. We go to the viewing the evening before, together.

As we enter the funeral home, Mary Anne and Jerry Bishop greet us at the door. No one speaks. They just nod. We walk forward to the next room. We walk slowly to the casket. Frankie lies beneath glass. I stare at him. I can't feel my body, it is numb. Sammy is blank. Dad is holding onto him. I just stare. Stare, through the glass, trying to picture Frankie smiling and laughing, as he always was. They didn't comb his hair right. That isn't how he wore it! I want to shout to someone, "THAT ISN'T HOW HE WORE HIS HAIR!" But I don't. It can't be fixed. He is beneath glass.

I think of him looking sly as a fox when he got caught soaping the church windows. And how he laughed when the boys came down off the school roof. He was always happy. So happy.

I feel his family beside me to the right. Their grief is like a dense fog in the room. I can't talk. I run out the door.

His family is distressed enough without seeing me being a blubbering idiot. There is a large bush beside the porch of the funeral home. I stand behind it so no one can see me. Bent at the waist and my hands on my knees, I whisper out loud to myself. "Breathe. Breathe. Breathe." I feel a presence beside me. It is Otto. I fall into his arms. I know we are just friends but I need his hug right now.

"It will be okay, Sophie. Let's go in together. I'll hold you up and you can hold me up."

I finally pull myself together and re-enter. I hug the family. Linda, Darlene, Janie and John. Then Frankie's mom and dad, Lizzy and Spy. I say nothing. What is there to say? What possibly could one say? Their cobwebs are plenty now, and will always be. I turn to see Otto just standing, staring. He is white as a ghost. "Come on, Otto. Let's get you out of here." I knew. I knew how hard this was for him.

Bishop Funeral Home, Main Street RV

The next day is the funeral. Every house on Main Street is flying the American Flag. They are there for Frankie. The town cared. They cared that we lost one of our own.

The service at the funeral home is first. There are so many people that many must stand on the porch. When that service ends, six men walk the casket to the hearse. Lizzy and Spy are to get in the first car to follow the hearse. Before getting in the car, Lizzy looks up at all the flags adorning Main Street. She smiles through her tears. "Look, Spy. Look at the flags for our boy."

A multitude of cars follow the hearse to the Catholic Church. We are among those. Sammy keeps his head down. Nobody is talking. I see Otto's truck in the line. The silence is deafening, yet necessary.

Dad keeps his arm around Sammy throughout the funeral. So many nice things are said about Frankie. There's music and prayers. At the end, the priest waves incense across the flag draped coffin. My Catholic friend told me that the meaning of the incense and prayers is sending a person off to heaven. He is in heaven. He is being honored as he should be.

When the funeral ends, everyone is still, and quiet. I look to the back of the church and Otto is standing there, like a statue, with an expression of tremendous grief and sorrow.

Dad looks at Sammy and smiles, squeezing his shoulder that he has his arm around. "A hero went home today, son. A hero went home."

Frankie......on his radio in Vietnam

Spy Brochetti

Yatesboro Man Killed In Vietnam

YATESBORO — A 21-year-old Yatesboro youth, Frank T. Brochetti, was fatally injured during hosile action while serving with the U.S. Army in Southeast Asia.

Mr. and Mrs. John Brochetti were notified by the Department of the Army that their son was killed at 5:10 a.m. on Saturday, April 8, by enemy fire during an attack on the base camp in which he was located.

According to preliminary reports the Yatesboro GI was assigned to a base camp called Nui Ba Den, which means Black Virgin Mountain. The camp is located in Tay Ninh Province, just north of Saigon near the Cambodian border.

CHAPTER THIRTY-FOUR
REVELATION
Spring 1973

A year passed. Grief is a funny thing. It never leaves, it just resides. Forever. But it changes form somehow.

Jackie was in the hospital a very long time. I run into her sister, Debbie, at the post office. "How's she doing?" I ask. She looks tired

"It's hard." She says as tears well up in her eyes. "She was in a coma for so long. Nine weeks to be exact. We talked to her every day when she was in the coma, even though she couldn't respond. They told us she could hear us. We told her about Billy, but we don't know if she understood. After she came out of the coma, she seemed to have lost so much memory. She is in rehabilitation now. They are teaching her to walk and talk again. We can only pray for the best."

"She'll be in my prayers, Deb." It sure doesn't seem fair to me. Two young people, one gone and one changed forever.

I try to keep busy with things so to not think about all the tragedy that has happened. I told Mom I'd help bake cookies for the church bake sale today. That will help.

It has been bothering me a lot that Otto never knew his mother. We are rolling out dough when I ask. "Mom, do you know anything at all about Otto's mother?"

She stops rolling dough. She puts down the rolling pin and brings the skirt of her apron up to wipe her hands. She falls into a chair. "Sit down, Sophie."

I am staring at her, as I sit. She knows something? All this time she has known something?

"I think it is time I tell you what I know."

I swallow hard and sit down beside her. "You know something?"

"Sophie, his mom ran to Kiser Wilson that day. Dastard had beaten her badly. Her head was bleeding and her right hand was broken."

"Otto told me about her running to Kiser. But how did you know it?"

"Because Kiser took her to your Aunt Dee in Erie. Aunt Dee had been a friend to Rosalie in church."

"Aunt Dee? Wait a minute!" I put my head down and shake it back and forth, trying to loosen the muck that just formed in my brain. When I look up, tears are rolling down Mom's face. "I don't understand. Why would you never have told me that, Mom?"

"You have to understand, Sophie. At the time, Aunt Dee was petrified. I was petrified FOR her! She was so afraid of Dastard. If he found out, he could be dangerous."

"But Dastard is in jail, Mom! Why did you still wait to tell me? All this time. ALL THIS TIME! Aunt Dee has been here for holidays and summer visits, and you all kept this secret? WHY?"

"Because I still didn't know anything. Aunt Dee had her only a couple hours."

"How or why did Kiser take her to Aunt Dee? I don't get it."

"Kiser had gone to Erie a couple times in the past to fish with your uncle, so he knew where Aunt Dee lived. He was so befuddled when Rosalie ran to him. He didn't know what to do, but get her out of the area. Rosalie's head injury was bad. She was dazed and confused. She couldn't tell Kiser where to go, so he went to Aunt Dee's house. Once he got her there, they found a note in her pocket of a cousin of Rosalie's in Cleveland. Rosalie probably kept that address in her pocket for years, knowing someday she would have to run. Poor creature!"

"Where is Rosalie, Mom?   Where is she?"

"I don't know. Aunt Dee doesn't know either. She got her to a doctor for medical attention, and then took her to that cousin of hers in Cleveland."

And that's it?   Aunt Dee didn't hear from her since then?"

"No, she didn't. I'm sorry."

My mind is spinning. Mom knew this all along. I cannot comprehend her not telling me sooner.

"Sophie, if his mother wanted to come back, she would have. What would be the sense in telling Otto this? He is better off believing she is dead."

I can't talk. I am staring at her. I take my apron off and fold it over the chair and walk away.

"Where are you going, Sophie?"

I turn back to look at her. "I am trying to NOT be angry. I am TRYING to understand, but right now I DON'T. I am going to Aunt Dee's!"

I go upstairs to pack a bag. I can hear Mom on the phone telling Aunt Dee I am coming. I hope I get some answers.

******

The drive was an hour and thirty minutes. Aunt Dee is sitting on her porch waiting for me. She comes down the stairs and across the grass as I pull in. Her arms go around me. "Sophie, it is so good to see you."

"Good to see you too." I walk up the stairs with her and we go into her kitchen. We both sit. "No sense in putting off this conversation, Aunt Dee. You know why I am here."

"I know, honey. And I am so sorry I didn't tell you that Kiser brought Rosalie here. I only had her a couple hours, but that would have been enough for Dastard to come after me. Even years later!"

"Tell me about her. When she got here, I mean. Was she hurt bad?"

"Very bad. Her head was bleeding. Kiser had wrapped gauze around her head to get her here. Her right hand was broken. He wrapped that too. She was so confused. She just stared, and the only words she said were 'my baby, where's my baby?' We took her to my doctor for stitches in her head and he splinted her hand. Then we took her to a cousin she had in Cleveland. She had the address in her pocket."

"What did she say to you?"

"Oh, honey, she didn't say much. She just stared into space. She was so distraught and confused. She just kept crying for Otto. She didn't even know where she was. It was pitiful."

"Do you have any idea what that would have meant to Otto, to know that?"

"Yes honey, but what would it do to him to know she wanted him, yet she didn't go back. I don't know why she didn't, so how do you tell a boy that yes, his mother thought of him, but not enough to go back for him. How do you say that? Isn't it better he thinks she is dead?"

"I don't think so. Not at all. He has spent his life wondering where she was. I don't think you made a good decision, Aunt Dee. I'm sorry. Did you talk to that Delores after you left Rosalie there?"

"Yes, one time. I called her. She told me that since the situation is so delicate, and the fear of Dastard and all, that she did not want to hear from me again. She just said she would take care of Rosalie. So, I never called again."

"Do you still have the address?"

"Yes, I do." She opens a small drawer of her hutch and comes out with a yellow piece of paper. On it is an address: Delores Frank, 100 Lakeside Avenue East, Cleveland. "Sophie, I never heard from her again. I am ashamed to say I never tried. I just left it alone after that.

Don't blame your mom and dad. I made them promise to never tell you about her coming here."

"I'm trying to understand, Aunt Dee. Really, I am. But poor Otto, all this time not knowing what happened to her."

"Sophie, let him think she is dead. If she never went back after all this time, she might as well have been dead. What kind of a mother would do that?"

"I can't do that, Aunt Dee. Otto is a man now, and he needs to know. Whatever the answer is, I'll help him through it."

I stand up and give her a hug. "I'm leaving now. I'm going to Cleveland. Thank you, Aunt Dee."

She doesn't answer. She just hugs me back and backs away. I can see her tears but I have no sympathy right now. I go out the door and into my car. I am nervous, but I must do this.

I drive the hour or so to Cleveland. The street is hard to find. It is in the city. Houses are so close to each other, I don't think a piece of cardboard would fit between them. Finally, I find the street. House numbers are counting down. One hundred six, four, two, and I see it. One Hundred Lakeside Avenue East is on the mailbox. I pull in and walk up the skinny curved sidewalk to the front door. Knock, knock, knock.

A thin lady answers the door, with a cigarette in her hand. Her hair is pulled back into a ponytail. She is badly wrinkled and the jeans and plaid blouse she wears gives her the look of the older lady wanting to be young again.

"Is your name Delores?" I ask.

"Yes, who are you?"

"You don't know me, but I am here to ask questions about Rosalie Black. My name is Sophie. I am a friend of Rosalie's son, Otto."

She stares at me. She flicks her cigarette out the door past me into her bushes. "Come in, Sophie."

As I enter, I feel like I am in the fifties. She either loves the style, or she is one of those lost-in-the-fifties ladies. I sit in a low plain padded chair, and she sits on her couch.

Conversation is hard but I must begin. "I know that my Aunt Dee brought Rosalie here, the day she ran away from her house. That much I know. What can you tell me about her?"

"Can I get you some tea?" she asks.

"No thank you." I wait.

She begins. "I hadn't seen Rosalie in years. Dastard never knew I existed, which is why she came here. Poor thing. Half her face was black and blue and she had been bandaged the whole way around her head. Dee brought her to me and explained what happened, but I couldn't get anything out of Rosalie. She just stared and fussed about Otto."

"Then what happened?"

"She seemed very confused. She kept calling for Otto! Where's Otto? Where's my baby, Otto! It was like she didn't know what happened, or that she was here. She just kept looking around my house for her baby."

I can see she is trying not to cry. She drops her head. "It was sad, so sad. She just wanted her baby. But she didn't even know where she was. She wasn't here but an hour or so when she went into a seizure. It was awful. Her eyes were rolled back in her head and foam was coming out her mouth. I got her on her side and called the ambulance. They took her to University Hospital here."

"Then what, Delores?"

"She never came back, Sophie. That bang on her head she took had caused her so many seizures, they had to medicate her to keep the seizures at bay. She went into somewhat of a vegetative state."

My heart is pounding. I must ask. "Did she die?"

"Would have been a blessing if she did, but no. She did not."

"Where is she then?"

"She is in a state-owned full care nursing home here. They see after her, but she is still in that state. I visit her, and occasionally her eyes will open and I think she recognizes me, but then I know she doesn't. She mumbles a couple words now and then. The state takes care of her, since she had nothing and all."

'I don't know how I feel about this news, Delores. I wanted to find her alive and well, even though it would be awfully hard for her to explain why she never came back in twenty-some years of Otto's life. There would be no excuse for that. I am trying to understand why you didn't tell Otto."

I thought about it, Sophie. Lots of times. I couldn't while Dastard was there. He'd be coming here after her and me too, probably. Then when I heard he went to prison for life, I thought about it. But Otto went away to that boy's home, so what was the sense to tell him. When he returned home, I thought about it again, and before I could decide he went off to the army. At that point, I quit thinking about it. It was better left alone. By now I figure he pretty much assumes she is dead. It would be better if she was, than for him to see her like this."

"How did you know about all this, what Otto was doing and all?"

"Kiser's brother, Fred. I knew him from years ago, when we were young. I'd call him and he'd tell me. I grew up out there in the country, you know. Dastard just never knew me."

"It feels a little better that you thought about it, at least. But you have no idea what this has done to him. Even in the state she is in, he needs to know. Can you take me there to see Rosalie, Delores?"

"Of course. It isn't far." She goes to a drawer in a tiny table in her entryway. "This is all she had on her, in a pocket of her dress."

She hands me three pictures. They are of Otto. He is just a baby in one, the next he is maybe eight months old, sitting up. In the third picture is him on her lap. He is maybe almost one. Her arms are wrapped around him and she is smiling. She is pretty. She has brown hair that falls softly around her face and cascades down her shoulders. "May I have these?"

"Of course, Sophie. I'm sorry I didn't have better news for you about Rosalie." She picks up her purse and walks toward her car. "Follow me, Sophie. It is only five miles."

We drive through some city traffic but soon are on a road leading out of the city. As we come upon it, I see the large porch with patients in wheelchairs. It is a sad looking place. It needs paint and the yard that once had a fountain and flowers is now in disrepair. Weeds are everywhere, the fountain is dry, and grass grows through the cracks in the sidewalk. I didn't expect much, since it is run by the state, but I had hoped for better than this.

We walk onto the porch and into double doors, then down a very long hallway. The place smells like urine. I hear a woman moaning and a man's voice calling for his mother. I try to block it out as I walk. Her room is the sixth door we come to. The door says 106. We enter.

She looks very frail. Her hair is still brown with just a few strands of gray. She would probably still be only in her mid-fifties. It's hard to tell. I go over to her and place my hand on hers. Her eyes flutter. "Rosalie! Rosalie, can you hear me?" Though her eyes, flutter, she does not respond.

Delores says nothing to me, but walks over to her. "This is Sophie, honey. She knows Otto. Otto, your baby."

I feel her body tense slightly. The fingers of her hand that I hold move. She mumbles something I cannot understand. That's all. I am so sad I did not get more. Yet, no matter how bad this is, I must tell Otto and bring him here. It will be hard, but it must be. He needs to know.

I don't stay long. It is a long drive home. "I will head home from here, Delores. The next time I come, I will have Otto with me."

"Thought you'd say that. Will you please tell him I am sorry?"

I think you are going to get the chance to tell him yourself, Delores.

I did not go straight to Otto's. It was late and I am overtired. I need to be awake and alert when I tell him. I decided a phone call was enough for now.

"What did you do today?" He asks.

"I'll tell you about it tomorrow, Otto."

"Okay, I guess. I worked in the barn all day, except for running to Dixon's for bread and milk. I went down the alley past the playground and there was a bunch of cheerleaders on the monkey bars. I suppose the yearbook was taking pictures. Lucky those don't get hurt!"

"I think young people's bones are made of rubber, Otto."

He laughed and we said goodnight. I didn't sleep well thinking about how to tell him. There is no easy way.

Cheerleaders on the monkey bars

I get up early and stop at Passerini's to fill my gas tank. I get to his house by 9 am. He is coming around the front of the house when he sees me. "Hi, Sophie! I was just in the barn working. Where were you yesterday?"

"Sorry, Otto. Something came up."

We walk onto his porch and sit together on his porch swing.

"What are you doing in the barn this early, Otto? What are you doing that is so important?"

"Just odds and ends. Anyways, it gives me something to do on the weekends."

He is back at his job in construction now and works every weekday, sometimes into the evenings. He has been much better lately. Not so jumpy. He still won't talk about the war and maybe someday he will. But at least, for now, it seems as though he has relaxed some.

"You seem quiet, Sophie. What's up?"

"I've got something to talk to you about. I don't know how to start."

"How to start? How serious is it? Just spit it out, Sophie."

I swallow hard. "I know where your mother is."

His eyes get wide and he stands up. He is staring at me. "Where? How do you know?"

"She is in a home in Cleveland, Otto. She is not well and hasn't been since the day she left you."

He goes over to the porch railing, placing both hands on it like he is going to collapse. He stares at the ground in front of him. In a low tone he asks. "Did you see her?"

"I did, Otto. I went there yesterday. I didn't know anything about her until I got to Cleveland yesterday. I was on a search for her. I couldn't tell you, in case I never found her. If I had known she was alive, I would have taken you with me."

He is still staring at the ground. "What do you mean not well? What did she say? What was her excuse for not coming back?"

I stand up to be beside him. "She said nothing, Otto. She can't speak. When your dad beat her up that day she ran off, she had a head injury. It caused her to have seizures. She lives in a state-run nursing home in somewhat of a vegetative state. The state takes care of her. She wanted to come back for you, Otto. She just couldn't."

"How do you know that?"

"Because the woman who had her for only a short time when she ran off, told me. She said she was in a state of confusion. Before the first seizure she had, she was looking for you, fussing about you." I take the three pictures out of my pocket. "She had these in her pocket, Otto."

He takes them. He studies each one. He looks at all three, then starts again, flipping one to the other. "She was pretty."

"Yes, she was, Otto."

"I never saw a baby picture of me." He smiles. He looks at me. "Who is the woman that had her?"

"It was a cousin of hers. Her names is Delores. She lives in Cleveland. She never let us know because she didn't want you to see her like this."

"That's not a good enough reason. I never heard of that woman. My mother cried out for me, Sophie?"

"Yes, she did. Delores said she was calling for you. Then she went into a seizure and that was the last she talked."

I can see he is trying to choke back tears. He is silent. He is thinking. "I want to see her. Today."

It is still morning, so it is still possible. I smile at him. "I just filled my car up with gas. Let's go."

We are in the car in minutes. We talk the whole way there. I must tell him about Aunt Dee too. The whole truth needs told now. He isn't mad at her. "I'm glad Kiser got her to your aunt. Kiser saved her life."

Just short of three hours we are pulling into the home. He is rigid. "This it?"

"Yes, Otto. I know it looks bad, but I think she is getting the proper care."

As we walk down the long hallway, he is silent. When we reach Room 106, he stops and puts his hand on the wall. "Give me a minute, Sophie."

"Take the time you need. Remember, Otto, she will probably not respond. And even if she does, she probably won't know you."

He nods and takes a deep breath. "Let's go in."

He walks ever so slowly to her bedside. She is sleeping. He puts his hand on hers. "Mom."

Her eyes flutter, then slowly open. Though she looks confused and somewhat blank, she mutters something. We can't make out what it is.

310

Otto pulled his chair beside her and held her hand for two hours. He talked to her, telling her about fixing up the house, and that he went to Vietnam, and that he owns a truck. He just talked. Rosalie's eyes fluttered and a couple times she tried to mutter something again. We couldn't understand.

He finally stands up. "We're leaving, Mom, but I'll be back! You can count on it, Mom. Do you hear me?"

There is no response but looking at Otto, he hears her response in his heart.

We walk out into the hallway and Delores approaches us. She had been waiting. She looks at Otto. "You are a handsome young man."

Otto does not respond. He just stares at her.

"Otto, I'm sorry. I'm so very sorry. I was trying. I just didn't know what to do."

Otto takes her hand. "Sophie told me. I will try to understand. I understand what fear is." He lets her hand go. "My mother mumbled when I first went in. Then she did it again a couple times. Do you know what she is saying when she does that?"

She smiles as she takes his hands. "Listen closely, Otto. The word is Otto. She mumbles it often."

His face falls into despair. "She's thinking of me and she doesn't know I'm here."

Delores smiles. "Oh yes she does, honey. Yes, she does."

We stay on the porch talking with Delores so she can tell him everything that happened. He listens intently. It is

311

getting to be late afternoon and we must get going. "Thank you for taking care of her, Delores. I do wish you had told me the minute I was old enough to understand. Perhaps you saved her from more harm, as my dad would have certainly come after her. I can't obsess about the past and what could have been. I am in the here and now. You do know I will be her guardian from here on out, right?"

"Of course, Otto."

He shakes her hand. "Goodbye then."

Her sad eyes meet Otto's. "You know, I love your mother, don't you?"

He just smiles and nods yes. We head home by four, stopping to eat at Roxy's Diner on 422. We each have lemonade with our wings and fries, though Otto is just picking at his. He is asking questions I have no answers for. "Do you think she suffered, Sophie?"

"Probably not, Otto. With head injuries, they say there is no pain."

"Do you think she knew I was there today? Like Delores said?"

"Yes, I do. I absolutely do."

"Do you think they take good enough care of her there?"

"Sure, they do. But, Otto, we can transfer her to a home in Kittanning. She'll be nearer then, and we can visit often."

"You think so? That would be great! But first, I'm going to have her evaluated. There is a new neurologist in Kittanning. Dr. Gershwin. They say he is really good."

When we get back to his place, he opens his door and gets out, but before he closes it, I ask. "You okay, Otto?"

He leans down to look at me across the seat. "I'm better than I was yesterday and the day before. Because of you. Thank you, Sophie." He smiles that soft smile of his that I love.

"You are very welcome, sir."

We both laugh and I watch him saunter onto his porch. As he is opening his door he waves. I give him a little *toot-toot* and head out the lane, smiling. The elephant has just lifted itself from Otto's chest.

CHAPTER THIRTY-SIX
THE TIDE TURNS
June 1973

Within in a couple weeks, we had transferred Rosalie to the Kittanning Hospital. We are there when she arrives by ambulance. Otto and I sit with her in her room and he holds her hand as he looks out the window. "Look, Mom. Do you see the bird on that tree branch out there?" She does not respond. "It's okay, Mom."

Dr. Gershwin comes in. He is very tall and distinguished looking. His hair is gray only at the temples. He introduces himself to us and shakes our hands. He sits in a chair beside Otto. "I am going to evaluate her tomorrow, son. We are going to start with an EEG to measure her brain activity. I have no answers for you until I look at that."

"I'm just glad she is here. The tests you are doing won't hurt, will they?"

"Not at all. Don't worry. We'll take good care of her. By afternoon tomorrow I will have results. Can I plan to speak with you here at 4:00?"

"Absolutely."

We continue to sit with her another hour. "What do you think the brain test will show, Sophie?"

"I'm not a doctor, Otto. But they must think it will show something, or they wouldn't do it."

"I'm going to pray a lot tonight."

"I'll pray too, Otto."

When we head home and arrive at my house, I ask him in. "You sure it's okay?" he asks.

"Wouldn't ask you if it weren't!"

Mom and Dad are working in the kitchen rearranging the items in the food cabinet.

I laugh. "You have to be bored to be doing that!"

Dad laughs too. "Well, we found a box of rice with little brown things in it. Not so sure it wasn't mouse turds."

"Oh Dad! Did you have to tell me that!"

"Don't worry, Sophie. Mice only like rice. We threw it out."

Otto and I settle into the couch to watch *The Twilight Zone*. It scares me but he likes it. In this episode, a little girl disappears into a wall. The parents call her and can hear her, but she is in the wall, somehow.

"I'm going to have nightmares, Otto!"

"It is make-believe, you know that, right? Or is that little girl just another soul you have the need to save?" He smiles. "Thanks for saving me, Sophie. And thanks for sticking with me as I figure this thing out with Mom."

"You don't have to thank me. I'm happy to be there. I'll go with you tomorrow too, so pick me up!"

He gets up to leave. "I'm tired. It's been a long day. Anyways, I need to leave so you can figure out where in the wall that little girl is!"

I give him a little loving shove and laugh. "Nope, I'm done saving people. If you think I saved you, okay. But I really think you saved yourself!"

******

Early the next day, I swing by the grocery store for milk. Don and Pat Dixon bought it, so now it is Dixon's Market. They are nice people. Otto loves going there, as Don gives him advice about cooking meat, and he gives him special attention in cutting what he wants. Pat and Don go to my church also, and have been friends of Mom and Dad's for years. I'm in charge at home for a couple days since Mom and Dad went to visit Ruby.

I walk across the street to Moore's Hardware. Otto needs some two inch nails so I told him I'd gladly get them. Chauncey and his wife, Janice, are both here today. Janice is always smiling. "Hi, Sophie. We hear you are helping Otto fix up his old place."

"I am. It might take a good while, but we'll get it done." I pay for my nails and head out.

Arriving back home, Theo tells me he wants to go to the football field so I drive him up. He also says he wants to go to the Landmark later. The Landmark opened down by the carwash in Yatesboro. They made it for teenagers, with game machines and a ping pong table. Theo goes there a lot with his friends. The boys are all into ping pong. Theo said there is this one boy, Ralph, who always has on white painter's pants. He also always has his own ping pong paddle hanging in the tab of his pants. "That's one serious ping pong player!" I tell Theo. He just laughs.

They play a card game also called Scopa. He seems to have a good time with all the teens and I don't think he is devilish, although I know he goes out to Ernie Smith's *Pearly*

Gates now and then with a bunch of kids. Who knows what goes on at the *Pearly Gates*!

A lot of the teenage boys that are a little older than Theo smoke pot at the boney dump. I sure hope Theo doesn't get into pot! I imagine if he starts hanging out at the boney dump, we'd pretty much know he was. The boney dump in Numine is no more. They somehow spread it out a couple years ago so it would stop burning. I ran into Leona though that lives near it and she said it is still burning in many areas where they spread it, even though it is just ash lying low to the ground.

Izzy is at her friend Barbie's house today for a sleep over. She seems to have two main friends, Barbie and Beth. Beth will be there too. Mom said she could. She is young yet but Mom knows the parents, so I suppose it is okay. I'm glad to have the rest of the day free.

I am ready when Otto picks me up at 3:00 pm. At Kittanning Hospital, we sit with Rosalie as Otto talks to her. She looks at him but doesn't talk, yet.   By 4:00 pm, as planned, Dr. Gershwin enters the room. He shakes our hands again. "I have good news for you, Otto."

Otto stands up to talk eye to eye with him. "Really? What's that?"

Dr. Gershwin smiles. "There is hope here. Her brain activity is normal. I am sorry to say that she has been kept sedated for twenty some years in order to keep the seizures at bay. I am faulting no one, you understand. The state run home had to do that to keep her alive. Had she kept having seizures she could have died. But nowadays, we have medication for seizures. Medications they didn't have back then. Right now, she has been on so many medications, the important thing is to wean her off them. Once we accomplish that, we will begin the seizure medication. Soon after that we are going to see a big change in her cognitive ability. She may be able to speak and be coherent. Whether she will ever walk again, I cannot say. It is possible she's been too many years in a bed. But I do see in her records where they did keep up a daily regimen of exercising her limbs. That may help. I still feel she will need to be in a home. But we will get her physical therapy and you just never know. It is going to be all up to Rosalie."

Otto's face is white. "You mean, she'll be able to talk to me?"

Dr. Gershwin smiles and places his hands on Otto's shoulders. "Yes, she should be. It's about time, don't you think?"

Otto starts to cry. He falls into his chair. I take his hand. "Otto, this is wonderful news!"

He can't talk. He just shakes his head.

******

Two weeks pass as we visit Rosalie every evening. Her progress day to day is incredible. Little by little her eyes stayed open longer and she started to say more words. He keeps talking to her, and every day she improves and says a few more words. She can say *hello, goodbye, yes, no, and I'm thirsty.* She started to put words together, and as time goes on she puts more than two words together, yet she has not given a definite response that she knows Otto.

We missed going for three days because Otto was working twelve hours a day on his job so I just waited for him. Today as we enter, they have her bed sitting up. We walk over to her. Otto takes her hand. "Hi Mom. How are you today?" He asks the same question every day.

She stares into his eyes. A faint smile lights her face. "Otto?"

He throws his arms around her. I am crying. This is a moment I will never forget. "Yes Mom, it's me, Otto."

She stares at him placing her hands on his cheeks. "But you're so big. Not a baby."

He chuckles. "I know Mom. I'll tell you all about it." He sits on her bed and begins to tell her what happened and the years that have passed.

She looks confused. Then her face saddens. "I missed it all. I missed you growing up."

"It's okay, Mom. We'll make up for it, won't we?"

She nods and her tears fall into her lap.

"No tears, now, Mom! This is the first day of the rest of our lives!"

I swear his skin has turned a new soft color of pink and his hazel eyes are more hazel than ever! The doctor comes in and sees the joy in Otto's face. "This has turned out better than we ever expected. Once she was totally taken off all the mediation, which we accomplished just four days ago, Rosalie became Rosalie again. I was just going to call you, she was fussing about you."

Otto smiles at her and takes her hand. "I've been fussing about you too, Mom."

Don and Pat Dixon, 2021. Owners of Dixon's Market

CHAPTER THIRTY-SEVEN
LOVE AND PEACE
July, 1973

Rosalie continues to improve and though she is unable to walk, her cognitive ability is quite good and she has wonderful conversations with Otto. The home that Otto transferred her to is quite nice, with outside gardens. Today we take her out to the garden in her wheelchair. It is a hot July day, but the shade of the maple trees is pleasant. Conversation is plentiful now. She looks up through the trees at a red bird flying and points. "See the red bird? Red birds mean good luck, Otto."

Otto smiles at her. "We've got good luck, Mom. You're back"

"You are such a wonderful young man, honey. I am so sorry I missed it all. I am so sorry,"

"It's okay, Mom. You are here now. You couldn't help it. We'll make up for it, okay?"

She smiles and nods. "You are such a good son."

"I hope I stay good, Mom. I'm so afraid the evil that was in Dad will come out in me someday."

She puts her head down and wrings her hands. When she looks up, her eyes are full of tears. "Oh, honey. You don't need to worry about that. Dastard was not your father."

I think Otto has stopped breathing. "What? What do you mean?"

"It is time you know the truth." She swallows hard. "Your true father was a wonderful man. I fell in love with him when I was sixteen, he was eighteen. My parents didn't allow me to see him, but I snuck out and did anyways. By the time I was seventeen and he was nineteen, he went off to the war in Korea. That was June of 1950. By July I knew I was pregnant. I was writing a letter to him to tell him, when his brother called me that he was killed in Korea. The officers had just left his house. It was the worst day of my life." She starts to cry.

Otto hugs her then backs off. "Tell me the rest, Mom."

My parents found my letter that same day and kicked me out. I was sitting on the steps of the Company Store late at night with only a bag of clothes when Dastard found me. He took me to his house. That is where I stayed, since I had nowhere to go. He made me promise to pretend you were his. Then, once you were born, the violence started."

"Oh my God. Mom, I'm so sorry. You couldn't go back to your parents?"

"They never spoke to me again. You have to understand that in those days it was truly a sin to be pregnant out of wedlock. The only important thing to them was that the town thought Dastard was your father, as he married me immediately. Lord forbid they should be disgraced! My father died within that next year from cancer and my mother had a stroke five months later and died."

"I'm sorry, Mom. That couldn't have been easy for you. But, thank God Dastard is not my dad!" He caresses her hands laying on her lap. "Who is he, Mom? Who is my dad?"

A smile came on her face of great love. "Robert Wilson, honey. Fred's twin brother. I loved him to the moon and back. He was wonderful and kind. He loved me too. He would have been crazy about you. Kiser and Fred never knew. I couldn't tell them. Dastard would have killed me."

Otto takes her hand. "It's okay, Mom. Of course, Robert loved you. Who wouldn't love you!" He got up and walked across the garden and leaned on a tree, thinking.

I go to him. "Otto, this is wonderful news."

"It is, yet I can't stand to think of her broken heart and what she went through just so I had a roof over my head."

"She's going to be okay, Otto. You'll see."

******

The next day I go with Otto to Fred Wilson's. Fred is just closing his barn door when he sees us. "Hi kids! Come in for a coffee?"

"Don't need coffee, Fred, but we need to talk."

We enter his house and sit around his kitchen table.

"You sure? I just made a pot!"

Otto is nervous. "Fred, I have something to tell you and I don't know where to begin."

"Well, just begin, kid!"

"Your brother, Robert." Otto stops. He is searching for words.

"What about my brother Robert?"

Otto looks at Fred and after a moment of silence he speaks. "Robert is my dad."

Fred stands up. "What? What do you mean?"

"My mother was able to tell me. She found out she was pregnant after Robert left for Korea. She was writing to tell him when she got the word he was killed. Her parents kicked her out, and Dastard took her in."

Fred walks over to his sink and looks out the window. The silence could be cut with a knife. He turns to Otto. Otto stands up. Fred walks up to him. "I knew there was something about you, kid. Just something, but I didn't know what. Now I know. It's that little dimple that comes onto your right cheek when you smile a certain way. Robert had that same dimple. It's your hazel eyes. Robert had the exact same hazel eyes. Hell, I've always been drawn to you and couldn't understand why I like you so much. Now I know. I just got a little piece of my brother back!" He throws his arms around Otto and they embrace. Fred is laughing. "You know you have to call me Uncle Fred now, right?"

We all laugh and have the cup of coffee that Fred offered. After pouring our cups Fred sits down. "I always wondered how your mother could have picked Dastard, when I knew she was crazy about Robert. Robert was crazy about her too. I just figured the grief of losing Robert got hold of her and she lost her senses. I never asked her. I couldn't even talk about Robert without crying. When he died, part of me died too. I turned to the bottle. I wish I would have talked to her now."

"It wouldn't have helped, Fred. She couldn't tell you. Dastard would have killed her."

"God bless her. Poor thing. And you. You've suffered so much, living with that beast. I'm so sorry."

"No need to be sorry." Otto smiles. "Don't be sorry.......Uncle Fred."

Fred smiles from ear to ear and walks over to a small table with a drawer. He opens the drawer and takes out a small velvet pouch. He unties the ribbon and takes Otto's hand palm up and holds the velvet pouch upside down. A silver chain falls out with a flat metal piece on the end of it with engraving. Otto studies it and looks at Fred. "It's your dad's dog tags, son. They sent them to me after he died. I think you should have them."

Otto wraps his hands around the dog tag and holds his head down. "If only I could have known him."

******

Saturday morning, I go to Otto's early and he makes me the pancakes I love. I've worn my favorite skirt and blouse. The skirt is a soft silk that falls gently around my hips and thighs and extends to my ankles. The soft feminine chiffon blouse that matches it is cream. I just feel happy, and I feel like dressing nice today.

"Let's take a walk." he proposes, mid-morning.

"Where we going?"

"You'll see!"

He grabs a bottle of wine and two glasses. "I can't drink wine before five o'clock, Otto!"

He laughs. "It's five o'clock somewhere!" He reaches into the refrigerator for a container with cheese and meat for us to eat. He grabs an old quilt off the back of the couch. Seems as though we are going on a picnic!

He grabs my hand as we walk up over the hill behind his house. I've never been up here. The trees are lush with green. There are apple trees, pear trees, and beautiful maples everywhere. As we round the top of the hill, there is a meadow beyond us. It is loaded with daisies and lavender. Butterflies hop from flower to flower. It is beautiful. There is a faint breeze and the whiskers from the daisies float past us. "It's beautiful up here, Otto! I didn't know this was here."

It's my land. My land now. My fake grandpap owned all this. Neither him or my fake dad appreciated the beauty of the land."

He lays the old hap on the grass. I sit down. "I want to just sit here and enjoy this, Otto."

"That's just what I thought you'd say!"

He sat down beside me, opening the wine and pouring us each a glass. As we sip and munch on cheese and salami, we talk about many things. After a short while, he starts to talk about the war. I am surprised. He has never talked about it. Now, it pours out of him. I listen intently, watching his face, hands and body as they react to each story he tells me. "In one battle, a tank came to get us out.

Three of us sat near the gun turret. There was the captain on my right, and my friend Lynch on the left. An RPG came in and blew us off the tank. The captain had his arm blown off. Lynch got shrapnel in his legs. I got nothing."

"Thank God, Otto!"

"It was hard to understand why I was spared, Sophie. The worst day was the day Bobby got killed."

"You wrote to me about him in one of your letters, Otto."

"I liked him a lot. He talked like a farm boy. He was so innocent and hard working. Nice guy. Awful nice guy."

"How did it happen, Otto?"

"Bobby and I were in a foxhole, putting out fires for the medivacs to come in for our wounded. We were shoulder to shoulder. He took a sniper bullet to his head."

He puts his head down. I can see the stress and the grief all in one. "We didn't expect that. The woods were so far off, to this day don't know how that was even possible. But those snipers were good at what they did, the bastards! Excuse my language. Worst day of my life. I remember clutching his head close to my chest and rocking. I just kept rocking, back and forth. The medics had to pry me off him. He didn't have a chance to survive that. And how and why did it hit him, and not me? We were shoulder to shoulder!"

"Because it wasn't your time, Otto. I'm so sorry. It must have been awful."

"Yes, to spend a year most days sitting in a jungle so thick, we couldn't see in front of our faces. Then I'd hear the mortars, and just wait and pray it wasn't coming down on me. I can't tell you how many times they hit the men beside me and around me. I've seen horrible things, Sophie. Horrible things."

No wonder. No wonder he came back different than he was before.

I take his hand. "But you made it, Otto. You are here now. You are okay."

He smiles as he looks at me. "You think? I don't think any soldier that went through that war will ever be okay."

He talks about the war for two hours. We each sip our wine as he talks. After two hours he seems done. So is the wine.

"I loved hearing about it, Otto. Thank you."

The insects are biting and I slap my ankle. I look at him smiling. "I hope when the insects take over the world, they will remember with gratitude how we took them along on all our picnics."

He laughs, and takes my empty glass and sets both down in the grass. "I love your humor, Sophie. What is your favorite season?"

"Fall. I love fall. The beauty of the trees, and rustling through leaves as you walk. It is magical."

"I kind of figured that is what you'd say. I like fall best too."

We have run out of conversation. I bring my face close to his, meeting his yes, "You've come a long way, haven't you?"

"Because of you, Sophie."

Our faces are being pulled together by a force of nature. When our lips meet, electric goes through my body. He is delicious. I don't want it to stop. He leans me back onto the quilt and kisses me with a softness and passion that fills my veins. His hands softly caress down my side as we kiss. My mind is racing. I thought we'd always be just friends, but my heart knew I wanted more! My body is alive.

As he pulls away, he is still very close to my face. "I love you, Sophie."

I start laughing, like a school girl. "What's so funny?" He is a little insulted.

"It's funny, because I LOVE YOU TOO! I just couldn't spit it out!"

He starts to laugh with me and we sink ourselves into a kiss of warm water washing our souls. Embracing, we lie there for a long time. He caresses my cheek as he talks, then turns onto his back with me cuddling into his shoulder. "I'm alive because of you, Sophie."

"Me? How so?"

He stares at the blue sky. "In Vietnam I prayed to God every day to bring me back to you. He did. It was my love for you that kept me going, and fighting for my life. I have loved you since elementary school. I wouldn't have made it without you. I was so miserable in my life, I came close to using Dastard's shotgun on myself at one time, but then I would think of you. You, at school, waiting for me to come to school. If there were days I didn't come, it was only because I was injured so badly my pain kept me home."

"Oh my God, Otto. I can't bear to think of it!"

"It's over now. You gave me life. A good life. And, now that I know Dastard is not my father, I can trust myself to love you. It's been eating away at me inside, Sophie."

I hug him and try not to cry. "You didn't have to be afraid to love me, because you are you, and no one else."

I feel his body melt into mine. He talks into my ear. "I love you so much. I have one more thing to ask of you."

I pull away so we are face to face. "Anything, Otto. What is it?"

"I need to go see Dastard. He is in the Eastern State Penitentiary in Philadelphia. That would be maybe four to five hours drive. I can get a hotel room for us. Will you go?"

"Of course, I'll go." Though I'm not sure what that means a hotel room *for us*. Not sure I'm ready yet. He sees my face.

"We'll get a room with two beds. Don't worry."

"I wasn't worried, silly!" I lied.

We spend the next hour in passionate embracing, with soft kisses. I am a helium balloon floating in the sky. His hands caress my body, but he asks for no more. I have an overwhelming feeling of ecstasy. It is perfect!

This is not what I felt with Buck. Not even before he was mean. Not ever.

I've never felt this. It is a hot bubbly bath and a soft breeze across my face all in one! He completes me.

******

The next week we take off for Philadelphia on Saturday morning. He has made an appointment to visit with Dastard at three in the afternoon.

After stopping for lunch on the way, we arrive just in time. As we park and walk towards it, I am nervous. "It is a horrible looking place, Otto. Look at all the barbed wire, and the bars on all the windows!"

"He deserves it, Sophie."

They take us into a small room and we sit at a long table. There are two hooks in the table. When they bring Dastard in, he is in handcuffs. He sits down across from us, and the officer attaches his handcuffs to a steel hook on the table.

Otto is glaring at him. Dastard's head is down. He looks much older. He is so thin, he looks sickly. His hair is gray now and his face hollow. He has grown a beard. When the officer who hooked him to the table is done, he stands behind him at the wall.

Dastard finally looks at Otto. "Hello, son."

"DON'T CALL ME YOUR SON!"

Dastard puts his head down. When he brings it up, I can see there are tears in his eyes. "I don't blame you for that."

"Do you know what you did to my mother?" Otto demands. "Let alone what you did to me!!! She has been lying in a bed for over twenty years now, because of the beating you gave her. OVER TWENTY YEARS! The life imprisonment you got is not enough punishment for you. YOU SHOULD HAVE BEEN PUT TO DEATH!"

Dastard is silent. Otto is silent. When Dastard finally speaks, his voice shakes. "I didn't know that. God forgive me."

Dastard then looks at me. "I remember you, Sophie. You grew up."

"DON'T TALK TO HER!" Otto shouts. "You don't deserve to talk to her!"

The room is silent again. The officer standing behind him doesn't know where to look. He stares at the ceiling.

"I can't change the past or what I've done, Otto. I can only say that I am sorry."

"Here's something you might like to know. All that money you left in the bank is mine now. I'm going to use it to get my mother well. How do you like that?"

"I'm actually glad to hear that. And again, I am sorry." Dastard replies.

Otto Is agitated. He is rubbing his hands. He stands up and takes my arm. "Good to know you are sorry. I can never forgive you. May you rot in hell." He takes my hand and pulls me to the door. He looks back at Dastard. "Oh yes, and here is one more little tidbit you might like to know. I know you are not my father!"

Dastard looks like he just saw a ghost. His eyes are fixed on Otto. "I raised you, no one else."

"YOU DID NOTHING OF THE SORT! You beat me within an inch of my life! You starved me! I hated you to the core of my soul. No, indeed, you are not my father. My father was a kind gentle man. He was a hero. You? You are only a coward. Only a coward would beat up little boys and women and do what you did. A COWARD! My father's name was Robert Wilson. ROBERT WILSON! Do you hear me? Robert is my father, NOT YOU! I will thank God every day for that."

It is over. Dastard keeps his head down. Otto has said what he needed to say. He has made his peace.

We drive around awhile and talk, have dinner at an upscale restaurant, drink a bottle of wine, then go to our hotel. It is getting late and though we are both tired, we can't stop talking. About everything. About Otto's childhood, about my childhood and how I came to live with Sam and Patsy. We never run out of conversation but we are running out of steam.

"Sophie, do you suppose if Mom ever starts to walk, that I could take care of her at home?"

"Absolutely you could, Otto. I would help you! And she is going to walk again!" He smiles and kisses me again. "I'm tired, Otto. Better get to bed."

"I agree." He says, putting his hands on my cheeks and giving me a soft warm goodnight kiss. "You get the bathroom first."

I turn on the radio. *I'd Love You To Want Me* is playing. How appropriate. I get into the shower. After I am done, he goes to shower. I crawl into my bed, turning onto my side, facing the wall. I think of all the things that happened today, and the good conversation Otto and I have had. I try to picture him as he was back in elementary school. So forlorn and forgotten. I smile as I think of the man he is today. I am starting to drift off to sleep, when I feel his body beside me. His lips kiss my neck. They are warm as velvet. His breath is hot.

"Can I just lie here?" he asks softly.

"Absolutely." I smile to myself, then I turn and kiss him with unleashed passion. He asked for no more than that, but the bull had escaped the pen. I am the bull. I want more. *It's Too Late To Turn Back Now* plays on the radio. Indeed, it is too late.

I chuckle. He stops. "What?" he asks.

"The radio. Do you hear it?"

He pauses. "Too late for sure. But, are you sure?"

"I'm sure. I'M SURE!"

CHAPTER THRITY-EIGHT
LOSS, DISCOVERY, AND PANIC
August 4, 1973

Otto got a call from the prison. Dastard died. They told Otto he had cancer. When Otto called and told me, he said it with no emotion. "He's gone now. I hope he is in hell, Sophie."

I didn't know what to say, so decided that nothing was best. "I'll be right out, Otto."

I haven't told Mom and Dad yet about Otto and me. I go to his place every evening now and every Saturday and Sunday. Dad raised his eyebrows yesterday when I was leaving and said, "Just a friend, huh?" He knows. I won't have to tell him.

Izzy wants to go along. I holler to Mom and Dad that she is with me, and we head to the car.

Otto is sitting on his swing waiting for us.

"Are you okay, Otto?"

"I'm fine. It's not like I'd miss him or anything."

"Still, he was part of your life."

"The part of my life I choose to forget. He is nothing to me, Sophie."

I understand. I sit with him awhile as Izzy plays with Thor. Thor is getting old now. He limps and he can't see well, but he loves Izzy. He comes to life when she is here. She is trying to get him to chase her.

"I'm going to pull those old rotten boards of that floor of the back porch today, Sophie. I want to replace them. Do you want to help?"

"Sure, I'll help." I quickly holler to Izzy to not leave the yard, and I go around back with Otto.

He takes the end of a board of the floor in his hand and lifts, it crumbles easily. "See what I mean? Rotten as heck!" He lifts the one next to it and stumbles slightly since it pops up so easily. He gains his stance as he stares at the opening that has just revealed itself. He seems puzzled. "What is that?" There is something under the supporting floor board, against the dirt. It has a strap. He takes a long stick and gets a hold of the strap and pulls. A purse comes out. "What the heck?" He is puzzled.

We sit down on the stairs of the porch. He opens it. There's a lipstick, a comb, a cloth handkerchief nicely folded, and red wallet. He opens it. Otto's face is white as snow. His hands are shaking.

Inside, there is no money, but there is a picture behind the plastic where a driver's license should be. A man, tall with light hair and light eyes. He is handsome. The woman has dark brown hair that falls to her shoulders, framing her petite face. She has dark brown eyes. She is pretty with a warm smile and she is holding a small girl, maybe a year old or less. There are two little girls standing, maybe two and three years old. I look closely. My heart jumps into my throat. "Give me that!" A chill runs up my spine as I grab it from him. I stare at it, consuming each person. I take it out of the wallet and turn it over. Written with pencil is: Jay, Stella, Delilah, Julia, Sophie. May 3rd, 1951. "Oh my God!" I start to cry. "This is my mother and father!"

Otto jumps up and starts to pace in the grass. His head is down. "Oh my god. Oh my God!" Finally, he drops to his knees. "This means that Dastard was the drunk driver! HE WAS THE DRUNK DRIVER THAT KILLED YOUR PARENTS! OH MY GOD!"

"Stop, Otto. PLEASE STOP! ANYTHING and EVERYTHING Dastard did has nothing to do with you! Nothing at all!"

"How can so much evil be in one person, Sophie. How? I am so sorry!"

"You do NOT need to apologize for him, Otto. He is gone. And do you see what this means? For the first time in my life, I see my parents! I have faces now to remember. They are no longer blank faces to me. It is wonderful!"

"Dastard is a murderer, not of one, or of two, but of three people! I think I'm going to throw up!"

"You must stop, Otto. Dastard isn't you! You had no way of knowing!"

Otto throws his arms around me. "I don't know what to say."

"Say 'I'm happy for you Sophie why don't you? I have faces now, and I never thought I would."

"It's kind of crazy how you find good in everything, Sophie." He goes into the house and comes out with a white bag and a soft linen pillowcase. He wraps the purse gently in the pillowcase and slips it into the bag.

337

He sits down on the step and places it at his chest, hugging it. "I'm just so sorry."

"No more of this sorry stuff, Otto. Let's get back to work! Let's get these old boards torn off here, I've got the energy of ten women now!"

He laughs as he gently places the bag with the purse aside. "You had that energy before."

We work diligently pulling the old boards off and preparing for new boards to go on come Monday morning.

When the last board is off, we look at our work proudly. I look at him and start to speak when suddenly, I hear a blood curdling scream.

"IZZY!" I start to run to the front of the house. I feel Otto behind me. Where is she? "IZZY! IZZY!"

"SOPHIE! HELP ME!"

She sounds like she is in a drum. We run to the well. SHE FELL INTO THE WELL!

"IZZY! LOOK AT ME! ARE YOU OKAY? ARE YOU HURT?"

She is crying. "I'M SCARED!"

I try to calm down and talk through my hysterical tears. "I know you are scared Izzy, but you are going to be okay. We are coming to get you. Now you just lay there! Keep still, okay?"

I turn in panic not knowing what to do. I see Otto racing towards me with a heavy rope. He quickly entwines it around the bar of the well that holds the bucket. He begins to descend. It is happening so fast. "NO, OTTO! We'll call the firemen to get her out!"

"You get into the house and call them; I may need them. GO!" He hollers as he continues to descend.

I race to the house, make the call, and race back to the well. He has reached her. He is talking to her and checking her out. "She's okay, Sophie! She isn't hurt. She is just scared."

Within minutes I hear the firetrucks coming. The firemen put some sort of a basket at the end of a cable and lower it down the well. Otto puts Izzy in the chair and she is lifted out.

I grab her with such intensity and hug her. She is crying and I am trying to comfort her. I look at her all over to be sure she is not hurt. She is not. It is a miracle.

I turn around to see the firemen pulling Otto out of the well in the same basket. He is covered in grass trimmings, same as Izzy.

"Is she okay?" He asks immediately.

"Seems to be. The firemen checked her out too. Oh, Otto. You are so brave."

"That wasn't bravery, Sophie. That was sheer terror. And at this point I have something to thank Dastard for."

"What would that be?"

"For making me put all those grass clippings and leaves down the well for years. It saved her life."

"You see, Otto. You've got to look for the silver linings."

The three of us melt into a loving embrace.

"I want to go home, Sophie," Izzy whispers.

"Okay, Izzy. Let's go. We need to tell Mom and Dad what happened." I am scared, and I feel horrible. I wasn't watching her. I'm going to have to admit it. I learned a very hard lesson today. A VERY hard lesson.

As I kiss Otto goodbye he smiles. "It wasn't your fault. We were both sidetracked. We should have been watching her."

"I know."

"She is okay, Sophie. You must not obsess about this. She is okay."

"I know."

"Sophie, when you come tomorrow, will you bring the key?"

"Sure, I will." But I am thinking where is it? I've had it so long; I don't know where I put it. So, after I apologize to Mom and Dad for being a horrible big sister to Izzy, I hope to find the key.

I sleep through the night, but with troubling dreams. The last one I remember is Izzy falling. I can see her falling down the well. It is like in slow motion. Her hands and feet are outstretched and her body is turning in circles as she falls. I am screaming to her, and she keeps falling. I awaken with a jerk and sit up in bed. My nightgown is wet from sweat. I run across the hall to look at Izzy. She is sound asleep. She is fine. I go to the bathroom, splash water on my face, and say out loud to myself, "get a grip!"

******

Before getting ready for church, I go through all my drawers for the key that Otto gave me. I can't find it. "Mom, did you see a key laying around here?" I holler.

"Could it be this one in the coin dish in the kitchen?"

I run to kitchen. "That's it!"

"What's it for, Sophie?"

"I don't know. Otto gave it to me long ago. He told me to bring it when I go today."

"Maybe it's the key to his heart, honey."

"I hardly think so, Mom. I didn't need a key for that. I opened his heart long ago."

She smiles. "I knew you did."

CHAPTER FORTY
BE MINE
August 5, 1973

I get to Otto's around 10:30, when church ends. I have the key in hand. He has the coffee hot as I enter and he has made me pancakes. "How do you know I didn't eat yet?" I ask him.

"Because I know you like my pancakes." He is right.

We sit over coffee and breakfast and chat a long while. "You know that Devivo boy that lost his arm when he was little?" he asks.

"Gary? Yes, I met him way back when. What about him?"

"People are saying he is one heck of a basketball player! That just goes to show you, there's nothing a person can't do once they set their mind to it."

"That doesn't surprise me about that boy, Otto. I picked out that trait in him when I met him years ago. He was swinging on the banisters leading to the gym, swinging way better than the other boys."

"Let's go out to the porch, Sophie!"

"Okay, and don't forget that I brought the key."

"Not yet," he says smiling. "I'll tell you when."

We swing and talk, watching the squirrels scurry up the trees. An Eagle comes flying above the house and we rush out into the grass to watch it. It is majestic. "A gift from God." He throws his arm around my shoulders and kisses my cheek.

"Indeed, it is, Otto."

It is nearly one o'clock. He keeps looking at his watch. "You expecting someone, Otto?"

"No, just wanting to know what time it is. So, where's the key?"

"In my pocket. You want it?"

"Just come with me, Sophie."

We walk over to the barn. "Now put the key in the padlock and open it."

I think that's funny. He works in this barn all the time. The key is for the barn? I don't get it. I am so glad that Otto removed all the chicken feet and deer horns that were hanging on the outside of this barn. They were creepy. I gently put the key into the padlock and turn it. The lock opens easily and I remove the padlock and push the barn doors open.

There, sitting in the middle of the barn, is the most beautiful gazebo I have ever seen. It is white and it is round with a peaked roof. There is beautiful soft material draping the front tied back with pink flowers. I walk around it, then step inside it. Every inch of it is perfect. I float my fingers over the carvings. They are intricate. It takes my breath away. I look at him. "Did you make this, Otto? It is wonderful!"

He is smiling. "I made it for you."

"Me? You made this for me?"

"Yes, you, Sophie. I started making it in high school. I knew then that you would never leave this area. You are a hometown girl. I wanted you to have something for your yard, so that every time you looked at it, you would think of me."

"Think of you? Where would you be?"

"I really didn't know."

"But, Otto, I don't have a house. Where will I put it?"

"We'll set it in the meadow."

"The meadow? I don't understand."

"Look up, Sophie."

I look up, and there on the ceiling it says *MARRY ME, SOPHIE!*

My hands go to my mouth. I look at him. He opens his arms. I run into them. We embrace as he swings me in circles, as I laugh like a little girl. He stops and puts me down. "I didn't hear a yes." He seems like he is not breathing.

"YES, YES, YES!"

He drops to his knee and takes out a small black box. When I open it, my tears are blurring my eyes. I stare at it through my fog. It is a diamond set in a square setting, with diamond chips on both sides. "It is beautiful, Otto!"

I move my pearl and jade ring that he bought me to my right hand. On my left hand, he slips the diamond. I sit down on the step of the gazebo and I take my crescent moon necklace off and lay it across my hand. "Look at that will you? Two love rings and a necklace that saved me. I don't feel deserving of all this love, Otto."

"If anyone deserves love it is you, Sophie! You were so easy to fall in love with. I loved you from the moment you told me to wear your mittens home in fourth grade. In my teens I started the gazebo for you. I gave you the key just in case something happened to me. I needed you to find it, even if it was not yet done."

"If something happened to you? What could possibly happen to you?"

"I still lived with Dastard at the time. Remember?"

"Oh my God, Otto. You thought he would kill you? It was that bad?"

"It was that bad, Sophie. It's over now. Let's forget about it." He hugs me tight talking into my ear. "I've loved you for a long time. When I started this gazebo, I dreamed of us together, yet thought it impossible. I just wanted you to have it. It was the little piece of happiness I had at that time, coming out to this barn and working on something for you. Praying it would be for us, even if was just a dream. It kept me away from Dastard. It kept me going. And now that I know he is not my father, I have the freedom to dream of a life with you."

"It isn't just a dream, Otto. It's real!"

He puts his hands on my face and kisses me softly. "I'd like us to be married October. It is our favorite time of year. The leaves should be beautiful. We'll be married in the meadow. We'll use Grandpap's money for the wedding, to make it special. We'll clean out the barn and rent white round tables and white chairs. We'll get caterers and hang white lights. I told you I was saving that for something special! This is it!"

"It sounds wonderful, Otto!"

He kisses me with such passion my toes are tingling. He consumes me, and I consume him.

"Some people search their whole lives to find what I found in you, Sophie. Every day I spend with you is the new best day of my life."

"Are you happy, Otto?"

"There are many ways to be happy in this life, but all I really need is you. I found the reason for my smile, the day I found you! Yes, I'm happy. VERY HAPPY!"

I melt into his body. Suddenly, I hear horns tooting. Toot! Toot! Toot! I look out. It is Mom, Dad, Theo and Izzy in one car. Aunt Bella and her three kids in another. Aunt Ina brought Uncle Doug and Red. Uncle Sid pulls in with Annie. Everyone is out of their cars, hugging us and cheering when I hear toot, toot, toot! It's Ruby and Charles! She has with her Dutch, Julia and Sammy. Lord how I've missed them!

Another car appears behind them with hands waving out all the windows. Brenda is driving. She has Judy, Renie, and Linda with her. Debra and Jax are in another car. Each

348

has a bottle of wine they are waving. I hear a roaring sound. It is a motorcycle. The guy comes to a quick stop kicking down his stand and gets off taking off his helmet. It's Ray.

I look at Otto and he is laughing. "You planned all this, didn't you?"

"Yep! It is our special moment. I wanted the people who are special to us to be here to share it."

We are all together. Here to celebrate, together. Friends and family. A mural of my life.

A white van pulls in. A man in a suit coat gets out and goes to the back opening double doors. I hear a lift lowering. He comes around the van pushing a wheelchair. It's Rosalie! Otto runs to her and places a soft kiss on her cheek. "Thanks for coming, Mom."

"I wouldn't have missed it, baby!" Her smile could light the sky. "I have a little surprise for you, honey."

"What's that, Mom?"

"Give me your hands."

Otto takes both her hands in his. The man in the suit folds the foot platforms of the wheelchair. Rosalie stands. Otto throws his arms around her and cries. "Oh, Mom. It won't be long now you'll be here with me and Sophie!"

The embracing continues amidst laughter and the sounds of chirping birds and the cry of a hawk from the west. Rosalie sits back down and Otto pushes her chair into the barn. Izzy runs onto the gazebo.

I can't help but laugh at Izzy. I walk onto the gazebo with her. I throw my arms around her and she cuddles into my chest. I smell her hair. I whisper. "Thank you, God, for keeping her here with me." I think of all those people in my life who lost siblings. I think of how I have spent my life fearing that it would happen to me. I wonder why God chose to save me from that grief.

I look up at the gazebo and the beauty of it. It takes my breath away.

Otto steps into the gazebo with us and puts his arms around us. Izzy sees a spider traveling along the delicate carving of the pillar and gently picks it up. "Look, Sophie. A spider!"

"You need to take him outside and let him go, honey."

"Why? Why do I have to let him go?"

"Because he needs to find a new cobweb to live in, dear. He won't find any cobwebs here. The cobwebs here are all gone from here."

Otto smiles at me as he strokes my face. "Indeed, they are. Indeed, they are."

IN MEMORY *Fear not, for I have redeemed you, I have called you by name,*
you are mine...You are precious and honored in my sight.
ISAIAH 43:1

Sue Ann Nagy   Died August 9, 1970 in Plane Crash

Frank Brochetti   Killed in Vietnam April 8, 1972

Billy and Jackie Pompelia on their wedding day
Bill killed in car crash April 5, 1972

James Schrecengost killed in car crash 1953

Butchie Doms

Debbie Doms

Paul Doms

Peggy Doms

Jimmy Lias killed by car Oct. 30, 1938

Jimmy Burns killed in WWII

DONNA JEAN MAFFEI

May 15, 1948 – December 10, 2005
My own personal tragedy.
My sister I lost. You still inspire me. I miss you!

A NOTE FROM THE AUTHOR

I was born June 9, 1950 in my grandmother's house in Yatesboro PA, a small coal mining town in Western Pennsylvania. I then grew up within one mile of the house I was born in and attended school at Shannock Valley High School. In 1968 I married my high school sweetheart, Michael Koma. We have two sons, two daughter-in-laws and seven wonderful grandchildren.

I worked most of my life as a high school secretary, but had different adventures as a hair stylist for seven years and a small restaurant owner for two years.

At age sixty-eight I decided to do what I like most, which is writing. It did not matter if I succeeded, but I needed to try. My love of home and family inspired me to begin writing the history of where I was born and grew up, in the Shwanee Valley.

My first book, THE CREEK DON'T RISE, was my first attempt at writing and took me two years to write. I fortunately had good people to help me. The positive response this book received was so uplifting, it lit my fire to continue writing.

I weave real memories into a fictional story that brings them back to life. I love capturing the history as well as tragedies of the past that I want remembered.

My second book, COBWEBS A'PLENTY, is the sequel to THE CREEK DON'T RISE. I plan to write the trilogy to be released 2023.

It is because of the memories given to me, that I can create the story. It is also because of the people who help me, that I succeed. I will never say I did it alone, as I did not. My hope is to write a book each year, *if the good Lord's willing and the creek don't rise!*

I still happily reside in my hometown of Rural Valley, in my homestead with my husband. Our greatest joy is family. We love our roots.

You may contact me at
mkoma.mail@gmail.com
to order books
or on Facebook: Mary Koma

Made in United States
North Haven, CT
11 March 2023

33928712R00196